"German? American? . . . In *This Must Be the Place* Winger avoids the braggadocio of typical expatriate fiction, telling a story rooted in universal human emotions—love, loneliness, grief, fear of change, and yes, hope—among people whose identity is more complicated than their citizenship."   —*The New York Times*

"Gracefully captures the odd emptiness of Berlin's streets as well as the subtleties of its inhabitants. . . . The odd-couple romance that inevitably forms between Walter and Hope stands in for Berlin's gloomy appeal . . . A smart, tasteful novel."
          —*The New York Sun*

"As smart and cosmopolitan as the twenty-first-century Berlin she chronicles so well, Anna Winger's *This Must Be the Place* is an essential love story for our confused and difficult times. Funny, touching, and unforgettable."   —Gary Shteyngart, author of
The Russian Debutante's Handbook and *Absurdistan*

"Cosmopolitan, funny, and breezy to read, the tale finds inspiration in the everyday but is always smart and never sappy."
          —*DailyCandy*

"Winger's novel bravely takes on themes of remorse, regret, and responsibility, both social and personal. . . . A writer worth watching."
          —*Booklist*

"Berlin is a city that lends itself to stories about how the past can often weigh down the present. The city—destroyed in war, divided for almost fifty years and now whole again—is itself a metaphor for renewal and overcoming fraught history. . . . But there is much that is fresh here, and it's a pleasure to read a story about finding oneself again not through romance but through friendship."
          —*The Jewish Daily Forward*

continued . . .

"Anna Winger's debut is a breezingly intelligent, emotionally hard-hitting, culturally insightful examination of people living 'abroad'—even within their own countries. Winger's post-Wall Berlin becomes emblematic of our global triumphs and our global malaise. This novel is insanely impressive—and it's also a plain great read."
—Heidi Julavits, author of
The Uses of Enchantment and *The Mineral Palace*

"An accomplished work . . . with characters who live and breathe and whose lives ring true."
—*Chicago Jewish Star*

"Intriguing . . . Winger deftly reveals [Berlin's] history and cultural significance."
—*Kirkus Reviews*

"Displacement is revealed as a permanent condition in Anna Winger's graceful and intelligent first novel. Her vivid characters—a German and an American—wander, half-lost, half-found, through a Western world where history is buried and all that once seemed permanent—from the Twin Towers to the Berlin Wall—is already gone."
—Danzy Senna, author of
Caucasia and *Symptomatic*

"Anna Winger writes about displacement and belonging, loss and connection with intelligent forthrightness and complex subtlety. As her protagonists, Walter and Hope, find their separate lives gradually and inevitably intertwining, their stories take on new layers of historical and cultural richness. Set in a modern-day, haunted Berlin, *This Must Be the Place* is a riveting, bittersweet, and bracingly unsentimental novel."
—Kate Christensen, author of
The Great Man and *In the Drink*

THIS MUST BE THE PLACE

ANNA WINGER

RIVERHEAD BOOKS

New York

RIVERHEAD BOOKS
Published by the Penguin Group
Penguin Group (USA) Inc.,
375 Hudson Street, New York, New York 10014, USA
Penguin Group (Canada), 90 Eglinton Avenue East, Suite 700, Toronto, Ontario M4P 2Y3, Canada
(a division of Pearson Penguin Canada Inc.)
Penguin Books Ltd., 80 Strand, London WCR 0RL, England
Penguin Group Ireland, 25 St. Stephen's Green, Dublin 2, Ireland (a division of Penguin Books Ltd.)
Penguin Group (Australia), 250 Camberwell Road, Camberwell, Victoria 3124, Australia
(a division of Pearson Australia Group Pty. Ltd.)
Penguin Books India Pvt. Ltd., 11 Community Centre, Panchsheel Park, New Delhi—110 017, India
Penguin Group (NZ), 67 Apollo Drive, Rosedale, North Shore 0632, New Zealand
(a division of Pearson New Zealand Ltd.)
Penguin Books (South Africa) (Pty.) Ltd., 24 Sturdee Avenue, Rosebank, Johannesburg 2196, South Africa

Penguin Books Ltd., Registered Offices: 80 Strand, London WC2R 0RL, England

Lines from "Can't Fight This Feeling Anymore" by Kevin Cronin are copyright © 1984 Fate Music
(ASCAP) (Administered by HoriPro Entertainment Group). All rights reserved. Used by permission.

First Riverhead hardcover edition: August 2008
First Riverhead trade paperback edition: August 2009
Riverhead trade paperback ISBN: 978-1-59448-383-7

The Library of Congress has catalogued the Riverhead hardcover edition as follows:

Winger, Anna.
     This must be the place / Anna Winger
          p.   cm.
     ISBN 978-1-59448-997-6
     1. Actors—Fiction   2. Married women—Fiction   3. Americans—
Germany—Berlin—Fiction   4. Berlin (Germany)—Fiction
     5. Friendship—Fiction   I. Title
     PS3623.I6624T48   2008   2008015129
     813'.6—dc22

PRINTED IN THE UNITED STATES OF AMERICA

10   9   8   7   6   5   4   3   2   1

FOR JÖRG

Ich habe dich gewählt
Unter allen Sternen.

I have chosen you
Among all these stars.

—ELSE LASKER-SCHÜLER

THIS MUST BE THE PLACE

PROLOGUE

The mothers pushed their babies past the building in the dark. Although the sun would not be up for at least another hour, the shops were open, as were the day-care centers, the kiosks selling cigarettes and newspapers. Students were riding bikes up the avenues to class. True daylight would last only for a few hours. By the time the schools let out, mid-afternoon, it would be dusk already. It was the peculiar lot of Berlin, given its Cold War island history, to hang on at the eastern edge of Western Europe's time zone. But in November 2001, twelve years after the fall of the Wall, its clocks were still set at GMT+1. It was a political, if arbitrary, position. Just up the Baltic coast in Vilnius or Tallinn, where the clocks read one hour later, working people would be coming home for dinner, while in Berlin they were still chained to their desks, as if they lived in Madrid, a thousand miles to the west, where it was light out.

When the building was constructed in 1911, it wrapped all the way around the corner from Schillerstrasse to Bismarckstrasse, then an elegant residential avenue lined with front gardens and horse-drawn carriages, not cheap supermarkets and traffic. Its architect had designed the apartments to be *Villenetagen*, villas on every floor, prime real estate, because Berlin's future had been promising in those days. Although most of the building had since been blown up or burned down, ninety years later its balconies and trellises, mullioned windows and inner courtyards designed to provide views from almost every room still hinted at the optimism of its origins. The back side of the original complex remained on Schillerstrasse, facing south. Its yellow-ocher façade needed a paint job, and the grand floor-through apartments had been divided up and nobody cared for the garden, but in the right light (and this was the right light: the blue beginnings of daybreak deep on the horizon) it was beautiful. Ninety years is not such a long time in the scheme of things: the life of a person, if they are lucky; a room just wide enough to touch both walls with outstretched hands. In other places, such a building might have seen only the soft swell of progress, but here? Ninety years of drama, followed only by this.

1

When Walter woke up in the dark he was alone in his bed, buried beneath a winter-weight duvet, afflicted simultaneously by a hangover and the residue of a nightmare (water at his ankles, the sudden suck of a tsunami, a tunnel, Christmas lights, an electric guitar). Four flights down, the traffic piled up every few minutes at the lights around Ernst-Reuter-Platz. Across the street, children waiting for the bell to ring in the schoolyard screamed. He reached around for Heike, but the space beside him was empty and the sound of water running in the bathroom sink confirmed that she was already up. He rolled over onto her side of the bed and burrowed into the pillows. He had accepted a guest turn on the popular soap opera she starred in only as a favor to her: recently the ratings had slipped. Her role, she claimed, was in danger and his name still carried with it a certain retro-chic cachet. But Walter had not acted in front of the cameras for almost twenty years. The idea that he might do so today seemed to him remote at best, and at worst, absurd. Eyes closed, he tried unsuccessfully to remember the last time he had seen Heike's face light up at the sight of him, or the last time they had made love in the morning even if it meant being late to work. Then he rubbed his eyes and worked on his cough. When she came out of the bathroom, he would say that he felt terrible. She would take pity on him. He could call in sick. It was a good plan until he made the mistake of answering the phone.

"Baum hier."

"Herr Walter Baum," the young producer replied. "Or should I say, Mr. Cruise. I would recognize your voice anywhere. I'm just calling to let you know that the car will pick you two up at nine. It's nice that you could join us today. And it will be fun for Heike too, of course."

"She's a good enough actress in her own right."

"Excuse me?"

"She doesn't need me there today."

"I don't understand."

"You shouldn't make her trade on her relationship with me to keep her job."

The long silence that followed was punctuated only by the uncomfortable sound of both men breathing into the phone.

"There has definitely been a misunderstanding," said the producer. "We think Heike is fantastic."

His incredulous tone clarified everything. Heike didn't need to trade on their relationship to get work anymore, more like the other way around.

. . .

Walter dropped the telephone on the bed and jumped up, pulling on the same clothes he had been wearing the day before.

"I'm going out to get bread," he told the bathroom door.

"Don't take too long," Heike replied.

But he was already in the elevator. When he rushed out into the lobby, raised voices were arguing in American English, blocking the doorway to the street. He stopped short behind a small woman in a trench coat. The man she faced just outside on the stoop was holding up a paper street map. Walter caught the angry flavor of their words immediately but not what they were talking about. He cleared his throat loudly.

The woman's face was delicate and pretty, her blue eyes red.

"*Guten Tag,*" said the man.

Walter pushed past them onto the street, where the winter air burned his cheeks but the view was immediately comforting: the same old linden trees lined the sidewalk, the same old cobblestones along the curb. The argument resumed behind him, but faded out as he walked toward the bakery. He had moved into his apartment in 1986 and had walked around the corner to buy bread for breakfast almost every morning since. The same old woman had been selling loaves of *Vollkornbrot,* sandwich rolls and poppy seed pastry, without any change in inventory for the past fifteen years. Once she'd made muffins to compete with a coffee bar that opened up a block away, chocolate and apple-cinnamon, with American flags on toothpicks tucked into them. But they languished on their doilies in the Plexiglas shelves. Walter had bought one just for the flag, which he kept, occasionally taking it out of his pocket to twirl between two fingers. After a while the red, white and blue paper had simply disintegrated.

In the twenty-four hours since he'd last been to the bakery, Christmas decorations had taken over like a fungus. Walter touched a gold pretzel hanging on a wreath by the door. They started earlier and earlier each year, he thought. It wasn't even December.

"What do you want?"

The woman who worked there was a typical *Berliner Schnauze*, unfriendly, but at least she was consistent: she never smiled. She asked questions in a voice hoarse from forty years of smoking, peering over the counter at her customers as if they were disturbing her afternoon nap. Walter pointed out a loaf of bread in the case.

"It sure is cold out," he offered while she wrapped it.

"Of course it's cold. It's almost Christmas."

He wanted to call her ridiculous. If it was almost Christmas, then it had just been Reunification Day, and would soon be Fasching; for that matter, it would soon be spring, and they both knew that wasn't true. She eyed him suspiciously.

"Where's your wife?"

"My wife?"

"You're usually here with a lady. The actress from the soap opera."

Ever since Heike had taken the role on the soap, which was set in a women's prison, her fans had been coming out of the woodwork. Married women of a certain age who, Heike insisted, felt like prisoners themselves. She had never been and would never be his wife, since she didn't believe in marriage. She couldn't even enjoy a Hollywood romantic comedy if it involved a wedding; whenever he'd dragged her out to one, she'd groaned disdainfully over her popcorn for ninety minutes and picked apart the happy ending before they'd even left the theater.

"She's not my wife," he said, accepting the paper package across the counters.

"That's too bad." The woman in the bakery shrugged, looking past him at the next person in line. "I love that show."

Outside, Walter watched the sidewalk disappear beneath his feet, holding the bread close to his heart.

"We think Heike's fantastic," he imitated the producer's tone exactly under his breath. *"And who the hell are you?"*

As he came around the corner, he saw the American couple still arguing on the stoop. Since he was hardly in a hurry to go back upstairs, he retreated gratefully to the other side of the street. Did they live in his building? Walter rarely crossed paths with his neighbors, mostly housebound geriatrics and traveling businessmen, not attractive young people from the United States. He sat down on the low wall around the schoolyard and looked around as if he were waiting for someone. He looked over at the couple as if simply checking the time on an invisible clock above the front door. The man was fully dressed in a suit, as if for work in an office, and shaking the paper map, now open to reveal an expansive tangle of pink and yellow streets. Although he was accompanied by a small blue suitcase, the woman wasn't even carrying a handbag. Closer inspection revealed that she wasn't wearing any shoes and her hair was wet, as if she had just emerged from the shower and wrapped the trench coat around her body like a bathrobe. The angry tone of their American accents was audible, but the words were just beyond Walter's grasp. How long had they been at it? Where did it start? Probably this began as a normal discussion: which way to go, which way was faster, when to leave. Maybe she was taking too long to get ready. Maybe the man was rushing her. But now it had come to this: he was yelling, she was crying. The woman grabbed the map away and threw it to the sidewalk.

Upstairs, thought Walter, Heike would be in the shower by now, washing her long brown hair. She would be wondering how the hell he was going to get ready in time if he didn't come home immediately. He pulled his jacket tightly around his body. The answer was that he would not be ready. The answer was that he would not be going at all. Why did she care so much if he ever acted again? She was too young to remember watching *Schönes Wochenende* in its original broadcast, of course, but she certainly appreciated the looks on people's faces when they went out in public together, that slow glimmer of recognition. She loved it when shy adult women came up to them in cafés to admit a teenage crush that had never died. Although the truth was that recently it had been shy men coming up to the table for autographs— hers, not his. *We think Heike's fantastic.* She pitied him, he thought.

The concrete wall was cold against his jeans, but Walter

stayed where he was, still unwilling to break up the scene on his doorstep. The American man had picked up the map off the ground and was tearing it into pieces; the woman was doubled over, weeping. Walter watched them with the tense exhilaration of a sports fan in the bleachers at the very end of a game. The last few moments of a fight were always the most dangerous. On the one hand, he wanted to yell something across the street, stop them before they went too far. On the other hand—he couldn't help it—he wanted to see them throw themselves off the precipice into a miserable abyss. His mobile rang and although he recognized Heike's number, he didn't pick it up. *Fantastic*, he thought, relishing the thought of frustration brewing in the shower four flights up. On the stoop, the woman cried and the man ripped up the map until his hands were empty. Then they looked at each other in silence for at least a minute. Then the man walked away. Walter inhaled sharply. Would she run after him? Should she? The pretty American did not move. She did not look down at the shredded pink and yellow paper at her feet. She smoothed her wet hair back and wiped her eyes, and although she continued looking down the street in his direction long after he was gone, she didn't call out to him once.

After a few moments had passed, Walter figured that he could walk right by and greet her normally, but it was cold out and suddenly he worried about her wet hair. If he came close enough, he felt, he would not be able to resist the urge to lift her feet from the cold ground and carry her across the threshold into the lobby. So he waited until she went inside. When enough time had passed that he was certain she had taken the elevator, he crossed the street, looked quickly over both shoulders, and collected the pieces of the paper map as carefully as he could, folding them into his jacket.

Heike was still in the shower when he returned to his apartment and entered the bathroom. Her mobile phone sat, wet, in the soap dish at the sink.

"I'm back."

"You're late."

He wiped away the steam from the mirror to examine the progress of his bald spot, a permanent yarmulke nestled into the close-cropped remains of what had once been thick, curly hair.

"Can you name a single famous actor in Hollywood who's bald?" he asked through the shower curtain.

"Are you getting ready?"

"One," he insisted. "Name one."

"Kevin Costner."

"He isn't famous anymore. I mean a great one."

"Jack Nicholson."

"He has power rails. Those are different. They imply virility and wisdom. I mean really bald."

"Well—"

"You can't. Because none of them are. Think about it: Robert De Niro, Al Pacino, Henry Fonda, Cary Grant, Tom Cruise, of course—"

"Aren't some of those guys dead?"

"But they were never bald."

When he had been famous in Germany in the early 1980s, his Dionysian mop had been Walter's trademark. But despite the daily application of expensive potion, by the end of 2001, a shiny pink monster was emerging from the hole in his head. He dropped his chin to his chest and strained for a glimpse of the back side. By the time his father died, in his forties, he no longer had hair on his legs or his toes. Walter was thirty-nine.

In middle age I will emerge anew, he said silently to himself. Smooth and hairless, like a baby.

Heike turned off the water and pushed open the curtain. She had the kind of figure that appeared shapely in clothes, but stripped of padding it was sharp, as if he might be injured on contact were his own body not so soft and forgiving.

"All the important actors were already famous in their early twenties," he told her. "Just like I was. At that point there was no way to predict if any of us would lose our hair. But look at me and look at them. All of them have kept it. All the big ones."

"You stopped acting before you started losing your hair."

"You're missing my point. In retrospect, it's as if these guys knew innatcly that they would keep their hair, and the knowledge of that gave them a comparative advantage. It's as if there were some hormonal connection between hair follicle activity and the development of enduring charisma."

Heike twisted a towel around her head.

"I can't do this," he said.

"Everything will be fine."

"I mean, this show is beneath me. The opening weekend of my last movie alone grossed more than fifteen million marks."

She stepped out of the tub. When she spoke again, her voice had dropped an octave.

"Think of your fans, baby. Everyone in Germany will watch the show when it airs."

"Just to see what I look like after all these years."

She shook her head.

"You have to let yourself evolve as an actor."

Allow himself to occupy a different space in people's minds is what she meant, thought Walter, a space off in the hinterlands, off the sexual radar. The middle-aged guy, innocuous neighbor, buddy, postman, high school teacher, killer; the character actor, not the heartthrob. He preferred to leave his celluloid persona uncompromised by the ravages of laziness and time. Was that so terrible? He thought of the American woman standing still in the cold on his doorstep a few minutes earlier and suddenly wished that he had swept her off her bare feet, right there, like the groom in one of the romantic movies that Heike couldn't stand. By "evolve," she meant she expected him to sacrifice the last golden vestige of his self-image in the interest of personal growth. *Fantastic*.

"I know you lied to me," he said.

"What?"

"You said you needed me on the show to boost the ratings. You begged me, as I remember it."

"I knew you wouldn't agree to do it otherwise."

It was true, but he would punish her anyway. For lying, for encouraging him, for giving a shit in the first place; for moving on with her young life while he wallowed in chronic indecision at the gateway to middle age.

"You lied to me," he said. "The fact remains."

Heike's wide-set eyes filled up halfway with tears and although they didn't touch, Walter felt as if one of his hands were wrapped delicately around her esophagus, one shoulder pressing hers to the wall.

"I can't do this anymore," she said.

Walter had been anticipating this moment since the day they met, but he did not respond. She squeezed past him in the doorway. The light blue of her eyes was the first thing he'd noticed about her, he thought; it was the thing he would always remember. When he turned around, she was dressed and throwing her things into a bag, smoking a cigarette held between her front teeth and wearing a tight white I LOVE NY T-shirt with a big red heart. Neither of them spoke until the downstairs buzzer rang.

"That's it then?" she asked. "You have nothing more to say to me?"

Don't go, he thought. But her figure was already receding down the hallway, through the front door, out into the world.

"The T-shirt is ridiculous. You've never even been to New York."

"It's a symbol, Walter."

"Of what?"

"Solidarity. Compassion. Something you know nothing about. What should I tell them when I get downstairs? They're expecting both of us."

"Just say I couldn't make it."

For the next thirty seconds he listened to the sound of her bag dragging along the wooden floorboards of the apartment, followed by the opening of locks.

"Bruce Willis," she called out, before slamming the front door decisively behind her. "Bruce Willis is bald."

2

Hope leaned back against the inside of her front door, quickly calculating what to pack. Facing down the long white hallway inside her apartment, she blinked as if driving into the light, trying to remember where she had last seen her passport. She had brought so little with her from New York that she could just throw it all back into the same suitcase and be out of there in five minutes flat. But she needed the passport. In the kitchen she found her handbag and dumped out its contents into the sink: the ticket stubs from her flight to Berlin, her wallet, a notebook, a pen, the wrapper she had saved from a German granola bar with the brand name Corny, the cover of a local magazine called *Zitty*, a dead U.S. mobile phone and some loose American change. No passport. She hit the counter with one hand and threw the bag on the floor. In the bedroom her suitcase was still standing in the same place it had been since she arrived a month earlier, like a child at a boring dinner party begging to be taken home. She stuffed it with her clothes, and by the time she sat down to close it, she was out of breath. Then she noticed her passport wedged beneath a standing lamp and the floor, and started crying again. It was one thing to leave, but she had nowhere to go. She sobbed into the arm of her raincoat not with regret for the place she might abandon, but from the realization that she had no clear alternative. When she imagined herself out in the world with her passport, she was unable to come up with a single viable destination. New York was no longer the home that she knew, and she could hardly return to her parents. In the past five months she had distanced herself even from her closest friends. Dave had turned out to be a pretty flimsy rug, she thought, but leaving him now felt like pulling out all she had left from beneath her feet.

The phone rang and she wiped her nose with the back of one hand. Only two people had the number: Dave and her mother, who called once a week to deliver cheerful midwestern edicts laced with palpable anxiety about Hope's life. But since it was two A.M. in Kansas City, it was not her mother. She let Dave wait long enough to worry that she was still outside, freezing her ass off on the doorstep where he'd left her, then rose from her seat on the packed suitcase and reached for the phone.

"You're home," he said.

She could hear the highway around his voice in the car.

"On Thursday night," he said, "when I get back, I'm going to take you to this great schnitzel place I heard about from a colleague."

Hope had to swallow the fury she felt rising in her throat. This is what he'd been doing since June, behaving as if nothing had happened. What was one more fight to him?

"Schnitzel."

"Breaded veal, Hope. It's a local delicacy."

"Great," she said.

"Good. My cell phone's fading out now."

When he was gone, she leaned against the wall and tried to calm herself down. Thursday night Dave would take her on a date. They would eat schnitzel. They would be polite to each other, as if they had just met, and make small talk about the Polish economy, the reconstruction of Berlin, the progress of the war in Afghanistan. Dave was perhaps the only person on earth who was able to spin even the war on terror in positive terms, she told herself. Everything would be fine. He would talk and she would not and after dinner they would have sex (habitual, results-oriented, precise). He would not mention the fight they had just had on the doorstep. He would not comment on the fact that although she spent most of her time in the bathtub, she had once again forgotten to wash her hair. He would not press for details about what she had been doing all week, alone, in this vast and empty apartment and she would try to make this work. They had been married for six years already. She thought: This is my life.

She left the suitcase packed on the floor and went into the bathroom, where the bath she had left to follow him down the stairs was already cold. She turned on the taps again, removed her clothes and stared at the pieces of herself reflected in the shiny white wall tiles. The bathroom was very large. There was a round bathtub in the middle of the room, a separate shower, a toilet and a marble counter containing two sinks, side by side. As she leaned back in the water, she

wondered if other couples actually brushed their teeth together, smiling at each other in the mirror through the
foam. She had never liked to be in the bathroom with Dave.
Even in the best of times, now difficult to recall, she had always preferred to be alone. Hope reflected that their New
York bathroom was so small that one of them would have
had to stand in the shower anyway, leaning over the other's
shoulder with a toothbrush to reach the mirror. Strange that
she had come all the way to Berlin to have a bathroom big
enough for two, a bathroom whose exaggerated luxury struck
her as distinctly American: the pièce de résistance in a fancy
house somewhere in New Jersey, not here. The only other
time she had been to Europe, on a summer trip with her
schoolteacher parents in 1986, the plumbing, in particular,
had seemed backward. In England, there were no showers at
all, only handheld faucets at the side of the tub. In France,
the toilets were often separated into little rooms, so that you
had to run down the hall to wash your hands. In some restaurants there had been only a hole in the ground. In Italy,
she had been fascinated by the mysterious bidets until her
mother showed her how to use one to wash sand off her feet.
There had been washing machines but no dryers anywhere,
as she remembered it. When she complained about having to
wear damp jeans, her father told her she was being culturally
insensitive.

"Europe is still somewhere between the First and Third
Worlds," he explained. "They're lagging behind us in terms
of technology and services."

But he was careful to point out that this did not mean
Europe was the Second World.

"The Second World refers to the one behind the Iron

17

Curtain. No one knows what kind of plumbing they have there."

Hope pulled her head under the water for as long as she could stand it, then came up, listening to the water running off her hair into the tub. Her eyes fell on the binding of a thick book she'd been using as a doorstop to the bathroom: *Hitler's Willing Executioners.* In place of a guidebook, Dave had given her a stack of books to read about the Holocaust and the roots of anti-Semitism. Books, he had suggested, that would help her understand Berlin. It was typical of him to decide that a good grasp of history would help her acclimate to everyday life, she thought. He was an economist, after all, interested in formulas and systems, the facts, not the emotional details. His tendency to break things down in rational terms had once had a calming effect, but now it enraged her.

"A fluke," he said about the baby. "Look at the statistics."

He had said this often during the past five months, as if his point just needed to sink into her brain for a lightbulb to go on. As if he truly believed that what happened would be easier to accept if she could just see it as the function of a mathematical equation. But Hope did not want to look at the statistics. She did not want to be a statistic; the one in a million who made all other pregnant women feel relieved. She wanted to grieve.

"What happened, happened," he'd said today. "It's been long enough."

"How can it possibly have been long enough," she'd replied, "when I never had the chance to say goodbye?"

It had become their usual routine: screaming at each other because there was no one else to blame.

"We have an opportunity to start over here," he'd said, again, before storming off.

For orientation about the culture, she preferred her textbook from German class to his history books, its lengthy descriptions of Christmas traditions and accompanying pictures of happy children. Sometimes she just flipped through the dictionary. Certain words were similar to their English counterparts: *Nervenzusammenbruch*, for example, was the word for nervous breakdown. Others, like *Schwangerschaft*, which meant pregnancy, or *Schmerz*, which meant pain, had no relationship at all. Still others, simple words like *Kind*, the word for child, meant one thing in English and something different altogether in German. Then there was a host of terms that had been imported wholesale from English: *brainstorm*, for example, or *midlife crisis*. Hope imagined people saying these words with a heavy German accent in the flow of an otherwise unintelligible conversation. Even if she spoke the language, she probably would not recognize them.

She let her hands rest on the stretch marks just above her pubic hair, purple stains against the pale skin that was still loose there, despite her flat stomach. She wondered if they would ever disappear and if then she would feel that it had been long enough to move on. But maybe there was no such thing as long enough, she thought. She reached for a bottle of conditioner sitting on the edge of the bathtub and ran one finger across the label. In New York she had isolated herself deliberately, unable to speak to friends and family whose concern for her felt like expectation, whose desire for her to bounce back had become an unbearable burden. It had seemed grotesque to be polite in light of what happened, so she just stopped talking to people at all. But here she had no other choice. She knew no one and couldn't speak the language. She was taking a German class but it was slow going. If only she had come to Berlin on that trip in 1986, she thought, she might have been prepared for how far away this city felt from the United States, and even from the rest of Europe, or from what she remembered of Europe (a charming parallel universe of familiar things made special: good milk chocolate, telephone booths with rounded corners, tobacco shops, double-decker buses, pink newspapers, women in high heels on narrow cobblestone streets). But the distance had a built-in benefit: nobody pitied her, or worried about her, or expected anything at all. She turned the bottle of conditioner over in her hands, thinking that here she might even welcome the benign company of strangers, if only for the chance to escape her own head. But where? The day before, she had gone into a drugstore and spent half an hour selecting the conditioner, unable to distinguish the name for it, *Spülung*, from that for shampoo, say, or shower gel or body lotion. She had asked the salesclerk at the front of the store for help.

"*Conditioner?*" She sounded the word out slowly, her best effort at a German accent. "Crème rinse?"

To illustrate the promises of the product, she had run both hands over her hair, which was anything but smooth and silky at the time, and the salesclerk had simply shrugged, uncomprehending. Later, she had returned to the hair aisle with her dictionary, but the word for conditioner was not in it. To identify this bottle, she had opened the tops of many bottles, smelled their contents, rubbed the liquids on the back of her hand, wondering finally if conditioner was even used in Germany. She had noticed a lot of fine, straight hair around, although apart from this it was much harder to generalize about the Germans than she had expected. She had yet to see a crowd of strapping, blond men, or a ruddy-cheeked Frau with pigtails, or anyone even remotely resembling Marlene Dietrich. If anything, she thought, the local population seemed harmless and exhausted, cautiously stooped over as they walked into the wind.

There were glimpses of beautiful architecture. The building she was living in was quite grand and old, but it connected to a cheap replica built much more recently. She had yet to wander far, but from what she had seen, the mix was typical and all the more dismal with so few people on the street. If her bathroom here was like somewhere in suburban New Jersey, she thought, then what she had seen of the rest of Berlin was more like Newark on a winter day than Rome or Paris, like the depopulated fringes of urban American. In a month she had not had a conversation with anyone except Dave, but people often asked her for directions. In fact, the very first day an older couple came up to her on the street and although she couldn't understand a thing they said, it was clear that they were lost. A few days later it happened again, this time a young woman with a backpack and a folded newspaper in one hand. After that, it was a family of tourists. First, they tried German, then a few rough words of English, but even in English she couldn't help them. She had no idea where anything was. This morning she had mentioned it to Dave.

"Why me?"

He looked up briefly from the small blue suitcase he was both unpacking and repacking on the bed.

"Why not?"

"I am so clearly a foreigner. I have no idea where I am or where I'm going. Why do they choose me?"

"Probably because you walk so slowly. You look like you have all the time in the world to talk. They don't want to stop someone who looks like they're in a hurry."

"Someone in a hurry is in a hurry because they have somewhere to go. If they have somewhere to go in such a hurry, it means they know their way around. That's the person to ask."

Dave closed his suitcase.

"The next time someone asks you for directions you should point that out," he said. "But I'm telling you: just walk a little faster and they'll leave you alone."

It was when he came in to say goodbye to her in the bathroom that he handed her the enormous map of Berlin, opening it up all the way as if to demonstrate its utility. It was different from American street maps. It was pink and yellow, folded in sixteen sections and covered with a bewildering scrawl of streets she didn't know, neighborhoods she'd never seen. The city was so huge it wrapped around from one side of the paper to the other.

"This is the map I use to get in and out of Berlin," he told her, folding it back up carefully. "But you can have it. The next time someone asks for directions you can actually help them."

"With that?"

She imagined herself whipping it out at the street corner, bending down to unfold it flat on the sidewalk, and trying to locate the nearest subway station, which is what they usually asked about, or where to get a coffee.

"Why not? Maybe you'll make some friends."

His total disregard for her experience made her so furious that she pulled herself up from the water and followed him down the stairs.

Now she leaned her head back and slowly washed her hair. Six months earlier, when Dave was originally offered the job in Berlin, she had willingly agreed to come with him. She knew as much about the city as anyone else, but it wasn't much: *Cabaret;* the War, the Wall; Ronald Reagan at the Brandenburg Gate (*"Mr. Gorbachev, tear down this wall!"*), heartbreaking news clips of freed people clambering over it. But the timing had seemed perfect. They had been living in the same place in New York, doing the same thing, for seven years. They were going to have a baby and she planned to stop working for a while. Anyway, she had liked the image of herself pushing a stroller on long, meandering walks through a romantic Euro-cityscape composed of fifteen-year-old memories of Rome, London and Paris. But in her fantasy of living here, she was able to read a menu. In the fantasy, it was always summer, not November. She was wearing a light trench for the occasional shower, not a winter coat. On weekends, they ate picnics of cheese and sausage on a blanket in dappled sunshine under a tree. In the fantasy, chic people on candy-colored Vespas cooed at the baby at stoplights because, of course, in the fantasy there was a baby. Dave had jumped at the chance to work on this project, the Polish Poverty Project, he called it, because he said it was a chance to wipe the slate clean. Privately, she thought he liked the idea that the very people who had once driven out his grandparents now needed his help. In any case, he had not explained that he would be gone all week, leaving her alone in Berlin. Hope looked around her at the bathroom thinking that six months ago she would never have imagined this; not the place nor the circumstances, not the reverberating sense of disorientation that afflicted her, like chronic nausea, whenever she got out of the tub. The fantasy of her European life had not materialized, but her American life no longer existed. She had to remind herself of this because it was easy to forget.

The clear water filled up with bubbles that floated on the surface, clinging to the sides of the tub. Six months earlier she would have been thrilled with this apartment. It was freshly painted white, a blank canvas, somewhere in some slick magazine just waiting to be filled with art and furniture. Because the dollar was strong, the same rent they had paid in New York now paid for this: moldings and parquet floors, a master bedroom and two bathrooms, even a beautiful nursery at the back. (The whole apartment was empty, but that room seemed emptier still.) The tiny place they'd shared in Greenwich Village for the past seven years had only two windows facing the street and three others facing the airshaft, but their friends had been jealous anyway because there was an extra little room for a baby. That the room had been more like a walk-in closet than a proper bedroom was irrelevant; it was separate space. It meant that they didn't have to move to Brooklyn to start a family. Hope squeezed her eyes shut and rubbed both hands across her empty belly. The baby's room would have fit three times over into the nursery here, maybe more, at least ten times into the whole apartment. Ten babies in Berlin. She examined her fingers, which were pale and almost colorless, puckered up like wet scraps of paper, and pictured the packed suitcase in her bedroom, her passport, the contents of her handbag loose in the kitchen sink. Where could she run to now? She never wanted to get out of the water. All summer in New York she had not wanted to get out of bed but there had been no bathtub. Now their furniture was still making its way across the Atlantic in a container, so here there was only the mattress on the floor, a table and four chairs. But there was this bathtub, this luxurious limbo between the horror of what had happened and the uncertainty of what might happen next. Hope let in some more hot water.

3

Other girlfriends had come and gone, but no girlfriend had ever left Walter at this time of year. Like a squirrel gathering nuts, or a wrestler sucking down for the season, he had always done what was necessary to make his relationships last until spring. After Heike left, he went into the bathroom and pissed for two minutes standing up. In the 1990s, there had been a nationwide movement instructing men to sit down: Women put up stickers in public restrooms, cartoon figures with little dicks hanging between their legs like tails. During the two years she had lived with him, he had not once stood up to piss. He had thus felt briefly defiant watching the wall tile behind the toilet, but two days later, the possibility of being alone through the holiday season ahead was starting to sink in. Walter lay in bed with the curtains drawn and catalogued the evidence that things were only getting worse: his growing paunch, his diminishing libido, the complete stagnation of Charlottenburg in favor of cooler, shabbier neighborhoods to the east, the advent of reality television, the continued popularity of electronic music, the bankruptcy of

Berlin. The war on terrorism had been the most recent example, now this. Most Berliners escaped midwinter to soak up ultraviolet light on cheap package tours to one of the Canary Islands; chicer locals spent the holidays at Raleigh Beach in Phuket. But Walter knew that he could not fathom such plans on his own. He turned on the TV and watched a square-jawed American commander deliver a status report, but the simultaneous translation from English into German was badly synced, making it impossible to understand what was being said in either language. He reached for the remote and pressed Play. The video of *Jerry Maguire* picked up exactly where he had left it the night before, right where Jerry enters the room full of bitter divorcées and makes the famous speech to win back his wife. As it played now, in perfectly synchronized German, Walter moved his lips to the sound of his own voice and watched Tom Cruise get down on his knees.

When he returned to Berlin from Los Angeles in 1985, Walter stopped acting, but to make money agreed to dub the voice of an up-and-coming American movie star. Tom Cruise had then just recently begun to distinguish himself in films. Other people had covered his few lines in *Endless Love, Taps,* and *The Outsiders;* the guy who usually did Rob Lowe had done *Risky Business;* but it wasn't until *Top Gun* came out in 1986 that Tom Cruise found his German voice. In the fourteen films he'd made since then, German audiences had heard Tom Cruise speak only in Walter's voice; they had never heard him speak English. American films were always shown dubbed in Germany, with specific native voices linked inextricably to the famous faces of all the movie stars, from Woody Allen to Julia Roberts. From the start, Tom Cruise was identified as one of the few celebrities admired equally in Germany by men and women, and as a result Walter had been making a good living doing voice-overs for commercials selling everything from luxury cars to laundry powder for fifteen years. To the advertising executives who hired him at a premium, the discrepancy between the aging German TV star before them and the all-American charisma his familiar voice conjured in the mind of their consumers was an inside joke.

"Voice of gold you've got there," they said, winking at Walter at the studio. "Men want to be Tom Cruise and women want to sleep with him."

Walter always chuckled along as if he were in on the joke; as if his diminished looks were a secret weapon or at least some sort of witty disguise. He told himself that even now he was better-looking than most of those guys could ever hope to be and he was laughing all the way to the bank, right? But the years had taken their toll. For a long time now his voice had been playing the hero while his body sat in the dark, eating ham sandwiches and candy bars and counting the cash.

He got under the covers thinking that he felt like a worm cut in half, whose head keeps moving forward while the tail end dances desperately in place. On screen, the women stared at Tom Cruise as his wife stood up slowly behind the couch.

"Ich lasse nicht zu dass Du mich weg wirfst," he said. "I'm not letting you get rid of me."

"We live in a cynical world."

"You complete me."

On screen, all the women were crying and Tom Cruise kissed his wife.

"You had me at hello," she said.

Walter made a mental note of key phrases that might come in handy if Heike called, although she was much tougher around the edges than the female character in the film. If he were to walk into a room full of Heike's friends and demand to speak to her, he reminded himself, she wouldn't dissolve into tears, or blush, or fall into his arms; she would take a suspicious step backward. She would think he'd lost his mind. When he got out of bed to switch the tape, he had to squint to make out the titles lined up in alphabetical order on his video shelf. The *Mission: Impossible*s were too action-oriented to provide the ego boost he needed now. He preferred the films whose drama was verbal, not physical, and thus driven by the sheer force and clarity of his dubbing. *Magnolia* was a favorite. *Born on the Fourth of July.* Finally he selected *A Few Good Men* and got back into bed. While it rewound to his favorite scene, he opened the paper to the two pages he read every day: *Leute von Heute,* People of Today, the day's gossip listed with pictures. Sometimes there was a profile of an up-and-coming celebrity, or pictures from a royal wedding, but usually just tidbits gathered from around the globe. Today, it reported that Jim Carrey, a Canadian, had applied for U.S. citizenship.

"I always felt growing up that America was a big brother, protecting us in the schoolyard," he said.

The article went on to say that he had just purchased a $42 million plane.

"You can do that when you're rich," he explained.

Walter turned the page and held his breath, as always: *Leute von Gestern*, People of Yesterday, the most popular section of the paper: an investigation into the current circumstances of the once famous, a daily dose of thrilling *Schadenfreude* at the miserable afterlife of someone who once had it all. With palpable relief, he looked down at an unflattering picture of Mickey Rourke, and pushed the paper aside. The final courtroom standoff between Tom Cruise and Jack Nicholson played forth. Walter pulled the covers up to his chin and listened.

When the telephone rang he took a moment to savor the flood of relief that filled his chest, relief so certain and sweet that it made the anxiety of the past two days almost worth it. By the second ring, he was angry. Did Heike actually think she could just come back as if nothing had happened? Actresses were all the same, he thought: histrionic and too easily indulged. He expected a pretty serious apology. There would be probation. She could not just take him for granted. By the third ring he paused the video and picked up slowly, taking his time.

"Baum hier," he said.

"You just didn't show up?"

It was his agent. She expelled the last breath of her cigarette.

"Klara."

"It was a great opportunity," she said. "A breakthrough role."

Walter picked up a glass ashtray that Heike had left behind on the bedside table and turned it over in his hands.

"Since when is playing a middle-aged high school teacher considered a breakthrough?"

"Not just a high school teacher—a murderer, a philanderer, a statutory rapist."

"Still."

"He murders a student he had an affair with to keep her quiet! Did you even read the script? It was the kind of role most actors would kill for."

He had been working with Klara since he was nineteen and she was twenty-five. She had been a casting director when she discovered him. When she started her own agency soon afterward he was one of her very first clients. At the time, she had been like an older sister to him, but since then the years between them seemed to have stretched exponentially. Success had catapulted her quickly forward into real adulthood while he lagged behind with tar on his shoes. Nowadays she was always slightly distracted; even on the telephone she seemed to be looking over his shoulder at someone more important on the other side of the room. She couldn't possibly be his sister anymore, he thought, maybe his mother. But Walter's mother had never been anything like Klara. She had never been old.

"Who did they get to replace you? What did Heike say?"

On the television screen Jack Nicholson's face, square under the military haircut, was frozen in a snarl.

"Actually, she left me."

"Good for her."

"I'm serious. She's not coming back here."

"Did she meet someone else?"

"Thanks."

"Isn't that how things usually go?"

"How do you know I didn't meet someone else?"

The American woman's map was laid out on the floor by his bed. Now dry, its pieces were wrinkled at the edges, like the half-burnt remains of newspaper kindling from a bonfire. It would take him forever to put it back together, maybe longer. Klara smoked.

"May-December relationships aren't easy," she said finally.

Walter had met Heike at the studio when she had a small voice role on *Eyes Wide Shut*. He had been in his element that day, the big fish in a very small pond. He was faster than anyone else. He needed only one or two tries to sync a line perfectly with the motion of the character's mouth. He was able to utter not only the words correctly but the breathing that truly distinguishes a personality. By the time it became clear that she didn't see him as a hero but rather as a project, she had already taken over his life.

"Reruns of *Schönes Wochenende* are on all the time now," Klara said. "Did you know that? According to the ratings it's actually pretty popular. I'm sure I can get you another TV gig."

"I start the new Tom Cruise next week."

"You can do something after that."

"A film."

"That would be a first."

"Not true. In Los Angeles—"

"I mean in Germany."

"But when was the last time a good film was made in German? I don't mean a little art house film seen and loved by ten people. I'll tell you when: before the war. Since then, the world hears the German language and thinks only of Nazis."

"*Das Boot* was in German."

"Exactly. And then Wolfgang Petersen moved to Hollywood to make *Air Force One*. You don't see him looking back."

Walter listened to burning tobacco on the other end of the line and eyed the map splayed out on the floor, reflexively trying to fit it back together like the wooden puzzles he had labored over as a child, whose pieces added up to a perfect medieval landscape.

"Ninety million people speak German. May I remind you that you make a living translating films from your beloved English into our unpopular language?"

"I'm talking about the world market."

"You're talking about the United States."

"They set the standard and Americans can't accept the idea of a sympathetic character who speaks German."

"Oskar Schindler—"

"Schindler had to speak English to be believable! Now that would have been a great opportunity."

Walter pictured Klara sitting at her desk overlooking Hackescher Markt through the plate-glass window, squashing out another cigarette butt as if it were a bug.

"If ninety million people isn't a big enough potential audience for you, I don't know why I bother," Klara said. "But if you insist on doing a film, I might actually have something for you."

He leaned back into the pillows and closed his eyes.

"A script came in recently for you from one of the film schools. It wouldn't pay, of course, but you don't need the money. It's good, and if the film turns out it'll make the rounds of the festivals."

"A student film?"

"The director's supposed to be quite talented."

On screen, the growth pattern of Jack Nicholson's hair was clearly visible, cropped short against his skull. Coming to a crest at the center of his forehead, his power rails dipped back on either side without any indication of further hair loss. Walter glanced down at Mickey Rourke's bloated cheeks.

"I'm not quite desperate enough to make a student film."

"You're not quite desperate enough to do anything. That's your problem."

He got out of bed and picked up one piece of the map off the floor. He recognized the name of one of the streets that crossed the paper, Bernauerstrasse, but could not remember if it had been in East Berlin or West. For that matter, he could not remember if it was in the northern part of the city or to the south. Even after almost twenty years in Berlin, he still got turned around. Maybe it had something to do with being surrounded by the Wall for so many years. It hadn't mattered much which direction you went in those days, there wasn't very far to go.

"No German actor has had a real career in Hollywood since Marlene," said Klara. "Why hire some unknown German guy and deal with all the accent trouble when there are a million American actors who look just like him?"

"I don't have an accent when I speak English."

She sighed.

"I can't get you work in English even if it is your mother tongue."

The VCR suddenly released Jack Nicholson from suspended animation and the military tribunal resumed at top volume.

"*Sie können die Wahrheit nicht ertragen,*" he yelled. "You can't handle the truth!"

"What is that?" Klara asked.

Walter scrambled for the remote control lost in the folds of the sheets and quickly squeezed Pause. This time, Tom Cruise's face filled the small screen, eyebrows knit together seriously, jaw clenched.

"Nothing."

"I have to get back to work," she said, "but here's something to look forward to: Tom Cruise is coming to Berlin, for the premiere of the movie in December."

"Tom Cruise."

"You've never met him, have you?"

Walter stared at Tom Cruise's face on the TV. He had stared at that face so many times, so intensely, that he knew its contours almost better than his own. But the idea of it attached to a warm, three-dimensional body seemed impossible. Through the crack in the curtains he could see the eggplant-colored sky outside, and the misery of the months to come unrolled in his mind like a carpet dropped carelessly downstairs: the decline of the temperature, the diminishing day-light hours, a terrible, inevitable descent into the hell of the holiday season. The decorations were already up at the bakery. Pretty soon all of Ku'damm would be alight with white lights, and the little Christmas markets would appear all over the city like elfin villages. Then next Sunday, the first Advent, the floodgates would open. Cookie-baking parties and colleagues setting up networks of Secret Santas, gas stations handing out cardboard advent calendars filled with chocolate; waitresses in restaurants in red stocking hats, local Bavarians calling out to him cheerfully, with the greeting *God Bless.* And in the diminishing December light, as the season picked up momentum, the people around him would retreat inside into their warm little worlds behind closed doors, to their Secret Santas and hymn concerts and their plans to roast goose with their families, opening presents, getting fat together on stollen. He closed his eyes thinking that he would do anything at all to get out of Berlin before Christmas. He had no children, no parents, no siblings, few close friends and Heike hadn't called all day. He was going to be alone through the holidays. He was going to grow old here alone in this room. Walter pressed his fingers against his temples in a futile effort to stop a sudden, urgent flow of tears. Sobbing into the orange insides of his eyelids then, he had a vision of the holiday season in Los Angeles: free candy canes by the cash registers, plastic decorations on summer-green lawns, poinsettia bushes grown tall as trees, people in flip-flops. Instead of endless Bach, there would be happy holiday songs for everyone on the radio: Frank Sinatra and Patti LaBelle, the Muppets! The democracy of Christmastime in California! The sky was blue there every day, as he remembered it. The sun shone even through the smog, even when it rained. Maybe things would have been different for him, maybe they still could be. He was not a superstitious man. He didn't believe in God or feng shui. He didn't throw spilled salt over his left shoulder or read his horoscope or knock wood. But he was desperate now. Like a drowning man grasping at driftwood, he reached out for the one shiny object he saw bobbing on the waves: Tom Cruise was coming to the premiere. Walter decided that it was a sign.

In the grand tradition of English-language names around West Berlin left over from the Army occupation (The John F. Kennedy School, Institute and Friendship Center; the Uncle Tom's Cabin Travel Agency, Riding Club and Nursery School; the Cruise-In Diner, the British-American Lifestyle Shop), Bodo's restaurant was called The Wild West. Its terrace spread around the corner of Knesebeckstrasse and Grolmanstrasse like a fan, facing the garden on Savignyplatz. In the summer its patrons sat outside and admired the view, in the winter they retreated to the yellow walls of the interior dining room. Walter had come up with the name the first time he met Bodo, when they were working together on *Top Gun* and the wall was still up in 1986. Bodo had at that time an incipient career as the voices of both Anthony Edwards and River Phoenix.

"I'm going to open my own restaurant," he told Walter between takes. "Only open for dinner so I can sleep late. Make all my money on wine."

"Here?"

"Why not? You don't think the front line of the Cold War is a good place to open a restaurant?"

"I like to think of this as the last frontier of democracy." Bodo smiled. "Even cowboys have to eat."

As the sound technicians cued the next scene, he threw his empty paper coffee cup toward a garbage can in the corner and made the basket easily. Manifest destiny, thought Walter.

"The Wild West," he said. "You should call it that."

By the summer of 1989, Bodo had enough money to open his doors. Although it was only four months before the Wall came down, no one in West Berlin could have foreseen the radical changes on the immediate horizon. In July, the restaurant's name and American comfort food menu and the rustic touches, like the ranch-style wooden fence around the outer edge of the front terrace, still made sense. The Wild West opened in July and was immediately popular with the actors, directors and film technicians in Bodo's professional circle. By 2001, when most of the other restaurants, galleries and clothing shops had closed up and moved east, abandoning Savignyplatz for the inexpensive real estate now available on the other side of the Wall, The Wild West remained, a cozy relic of stability in an ever-morphing city.

Emboldened by his conversation with Klara, Walter got out of bed and went down to the restaurant for dinner. Bodo quickly came to greet him across the room. He still looked exactly the same as he had in 1986, like a welterweight boxer, blond and fit, light on his feet.

"Look who's here," he called out.

Walter allowed himself to be embraced and climbed onto a stool at the bar that extended across the left-hand side of the restaurant. Elton John crowed over the ceiling speakers. Bodo had a small yellow ribbon attached to his shirt collar with a safety pin. He leaned his back against the wooden counter.

"Let me buy you a drink."

Walter requested a *Weissbier*. "What's with the ribbon?"

"Showing my support for the troops."

"The American troops?"

"Saved our asses once upon a time, didn't they? My mother never stopped talking about the airlift."

When the Soviets cut off road access for nine months in 1948, the American Army delivered packages of food to the starving citizens of West Berlin in planes. Although in fact the planes had landed at Tempelhof airport, Walter had always imagined the food literally falling from the sky: candy into the mouths of children, people standing all over the city with their arms outstretched. He pictured himself waiting in the rubble along Ku'damm, looking up at the heavens. When his beer came, he drank half of it down in one gulp.

"Heike left me."

Bodo nodded.

"She came in last night and gave me these to give to you." He reached over the bar and pulled out a ring of house keys. "Are you okay?"

The keys were cold against the palm of Walter's hand. Many questions presented themselves simultaneously. What did she say? Who was she with? How did she look? Where is she now? He asked none of them. Instead he pushed his empty beer glass toward the bartender, who refilled it and handed it to Bodo, who carried it over to a table out of earshot by the window. They both sat down.

"I'm going to California," he said with finality, as if he had already bought the tickets and packed his bags.

"Going to California?"

In heavily accented English, Bodo sang the title of the Led Zeppelin song, badly. Walter moved around the silverware set at his place. They were exactly the same age, old enough to remember playing air guitar to that song when it first came out.

"When?"

"Soon."

Walter sipped his second beer. A waiter came and he ordered a hamburger.

"Because of Heike?"

"Because a good opportunity just came up and anyway it's time for a change."

He was hesitant to get into details because the rhythm of his friendship with Bodo had long been established: Bodo was the one with the big ideas and Walter was the listener. Bodo took action while Walter plodded predictably forward like a pilgrim toward what felt like an increasingly ephemeral destination. In the fifteen years they'd known each other, Bodo had achieved impressive notoriety as the voice of River Phoenix, gotten married, retired from dubbing on the heels of Phoenix's dramatic death from a drug overdose, had two children and refused to come out of retirement when Anthony Edwards's career took off in Germany with the TV show *ER*, graciously offering the part to a younger, less experienced actor who had since made a great deal of money doing voice-overs for a derivative, safety-oriented pharmaceutical campaign (*"I'm not a doctor, but I play one on TV"*). Throughout, he had maintained a successful restaurant in West Berlin despite the fact that everyone else had moved to Mitte. Walter, meanwhile, had been living in the same rental apartment he took over from a friend in the summer of 1985 when he returned from his first, failed stint in California. He had been doing Tom Cruise since early 1986, had had a series of unsuccessful relationships, gained fifteen kilos, lost his hair, kept his considerable earnings in a simple savings account that accrued a paltry floating interest rate of 1.5 to 3 percent a year and had eaten almost the same meal, at the same restaurant, almost every night since it opened. Over the years, Bodo had suggested endless possibilities to Walter: summerhouses on the Baltic Sea, new-economy investments, Pan-Asian restaurants and other explorations into the world of ethnic cuisine. Walter had never, on his own, offered up a plan like moving to another country, in particular the very country where they both knew he'd lost his way once.

The confidence he had felt when he was alone with Tom Cruise at home on Replay was fading now like a daydream.

"What kind of opportunity would take you, of all places, back to California?"

Walter looked into his beer for support.

"In December, Tom Cruise is coming to Berlin for the premiere of the film I start next week, so I'm going to talk to him about getting started in Hollywood." The plan solidified in his mind as he spoke of it aloud. "He's a producer now. Maybe he can use me for something. Otherwise he can introduce me around. He has connections to the right people."

"I'm sure he's only coming here now to lend his celebrity to the cause."

"What cause?"

"Scientology isn't recognized as a religion here. They've been lobbying to receive church tax status."

"I'm not interested in religion. You know that. That's his private business."

"Then why?"

"Why what?"

"Why should he help you?"

"Sixteen percent of his box office comes from the German-language screenings. Do you know how much that is, total, since 1986?"

"No."

"Three hundred and twenty-eight million dollars, give or take."

"You've already been paid for your work."

"It's not about the money. I want to work again as a real actor. Somewhere else, somewhere I don't have to deal with everyone remembering me from before. Look, I'm still talented. I just need the right project." He realized that this last statement sounded particularly pathetic, but strained to keep his confidence afloat. "I'm not some crazy, delusional fan. Tom and I have a professional relationship. I feel like I know him. I'm sure he'll help me out."

Bodo motioned to the bartender for a cigarette.

"Everybody feels like they know Tom Cruise. It's his job to make us feel that way, isn't it? It isn't real. He isn't real."

Only recently Walter had been thinking the same thing.

"Of course he's real," he said now. "Look beyond the celebrity thing. He's just a guy like you or me."

"People that famous are not regular guys."

"I know a thing or two about celebrity, Bodo. I've been there, you know. I never stopped being myself."

"What, during *Schönes Wochenende*?" Bodo smoked, considering Walter's head as if it were a piece of fruit whose edibility was in question.

"I realize that you're going through a tough time," he said after a while.

"That's really not the point."

"Okay, then: I respect that you have a professional relationship with him. But owing to that relationship, he cannot take you to California, because he needs you to stay here and do his German voice, right?"

Walter's hamburger arrived.

"But even if that weren't the case," said Bodo, "what makes you think you're going to meet him when he comes to the premiere? What makes you think he's even aware of you at all?"

Walter silently fished bits of bun from his teeth with his tongue. In sixteen years this thought had never crossed his mind. Of course Tom Cruise was aware of him, of course he knew his films were regularly dubbed into German, right? Bodo dropped his voice now to a much lower register.

"Dubbing is behind-the-scenes work, man," he said. "In Germany it's a big deal to be doing the voice for a box office star. Around those moles at Deutsche Synchron you get credit for that sixteen percent. I won't argue with that, it's an impressive statistic. But when Tom Cruise comes to town, it's his show. No one is going to say, 'Hey Tom, here's the man responsible for all those hits in Germany.' They're going to keep you as far away from him as possible. Remember that story you told me about Disneyland? About that guy you worked with there, the one that played the suited character. Goofy?"

Walter put down the burger. He wished he had never told Bodo that he'd worked at Disneyland when he lived in California. His year as Prince Charming, a face character in the Cinderella Panorama, was something he tried to forget. Given the chance, he'd happily erase everything that happened that year from memory, but because he'd told Bodo about Disneyland during a drunken late night long ago he was stuck with it, like a stubborn stain on a favorite shirt.

"What story?"

"About the family who were led out the back by mistake and saw the actor playing Goofy with his head off, smoking a cigarette. You told me they sued Disneyland for emotional distress because their kids were so upset to learn that Goofy wasn't real."

"What about it?"

Bodo held the filter of his cigarette like a joint. He took a last toke before putting it out.

"They won, didn't they?" He exhaled. "Not to be harsh, buddy, but in this situation, you're the guy in the Goofy suit. Nobody wants to know where that voice is really coming from."

4

Hope looked down at the schnitzel laid out before her by a middle-aged waiter who didn't even crack a smile. On the plate with it were a soggy cucumber salad and roasted potatoes.

"Besides the English," Dave was saying, "Germans were the biggest immigrant group to the United States. It's funny, because people so rarely refer to themselves as German-American. I think they gave that up during the First World War. But if you look around us here, we'd blend right in."

She looked around the dimly lit restaurant. Twenty empty white-draped tables spread out from where they sat in the center. The only other people in the room were an old couple who had not said a word to each other in twenty minutes, which meant that they could not possibly be Americans, she thought. Americans talked throughout the meal, nonstop, as if the whole point of going out to eat was not nourishment but conversation, as if silence were dangerous, or at least an admission of failure.

"If you want to see the German roots of American culture," she said, "just look at this food."

"What about it?"

"Chicken patties and french fries."

"This is veal."

"I'm telling you, we ate more or less exactly this once a week when I was growing up in Missouri."

Dave groaned in protest.

"Everything else we ate too," she insisted. "Now that I think about it. Frankfurters, hamburgers. Even their names are German."

"The greatest legacy of the massive German immigration is the hot dog?"

"It is our national dish."

He leaned forward, so that his nose was very close to her face.

"This is a nice restaurant, Hope. I just wanted to take you somewhere nice."

The winter after their wedding, they had spent one week in the British Virgin Islands on a belated honeymoon, a gift from his parents who, once they got over the initial shock of the marriage, tried to make amends. The native islanders and other tourists there had been completely exotic to both Hope and Dave, so that the usual black and white differences in their own backgrounds, often the subject of tension and dismay, were reduced to inconsequential shades of gray. They had entered into a kind of cozy bubble, as she remembered it now, in which their only point of reference, their only reality, was each other. It had been an awfully nice way to experience a foreign country. The young, tanned couple in the Virgin Islands would have snuggled up against the strangeness of it all in Berlin: the unfriendly waiter, the cultural history of the hot dog, the soggy cucumber salad. As it was, what might have been grounds for reconciliation was having the opposite effect. She wondered if the problem with Germany was the very fact that they could blend right in here. She wondered if it was the inevitable fate of a childless couple to grow apart.

The waiter returned to refill their wine. Hope watched the neighborhood out the window for signs of life. Earlier, she thought she'd recognized a man walking by as the neighbor who had walked through their argument at the beginning of the week, but his short, thick frame was hunched over his pockets and she didn't see his face. He had disappeared into another restaurant across the street. Not another person had walked by since.

"This is a ghost town," she said, when the waiter had gone. "Where are all the people? They aren't out on the street, they aren't home watching TV. It's not even eight P.M."

"Maybe they're working."

"So late?"

"Most people do work past three in the afternoon."

She might have retorted that most people did not have to get up at six, as she had done every morning in her seven years as a third-grade teacher, but she didn't take Dave's bait.

47

"It must have been busy here once. That's all I mean. They would never have built all these big buildings if there hadn't been people to live in them. Now the neighborhood seems abandoned."

"Most places seem abandoned compared to New York."

"Maybe. But it must have been different here a hundred years ago. I would have liked to see that. Wouldn't you?"

In the past, they had liked to discuss the New York of various bygone eras: Fifth Avenue by horse-drawn carriage in the 1870s, Central Park during the Summer of Love.

"I don't think so."

"Why not?"

Dave wiped his mouth with his napkin.

"Because I like my Germans guilty," he said.

"What is that supposed to mean?"

"They're nice to me now."

Hope let her head fall to the side and stared at his neck. In the past she had often slept with her face buried into the soft base of his hairline.

"Fifteen minutes ago you said we could blend right in if we wanted to."

"I guess I meant you. If you never opened your mouth no one would know you were a foreigner here. In my case, they wouldn't necessarily see that I'm Jewish, but a hundred years ago I would have felt a lot different from everyone else."

"Now you don't?"

"I do, but now it works to my advantage." He laughed. "Let's just say that for me, at least, this is the best time yet to be living in Berlin."

He likes it here, she thought. Her surprise was not so much an indictment of the city but a realization that his experience here was completely separate from her own. In New York they had had different jobs but a single shared domestic life. They had cooked together, seen friends together. Now, he had been in Berlin for three months, since July, and she for one, since October. But the two months apart in the middle, August and September, had created a space between them. He liked it here, but she didn't know why. He went to work, but she had no idea what he did there. He spent days away, and she didn't even have a mental image of how he spent his time. When he practiced his German, long-winded soliloquies on waiters or the super, on anyone who would listen, she could not understand a word he said. It was as if they had been apart for a year or more, or worse: as if the only thing that had been keeping them together for the six years previous had been the rhythm of daily life which, now upset, could no longer provide the necessary glue.

Dave's phone rang, startling both of them. It vibrated loudly against the table, where it had been sitting throughout the meal, and danced up to the edge of his plate.

"Work," he whispered, visibly relieved to have an excuse to step outside. "I have to take this. It'll just take a minute."

She watched him through the window. Pacing the sidewalk, he moved one hand in a circle for emphasis, smiling, and for a moment she felt jealous of the colleague on the other end of the line. Because the look on his face reminded her of an evening, late into her pregnancy, when they already knew that the baby was going to be a boy. At the Chinese restaurant around the corner from their New York apartment, they had each made up a list of names, then traded the lists facedown across the table, lifting the edges of the paper with trepidation both exaggerated and real. Out there on the telephone now, pacing the cold Berlin sidewalk, the look on his face was exactly as it had been that night in New York, when they finally turned over their lists to reveal the very same first choice.

"Wein?"

She let the waiter finish off the bottle into her glass. Still on the phone, Dave stood flush up to the window, only a few feet away, and she found herself mesmerized by his features, at once totally familiar and yet strange, like a pair of shoes whose shape has changed with use. She stared at his features and wondered, yet again, what their son's face might have looked like. When there was no more wine in her glass she tapped lightly on the window.

"I'm going home," she mouthed, pointing at the door.

She expected Dave to protest, to hang up and come back inside, order another bottle of wine, dessert, a coffee, but he just smiled back and made an enthusiastic thumbs-up.

"See you there." He enunciated each syllable with exaggerated relish, like a mime on the street.

Hope could sense the waiter's worried eyes on her back so she turned to him and pointed to Dave's jacket, which was still hanging over the back of his chair.

"He'll pay," she said in English.

The word for money was the only relevant one that came to mind. It came out like an afterthought.

"*Geld*," she said as she put on her coat. "*Mein Mann.*"

The waiter must have understood, because he didn't try to stop her.

5

The men's bathroom at The Wild West had film stills from Westerns hanging in frames all over the walls like family pictures. Walter splashed cold water on his face and put his hands on either side of the basin, leaning forward to catch his breath. As the water dripped off into the sink, he looked up into the mirror above it and examined his own reflection. The monster stared back at him aggressively over the edge of his hair, a few days' gray-flecked stubble coated his jaw and a second chin peeked out beneath it like a drop shadow. His skin was pale. His round eyes and thick eyebrows sagged together over dark circles: smile-shaped scars etched into the tops of his cheeks. He ran two fingers along them, pulling the skin smooth from his nose out to the edge of his eyes. On the wall to his right were framed photographs of famous cowboys: John Wayne, Henry Fonda, the Marlboro Man. Included in the collection was a picture of himself aged nineteen in character, sitting on a horse. A cigarette was hanging off his bottom lip.

. . .

In 1980, Walter was discovered at the proverbial soda fountain, plucked from oblivion in his small village in the Alps to join the cast of the popular television drama *Schönes Wochenende*. The title meant *Have a Nice Weekend*. The soda fountain, in his case, was a large outdoor public swimming pool filled with screaming children, one of thousands dotting the West German landscape like shiny blue plastic bobbles against the green. He had just finished high school and was working for the summer as a lifeguard until his fifteen months of compulsory military service began in September. Outside of work, he spent most of his free time lifting weights in his father's basement and listening to Journey's first album, *Departure* (specifically the song "Any Way You Want It"), rewound again and again and played at top volume. His ambitions, insofar as he had any, were to be a student for as long as possible and thus avoid working altogether. He had no prior acting experience. When Klara came up to him in his lifeguard chair and invited him to an audition the following week, her frosted hair teased up like a feather boa, she stood out gloriously from the crowd. Everyone at the pool noticed when she handed Walter her business card.

"All that weight training's finally paying off, Pretty Boy," the other guys said afterward.

They were impressed, of course. Walter himself was impressed, but he wasn't surprised. Instead he had felt something rising in him like the slow swell of a warm tropical tide. It wasn't arrogance or greed or even vanity so much as satisfaction. He had been waiting for someone to come along and recognize his potential. He had average grades and no unique talents to speak of; he was short in a country of very tall men; but he was going places. Turning Klara's card over in his hand that day by the pool, he knew that somewhere deep inside himself he had always expected to be famous. Years later, in his thirties, he happened to read a magazine interview with Gwyneth Paltrow in which she said matter-of-factly that she always knew she was going to be famous too.

"Ask anyone else who's famous now," she said in the article. "They'll tell you the same thing."

Reading this he felt an uncomfortable combination of self-recognition and shame. That feeling wasn't prescient at all; most people expected to become famous. The few who actually did could claim to have predicted it, while everyone else was still waiting for their moment to arrive. The problem was that if it came, there was no way of knowing how long it would last.

Schönes Wochenende had made Walter famous right away. At the end of that summer, he moved his legal residence to West Berlin, an island of democracy in a sea of communism that garnered a special privilege: its male citizens were relieved of the military service required of all other German nineteen-year-olds. Although the show was shot in the countryside near Munich, by moving officially to Berlin at eighteen, he was allowed to go directly into television. There were only two channels in Germany in those days. They showed primarily detective shows, American imports like *Dallas* and old movies. *Schönes Wochenende,* about a city family from Munich who moved full-time to their weekend house in the countryside, was one of the few dramas actually produced in Germany, and the majority of viewers tuned into it each week. Walter's character, Hans, was the troubled son of a local farmer who seduced the city family's daughter, Julia.

"The James Dean character," the producers told the press, spinning a frenzy that lifted Walter up like a tornado.

They made sure that when Hans fixed his blue eyes on Julia, teenage girls all over Germany swooned. In cities he could hardly walk down the street without a swarm of young fans trailing perpetually just a few steps behind. Even their mothers asked him for autographs. He perfected a dazzling smile and patiently signed his name on proffered subway tickets, the insides of book covers, T-shirts and, occasionally, the pocket diaries of particularly lovesick thirteen-year-old girls. The seasoned television people around him commented among themselves that for a nineteen-year-old kid from *am Arsch der Welt*, the ass of the world, he took his newfound fame impressively in stride. But the truth was that he was used to being treated differently in his hometown. First, because his mother was American, then because of the tragic circumstances surrounding her death. He could speak in local dialect, he could draw a map of the forests around his village in his sleep; he was born there, but from the beginning he was set apart. And now, he had not been back in almost twenty years, since his father's funeral in 1983, when he quit the show at its peak and left for California.

Although he rarely used it outside of the house, Walter had learned to speak English first. Later on, as a teenager, he picked up vocabulary from song lyrics. Neon lights in the fog, the words rose up to him through the dense rock ballads of the late 1970s and early '80s. In 1983, he arrived in Hollywood with nearly perfect English, but casting directors had trouble looking past his origins. In two years he got only a one-liner bit part as an SS guard in a World War II film. Still, it was a bona fide Hollywood production: quasi-famous principals, elaborate Warsaw ghetto sets, M&M's at the craft service table separated by color into individual bowls.

"You do not even exist," he said to a skinny Jewish prisoner, who was played by an Italian-American.

Then he spit. His scene took fourteen takes because his accent was too good.

"Make it sound more German," the director said. "Think Arnold, c'mon."

Maybe what Klara said was true and he had never had a chance there, but at the time it felt like a step in the right direction. Maybe things would have been different for him. He would never know. In the end, his time in California was cut short before the film came out in the theaters. He left town too soon to find out what might have happened next.

Walter pulled some paper towels out of a dispenser next to the sink and mopped at his damp face without taking his eyes off the picture. He was still trying to conjure the feeling of the young man sitting before him on a horse. The picture had been taken for an article on up-and-coming stars in a German celebrity magazine. He remembered the shoot, the feeling of the warm horse beneath him and the smell of manure at the farm, as if he were touching it all to his fingertips through very thick gloves; the distance traveled since then felt much longer than twenty years. It had been freezing that day. The cigarette had been added to explain the cloud of breath around his mouth. Drying his hands, Walter counted off the dates in his head. The picture was taken in February 1981, which meant that he had been on *Schönes Wochenende* for only five months at the time. Acting was still an adventure to him then, not a career. He threw the wad of used paper towels into a bin under the sink, finally seeing himself clearly at nineteen.

"*Ich war so glücklich,*" he said under his breath. "I was so happy."

He touched the picture lightly as if he might recapture the sensation through the glass, but it struck him that *glücklich*, the German translation of the English adjective *happy*, was also the word for *lucky*. This conflation of what are considered to be two distinct emotions by Americans had caused him many dubbing problems over the years. Now he pulled apart the German word and reimagined the same statement in English. Not happy. *Lucky.* That was it: sitting on that warm horse twenty years ago in freezing cold weather, playing it up for the camera, he had felt lucky. It was something he had rarely experienced since.

He left The Wild West without finishing his dinner. He waited until Bodo was distracted by something in the kitchen and paid his bill without saying goodbye. The streets of his neighborhood were quiet: an old woman was walking a little terrier on the block up ahead, shuffling her feet and speaking to it under her breath. In the playground at the corner teenagers lounged over a rusty jungle gym, smoking. Ornate art nouveau façades, built before World War II, switched off every few buildings with the practical concrete apartment blocks built in the 1950s to fill in the bombed-out blanks. Orange light glowed in the windows of other people's apartments as if to underscore the dark emptiness awaiting him at home. When he'd first moved to Charlottenburg sixteen years earlier, the streets he walked now had been busy with nightlife. But since the inclusion of its eastern half, the city had completely shifted its topography, pushing Charlottenburg to the western fringe, so that he might as well have moved to the suburbs. In 2001, the only reason anyone who was anyone ever came back to the old neighborhood was to eat at The Wild West, and when they ran into Walter there they feigned disbelief that he still lived around the corner. He was sure they laughed about it once he was out of earshot.

"What better place for that relic of the 1980s," they probably said, "than Charlottenburg?"

Gone were the bars and crowds of his youth, and in their place only hair salons and jewelry stores, women of a certain age who wore tent dresses and dyed their hair bright red, and yuppie families with children. On his way home from Bodo's, Walter occasionally still saw ghosts of the artists and musicians he'd partied with in the 1980s, but not tonight. At Zwiebelfisch, the pub where he'd spent many a drunk early morning after dancing all night at Dschungel, two old guys sat alone with their beer by the window. At the jazz bar A-Trane, the only local nightclub to survive the change, musicians warmed up before an audience of four. He looked in automatically but continued toward home, pulling his jacket collar up against his neck.

. . .

He took his mobile phone out of his pocket and checked for messages but there weren't any. The display told him only that it was 9:17 P.M. When he'd lived with Heike, the weeks had gone by quickly: Monday to Friday, Friday to Sunday. The past few days now seemed longer to him than the entire two years they were together. Her house keys jingled in his pocket as he walked. Finally liberated from the shackles of his bad attitude, she was probably out at a club in the East with some skinny guy her own age. He pictured a room of young people in I LOVE NY T-shirts, rocking out to show their solidarity with heartbroken widows and children five thousand kilometers away, then stopped at the corner of Schlüterstrasse, dizzy and out of breath. He bent over and inhaled deeply. In a third-floor apartment above his head he could see the silhouettes of a couple getting ready to go to sleep and felt a sudden, urgent longing to join them. He could just curl up and sleep at the foot of their bed, he thought. They could sing to him. He wondered if they knew any American lullabies. His mother's singing voice had been higher than her speaking voice but clear and pretty. *"The river Jordan is deep and wide."* That's how it went. *"Milk and honey on the other side."* By the time the light upstairs switched off and the window went black, tears were burning at the back of Walter's eyes.

His gaze fixed at street level, he forced himself forward to the next block, where a policeman paced in front of what appeared to be a residential building, hands clasped behind his back. He was the same cop pacing most Friday evenings in this spot, half asleep in his silly green uniform and cap. Only in Germany did the government play down the authority of the police by making them look ridiculous. In that outfit it was hard to imagine this man tackling terrorists or dismantling a bomb. That his very presence was more likely to attract attention to the synagogue hidden behind the front door than protect it was something the city never seemed to consider: it was a matter of pride and principle that Jewish organizations deserved state protection. Walter leaned against a wall and wiped his eyes. The door of the synagogue looked like any other, but it was just a false front, like a city backdrop on a film set. Only once had he ventured close enough to see the freestanding building inside, its stained-glass windows and a small front garden. To be allowed in you had to show identification and register with security, which he had never done. He had only hovered here at the edge of the block, listening closely for the cantor's melody. He liked to imagine an old woman standing alone in a cool dark room, singing with her arms out and her eyes closed, but he was unable to picture the congregation. The only local Jews he was aware of were the glamorous Russians who double-parked their cars on Fasanenstrasse while they ran into Gucci, people who surely had something more exciting to do on a Friday night. The very thought of joining the mysterious men and women inside the temple made him feel ashamed. How many of his acquaintances claimed to have had a transformative experience in Israel? How often had he heard someone refer to himself or herself as twelve percent or even five percent Jewish? What did that mean? It was a contemporary German cliché, he thought, to wish for salvation if not merely comfort, or acceptance, from Jews. The cop came back Walter's way and thrust out his chin, to remind him that he had no business here.

As he headed home reluctantly down Schlüterstrasse, Walter had the eerie feeling he was leaving his last contact with civilization behind. It was cold and dark and few cars came up the street. Glued up on the wall to his left were a slew of posters advertising dance parties in Soviet-cool spaces in the East, abandoned offices of the GDR government or rooms that once housed the airline of the former Czechoslovakia. Heike was probably at one of these parties tonight. The wide shot: her lithe body snapping like a rubber band to a throbbing electronic beat. The close-up: beads of sweat dripping down into the silky hollow between her breasts. The hamburger he'd eaten earlier backed halfway up his throat. The poster at the end of the wall caught his eye because it stood out from the rest in its graphic simplicity. Against a plain black background, a pale woman was holding two fists up high like a champion. The frame cut off just above the nipples and below her cleavage. She was looking out at him from under low-tilted brows, and he walked toward her as the tears came, pressing his face into the smooth, cool paper. Only after he had been crying for a few moments did he notice that the old woman he'd seen up the street was staring at him, muttering to her dog and shaking her head with disapproval. He looked up at the poster he was hugging and realized it was an ad for porn. Above the woman's head it said, in English, in red capital letters: TIME FOR ACTION! He ran the last few steps home.

· · ·

The bright light in the lobby of Walter's apartment building caught him by surprise, then he saw the American woman from the stoop waiting by the elevator. She was wearing the same trench coat, but clothes underneath it now, and shoes. He was considering an immediate retreat when he heard the humming. It was a familiar tune, but he couldn't put his finger on it. The lobby, a once luxuriously appointed place, had seen better days. The marble steps were worn down in the middle from almost a century of footsteps in exactly the same place, ceiling details were obscured by dust; but the acoustics were perfect. The cavernous space gave the woman's high-pitched humming the clarity of a violin solo performed in a concert hall. Walter swayed back and forth at the threshold, soothed by the music, wondering if he was imagining things. In his hometown, people in crisis were often comforted by visions of the Virgin Mary in breakfast cereal or dishwater bubbles. If he prayed, he thought, he would have prayed for this. He straightened his jacket, took a few careful steps closer toward her and unpacked his best attempt at a dazzling smile.

"*Guten Abend,*" he said. "Good evening."

She was lovely. Her nose was long, slightly too large for her fine-boned face. Delicate laughter lines spread out from her deep-set eyes. At work he'd made a private study of how different languages and even accents formed their speakers' mouths over time: the mouths of the British bent down at the sides, the Italians' stretched back from the middle, and those of the French curled forward like they were blowing irritated kisses; Germans pulled their mouths together like they were nibbling little seeds between their front teeth. Even if he hadn't already heard her speak English, he would have known this woman wasn't German, because her full lips turned up at the corners as if she were smiling inside about a private joke, as only American lips did. She nodded at him and continued to hum, and the desperation he had been feeling moments earlier gave way to high-pitched enthusiasm. This woman came from California, he told himself. She had a tawny-skinned, wholesome look about her that immediately conjured the feeling of someplace warm. A whole life flashed through his mind in Super 8: there she was waddling across the fresh-cut lawn in Pampers and ringlets, giggling in a classroom, dancing at a bonfire beach party, making out with a boyfriend in a VW Cabriolet.

The elevator opened and he followed her into it, recalling the calm look on her face a few days earlier as she watched the man walk away. Her boyfriend? Her husband? Her brother. The elevator was small and old-fashioned. Once inside, Walter was close enough to smell her hair, or whisper in her ear if he leaned forward, or bury his face in her neck. She rested her eyes on the middle distance between herself and the door, and in his head he followed the tune she was humming like the ball in a karaoke video. He was able to anticipate the upcoming notes and even the lyrics, but still unable to name the song, a pop hit from years ago, the kind that lived on forever at the supermarket. Her version was nice, he thought, the acoustic original pared down to the kind of simple melody hippies used to play on guitars. When the old elevator lurched into its ascent she stopped humming. Then she continued out loud.

"Forgotten what I started fighting for," she sang under her breath.

It was clear she hadn't noticed that the song slipped out her mouth. When she took a long pause to inhale, he held his breath. They were so close to each other they might have kissed. The elevator creaked slowly past the first floor, then past the second.

"It's time to bring this ship into the shore," she sang, *"and throw away the oars. Forever."*

The next line lingered on Walter's lips. If this were a musical, he thought, they would break into a duet at the chorus. They would start off a cappella in the elevator, like Gene Kelly and Debbie Reynolds. The orchestra would join in as they danced onto the landing, singing together. *I can't fight this feeling anymore!* As they twirled down the hallway, the neighbors would stick out their heads, then slam their doors in unison. Walter and the beautiful woman would just laugh, snapping their fingers, swinging their hips. The number would wind down at her front door. Arched back, dramatic kiss. In fact, they were still standing side by side in the elevator, but he grinned at her anyway, and when she saw his smile she stopped singing abruptly, covered her mouth with one hand. She was embarrassed! He wanted to tell her not to be. He wanted to say it was beautiful, but the English words escaped him. *Tom Cruise has never made a musical,* is what he was thinking. They could talk about that in California. They could develop the project together next year. Walter was still considering whether or not the singing parts should be dubbed into German when the elevator reached the third floor and the woman stepped out.

6

Hope woke up late and went down to the end of her street to a Starbucks look-alike called Balzac, where she ordered a cup of coffee. That Balzac had its menu board in English (the unique nomenclature of Starbucks English) and a take-out system that required little contact with its employees meant that she often bought all her meals there, listening to the same collection of hits from the eighties that played on shuffle over the loudspeakers. Today, she had walked in to "Careless Whisper," followed closely by "Total Eclipse of the Heart." Normally she took her coffee to go and drank it back at the apartment, but after what had happened the night before she determined to stay. She was clearly spending way too much time alone. How long had she been singing out loud? Maybe she'd been doing it on and off for days, on the street and in her German class, in her sleep. She found herself an armchair by the window with her coffee. The night before she had rushed into her apartment from the elevator and done something she rarely did anymore: she called her mother.

"At least he smiled," said Hope. "If he hadn't smiled I wouldn't have noticed. I might have just gone on singing for days."

The song had been stuck in her head for a week: "Can't Fight This Feeling," an REO Speedwagon hit from high school that she'd never liked, even when it was popular, but like most of the Top 40 hits from her youth she remembered all the words. She hadn't heard this particular song for fifteen years, but in Berlin it was on all the time.

"What about Dave?"

Dave had come home after she was already asleep and left the house before she got up.

"He's busy, Mom. I don't see him much these days, and since I rarely speak to anyone else, the sound of my own voice is becoming unfamiliar."

"After what you've been through anyone would be distracted."

"Or maybe I'm going crazy."

Her mother's preternaturally positive personality did not allow for a lot of soul-searching. She preferred solution-oriented conversations, which is why Hope had been avoiding her until now.

"Nonsense. You just need to make some friends there. Actually, you really only need one friend, in my experience. This is what you do: Tomorrow go to the busiest place you can think of—I mean a nice, busy place, not the train station—take a seat and look around. When you see an attractive woman who looks friendly, introduce yourself."

"What if she doesn't speak English?"

"Everyone speaks English. A nice girlfriend in the neighborhood will do you a world of good."

. . .

So it was that Hope found herself holding a cup of coffee with both hands and looking around at Balzac for a friend. The median age of the patrons was about twenty-two, presumably due to the university across the street, and she tried to count how many of them were smoking. Too many, so she counted how many were not smoking instead: four, including herself. Germans smoked like they thought it was good for them, she thought. "Uptown Girl" played over the loudspeakers and she watched the students at a table to her left. They were unbelievably young and yet old-fashioned: inexpensive clothes and obvious makeup, big hair, acne. In New York, it had seemed to her that college students were much more sophisticated nowadays. They owned companies already, wore designer clothes, had perfect skin. The students at Balzac reminded her instead of her own college friends years ago, hanging around in lazy groups of four or five, fixing each other's makeup. Occasionally, one or the other would burst out into laughter so hysterical that she had to double over completely to recover. Hope drank her coffee and turned to face the tall, curved window stretching around the entire front of the café, like a movie screen, capturing the street corner in action. People blew by in both directions clutching newspapers, briefcases, handbags and groceries, illuminated as if deliberately by pale northern light. A man carrying his small daughter on his shoulders caught her attention. The girl was bundled up in a pink jacket and a hat and asked to be taken down. When she hit the ground running and tripped on the sidewalk, Hope's entire body jerked forward as if to pick her up, spilling hot coffee on her thighs.

She winced in pain, but it was the girl's father who reached for her outside, who dusted off her knees and used the inside of his coat cuff to wipe her tears. Hope forced herself to close her eyes until they were gone.

She wiped up the spilled coffee with a napkin and tried to concentrate on the task at hand. She didn't see a friendly-looking woman to pick up anywhere and befriend. But if not here, then where? There were fifteen other students in her German class, but on the first day, when they went around in a circle to give their names and their countries of origin, it had not been lost on her that both past and current enemies of the United States were well represented: *Vietnam, Russland, der Irak.* To her right had been two men from *Saudi Arabien,* to her left another from *Marokko.* She was the only woman in the class with the exception of a very young one from *Kuba,* married to a German pensioner three times her age. When the introduction circle had arrived at Hope's place, she had cleared her throat.

"*Ich komme aus New York.*"

The announcement had been followed by a pause in conversation. The teacher nodded sympathetically and the other students looked away, as if she had admitted to a terrible handicap that made them feel disgusted, helpless and guilty all at once. In the days since, they had all settled into regular seats and stayed as far away from her as possible. Since the majority were men from the Middle East and northern Africa, they took the front and shared a single Arabic–German dictionary, the Russians formed a group in the middle row and the two men from Vietnam—brothers, apparently—

sat together. She had taken a place at the back with the Cuban teenage bride who dropped out after the first two weeks. These days, she sat alone.

She pulled her textbook out of her bag and opened it up to the Christmas calendar that was her homework. Much to her parents' dismay she had not actually celebrated Christmas since she met Dave, but even as a child it had never been her favorite holiday (uncomfortable dress, turkey and stuffing the second time in a month, boring television). She had always preferred Halloween and Easter (trick-or-treating, egg hunts, active holidays with things to do) but the textbook made German Christmas seem interesting. Pictures were laid out along the month of December. There were many more days to celebrate here than she remembered in the United States. One picture showed a pine wreath laid flat and decorated with four large candles. The book said that Christmas trees were only decorated on the evening of the 24th and then with real candles, not electric lights; it said that Sankt Nikolaus came on the 6th to bring children candy, and the *Weihnachtsmann* came with presents the 24th, although the difference between these two characters was unclear. Both were old men with beards, red hats, big bellies. Her favorite picture was of a girl kneeling down before a shoe filled with candy. The American version of the same picture would have shown one of her own third-grade students, she thought, his or her brightly colored sneaker stuffed with candy bars, the Velcro closures hanging open. Somehow the simple laces of the brown leather German shoe suggested that an idyllic childhood was still possible here, if no longer in New York. She hoped so, because like the rounded edges of phone booths in Paris, or the pink of the Italian newspaper, the German Christmas rituals outlined in her textbook satisfied her expectations of Europe. She was comforted to have found something charming here.

On her way to class she carefully followed the street signs leading south, marking off the corners she recognized in an effort not to get lost. She had been in Berlin for a month and it had been overcast every day so far, dry and cold. The sky was gray and the buildings were gray. There were so few people on the street, and so few stores, that the streets were similar one to the next and she often got turned around, mistaking north for south or east for west. She was used to Manhattan's grid. Here, when she got lost, she could not just flag down a yellow cab, because there were no yellow cabs in Berlin, only the occasional curbside group of cream-colored Mercedes waiting for phone calls. So she walked slowly and paid attention. Dave had mentioned that most of the streets in their neighborhood were named after famous educators (he was appealing to her vanity, she thought, but as she had never heard of Mommsen, or Leibniz, or Pestalozzi, the names didn't stick). She clung to the few she remembered, like Kant, searching out memorable landmarks. At the corner of Kant and Leibniz was a sex shop, its exterior covered with life-size photographs of women in black leather bikinis, carrying whips. The photographs were lit from behind like ads in an airport, so that even in the dark, Hope could see this corner glowing from a few blocks away. Now, as she came around it, a man in a black coat approached her. His hair was cropped short and he wore a small black leather cap.

"Excuse me," he started in English, enunciating his words, "do you know where I could find——?"

"You're American," she said, grasping at his familiar accent.

"No. Well, yes, but I'm giving it up."

As he turned his head fully toward her, she noticed that he had only one ear. On the other side of his head were only a hole and a scar. He was tall and she had to look up at him.

"I'm from L.A. but I'm applying for German citizenship now. I'm finished with the States."

"Why?"

He turned his head again, so that the good ear was aimed her way.

"Why? Because I don't want to be liable for their foreign policy."

Hope held her handbag close.

"Whose?"

"The American government's."

"I don't understand."

"As an American citizen you are automatically an ambassador when you go abroad. You're a target. You're putting yourself in harm's way, don't you know that? Global politics are personal now. It's all personal."

She examined his face, pink in the reflected light of the photographs. That she could recall, the only two people to famously lose an ear were the painter van Gogh and the teenage son of the Getty family who had been kidnapped in Rome in the 1970s. It had been a big story one summer. The kidnappers had sent his ear back to his rich parents when they refused to pay the ransom.

"I have never lived abroad before," she said. "I guess I've never thought much about how America looks from the outside."

"Just be thankful you got out when you did."

"Of the United States?"

"Well, yeah."

It was one thing to travel, she thought. It was another to give up being American altogether, which seemed illicit and impossible, like some kind of dirty joke. Even if you lived abroad for the rest of your life, you still had to file a U.S. tax return every year. Dave would have dismissed this guy as a nutcase.

"How do you know that I got out in time?"

"You're here now, aren't you?"

When Hope tried to picture herself as a member of some other national tribe, only stereotypes came to mind: the French Hope with a beret and cigarette, the Argentinean Hope dancing tango. The idea had nonetheless been introduced. Had she not raged at the American government? How much time had she spent pondering the bewildering fact that it was illegal in the United States to issue a birth certificate and a death certificate on the same day? She had been over the details at the hospital and at city hall. It had all been explained to her, but it still didn't make any sense. She had received the death certificate, the ashes, nothing else. And yet, how could someone die without ever being alive? If a death certificate marked the end of a life, then didn't that life, however short, deserve validation?

"Think of this as an opportunity to start again," said the one-eared man.

She nodded, because Dave had been saying the same thing to her for weeks but she liked it better coming from a stranger. She wondered if Americans on the streets of foreign cities routinely spoke to one another this way, cutting right to the chase like estranged members of the same screwed-up family. She was late for class but considered his point. The global might be personal now, but how about the other way around? In September, when she came out of her downtown building to see people covered in white powder running for their lives, she had not been entirely surprised to find the outside world finally reflecting her inner chaos. Maybe Berlin was an opportunity to start again. In the photograph shining beside her, a woman in blond cornrows and leather touched her tongue seductively to her upper lip. The man put his hands in his pockets.

"Anyway," he said, "do you know where I can find an ATM machine?"

Hope laughed, because she actually knew the answer to his question, and pointed out the bank at the northwest corner of Savignyplatz.

As she walked the last few blocks to class, the REO Speedwagon song came back into her head and she sang along quietly under her breath. *Even as I wander, I'm keeping you in sight.* Maybe it had been so long, that this kind of music was actually cool again, come back in a sudden wave of misguided nostalgia. *You're a candle in the window on a cold, dark winter's night.* Then again, it hadn't really been cool the first time. It had been popular, inescapable for a while, and then it had disappeared. Maybe it had just moved to Berlin to start over? The young tan couple in the Virgin Islands would have had a good laugh over this possibility, thought Hope, but now she could hardly imagine such a conversation with Dave. She wished she had asked the one-eared man for his phone number. The only other person she could think of was her neighbor from the elevator. He wasn't the woman in a busy place that her mother told her to look for, but he did smile when she sang. She could track him down and ask him. Maybe the cheesy music of her youth, long given up for dead, had been playing in a loop over the loudspeakers at Balzac every day since the last time she heard it on American radio fifteen years ago. Maybe all those musicians survived and were living on here in Berlin. The image of them all on the plane made her feel almost optimistic: Bonnie Tyler and Bryan Adams and Billy Joel, Cher and Steve Perry all piled into economy class like a summer school glee club trip. Bryan Adams had an acoustic guitar in his lap. Billy Joel was playing air piano against the backs of the seats. The others snapped their fingers and hummed, eyes closed, keeping the beat, rocking and rolling across the Atlantic. The party plane to Berlin, thought Hope. She was there too, of course, in layered hair and braces, her favorite red jacket from high school with the diagonal zipper, lip gloss, while behind them in the distance, smoke was still rising from the ground in New York.

7

"You're brilliant, you're good-looking, you are handsome."

The original English feedback played into Walter's earphones. On the cinema-size screen above his head, Tom Cruise's toothy smile collapsed backward into the serious expression that preceded it. His character in *Vanilla Sky* was having a conversation at a party that involved many nonverbal cues: raised eyebrows, widened eyes, licked lips. He gesticulated with his arms. His spoken contributions were each cursory and precise, the hardest kind of dialogue to dub accurately into German, which requires more words than English to say the same thing. The translations kept running on too long, so that Walter was still speaking over the grinfinale of the scene. He worked at the words like a masseur kneading a knot in someone's back, pushing and pulling until tight muscles relaxed into the limited space between two shoulder blades. Tom Cruise made the same movements again and again above Walter's head.

"Du bist intelligent, du siehst gut aus, du bist—" Walter stopped midsentence and swore under his breath, *"Scheisse."*

He was standing in complete darkness at a lectern with a microphone. A spotlight shined on the script.

"I'm going to kill *You're good-looking*," he said to the darkness. "It doesn't fit. It's expendable."

"Actually, let's discuss it."

The director was sitting in a mixing booth up a spiral staircase. The six studios at Deutsche Synchron were all the same: large screening rooms downstairs where the sound was recorded, and mixing cabins upstairs where engineers synced it with the precision of air traffic controllers. Dark purple carpet and confetti-flecked wallpaper ran throughout the entire facility. Fluorescent lamps cast the sun-deprived employees in unflattering light. But the unfortunate décor belied the fact that Deutsche Synchron was the most successful dubbing facility in Germany. In the long hallways separating one studio from the next, the posters from Academy Award winners and Hollywood blockbusters hung proudly in plastic frames.

Walter turned to look up over his shoulder at the window into the cabin above. Dubbing actors usually covered scenes together in repertory, standing around a semicircle of microphones with the director in the middle. But it infuriated Walter to wait through other actors' more frequent mistakes. When Klara renegotiated his contract after *Mission: Impossible,* he had elected to record his lines alone. The director, until now, had been Rainer Brandt, voice of Tony Curtis and famed translation dramaturge, an industry legend who treated Walter like a favorite son. When Walter suggested changes to the German translation, Brandt never said, *Let's discuss it.* He said, *Fine.* He said, *Do it.* But Brandt had backed out of *Vanilla Sky* last minute, pleading exhaustion.

"I'm leaving you in good hands," he told Walter. "The latest *Wunderkind.* He's full of energy, this one. Going places."

Walter had met the wunderkind this morning, a skinny young man wearing leather pants, an I LOVE NY T-shirt, a red bandana at his neck and pink-tinted sunglasses. It was almost completely dark inside the studio.

"Orson Welles," said the kid to Walter, holding out his hand.

Walter shook it limply. He wished he could go back to bed.

"Orson Welles?"

"You know, Rosebud."

"Right."

"It's my nom de plume. I want to keep my money work separate from my real work. Only use my real name where it counts."

"Your real work?"

"I'm developing my first feature at the moment. Start shooting next month. That's why I'm doing this now." Orson rubbed two fingers together in the air. "Good money, this dubbing racket. Pays the rent. But as a filmmaker I think all films should be seen in the original. Did you know that in Mexico there's a law against synchronization? Their native industry is huge since all the foreign films are subtitled. Call it the upside of illiteracy."

"Most Germans can read."

"Maybe, but the work we do here, in this studio, is so good that audiences can't distinguish between what is original and what's dubbed. They feel like American films are German films. It's killed the local business because we don't have the money to compete with this Hollywood crap, I mean, how much do you think this movie cost?

"*Vanilla Sky*? I don't know. Fifty million dollars?"

"My film is going to cost twelve thousand deutschmarks. It's a great story, believe me, but it's been a bitch to get it made. Sometimes I really feel like I'm shooting myself in the foot here."

They retreated to their separate quarters and Walter wiped a thin film of sweat from his forehead with a napkin. How many times did he have to listen to a novice dismiss dubbing as a money job? Orson Welles? The kid talked about making a feature with the casual assurance of someone planning to mail some letters at the post office. We'll see about that, thought Walter. No one went into dubbing with his eye on a lifelong career. Actors, directors, sound technicians, everyone at Deutsche Synchron was supposedly saving up to get out of dubbing and into something else. But when they were still there ten years later, they didn't mention their real work anymore. Walter adjusted his headphones and tested the sound. He had gotten into dubbing for the money too, of course. But after *Rain Man* he'd learned to respect it as a craft. He'd recorded almost every scene with Joachim Kerzel, who'd been doing Dustin Hoffman since *The Graduate*. The autistic brother's genius was only believable because of the voice that Kerzel gave him (the irritating monotone, the perfect repetitions, the funny little moans). His performance raised the bar. When Walter took the *Top Gun* job, he'd never intended to spend the next sixteen years at the dubbing studio. But after *Rain Man* he decided to be good at it, and it still gave him a certain satisfaction to know he could do one thing better than anyone else.

Two hours had passed since his introduction to Orson and they had only made it through four lines of the movie. *Let's discuss it.* Walter looked up impatiently as Orson came out at the top of the staircase.

"I feel like Rapunzel," he joked, shaking his long ponytail over the edge of the banister.

"What do you want to discuss?"

"Well, if we have to make it shorter, keep *You're good-looking* and kill *You are handsome.* They mean essentially the same thing, but good-looking is slightly more complex. It has an inside-outside quality that really points to the theme of male vanity in this film. It's more emotionally accurate to the character's story in the end than *handsome.*"

Walter willed himself to argue with Orson, but he could not muster the necessary energy.

"Have you ever actually been to New York?" he asked instead.

"Once, why?"

"The T-shirt."

Orson looked down at himself.

"I'm selling them to help raise money for my film. They're really popular right now, you know, everyone here wants to be a part of 9/11. People were ordering them over the Internet from New York so I had some made up at a T-shirt place in Friedrichshain and now they can buy them from me. You want one? I'll give you a good deal."

"I've never even been to New York."

"That doesn't matter. Show your support for the American people."

I am American, thought Walter.

Orson shrugged. "I'm pretty damn suspicious of the whole situation, myself. I'm just wearing the T-shirt to promote sales. You have seen the original film, haven't you?"

"Which film?"

"*Vanilla Sky.*"

"No," Walter admitted.

"Didn't they send it to you? How are you supposed to anticipate the tone of the dialogue if you don't know what happens next?"

The truth was that watching the original with Tom Cruise's real voice in it ruined the illusion not only for millions of German-speaking fans, but also for Walter. He liked seeing the film first in segments in the studio, watching the story build in fragments of dialogue like a crossword puzzle coming into focus.

"I was out of town last week," Walter lied. "I only got back last night."

Orson gave him a long look and went back into the cabin upstairs.

"*Du bist intelligent und du siehst gut aus,*" Walter said into the microphone, eliminating *handsome,* as directed.

But when he read the new few lines on paper and listened to the English playback, he was infuriated.

"Excuse me. The German translation here is totally off. When Tom Cruise's friend tells him he has a *shit-eating grin.* That's a fantastic term in English. The translation just says he's smiling. It misses the point."

"The point is that he's happy."

"No, it's more than that. *Smiling* doesn't come close to the true essence of a shit-eating grin."

"Describe it, then." Orson was standing on top of the stairs again.

"What?"

"That essence."

Walter thought it over. "Pleased with oneself, as a child might be after eating his own shit when he knows he shouldn't."

"That is unbelievably disgusting."

"That's the genius of American English right there."

"No. That proves Americans are as crazy as everyone said they were when I was growing up in East Berlin. But have it your way."

They moved on to the next segment, a long voice-over spoken in retrospect, while on screen, Tom Cruise flirted with a beautiful brunette. Alone in the darkness, Walter closed his eyes and let the English feedback form patterns on his brain, elaborate plaids of syntax, breath and emotion— so that the German translation coming out of his mouth would follow the same contours; when it worked, he felt like he was speaking in tongues.

"*Moment mal,*" Orson's voice boomed over the speakers, interrupting Walter's concentration. "Cruise's character is wearing a mask when he's saying this voice-over. And he's had some damage to his mouth, which makes him talk differently. Of course, you wouldn't know this, since you haven't seen the film."

Orson paused here to make sure his point was understood.

"But we have to make your voice sound like his does.

How about you stick one finger in your mouth, and put your other hand over the whole thing, while you speak."

Walter inserted one finger into the corner of his mouth and pulled delicately at the edge of it. He held his other hand against his nose. As it rubbed up against his nostrils he smelled coffee and the residual rank of the old lectern's years in use. His finger tasted sour and leathery, like the wheel of his car. He tried the first line again.

"Too much," Orson's voice filled the room. "Hold your top hand a little further out. And stick the finger deeper. Really pull at the side of your mouth. Make it difficult to speak."

Walter moved his hands around, trying the line different ways, but it either sounded too muffled or not muffled enough.

"I have an idea." Orson came down the stairs, untied the red bandana around his neck and shook it out. "Try this."

He folded the bandana in half diagonally and reached one arm back to tie it tightly around Walter's mouth and nose like a surgical mask. Then he took Walter's left hand and hooked the forefinger over his bottom lip, pulling it down till it turned inside out. The finger still tasted bad and now it was wet with saliva, but the bandana smelled lightly of patchouli oil: better than the scent of his own unwashed hand. Orson patted him on the back and came around to face him in the darkness.

"Okay. Hold that. Can you do that for me? Now imagine that underneath this mask your face is damaged and your heart is heavy and you've lost the woman you love. Try again."

When Walter said the line again, through the pitch-perfect muffle of the bandana, he had to blink back real tears.

. . .

Work progressed in the afternoon. The dialogue picked up and they moved through it beat for beat. Tom and the woman left the party, went back to her place and circled each other fully clothed. It was nice, Walter liked imagining what might be around the next corner instead of seeing the usual panting climax laid out for him immediately. For a full half-hour he didn't even think about Heike, until the original voice-over called Tom's woman *the last semi-guileless girl in New York*. The opposite of Heike, he thought, turning off the spotlight at the lectern and walking into the middle of the studio with a portable microphone. At first he'd been pleasantly surprised that his long-faded celebrity could still win favor with a beautiful young woman, but quickly he worried that it was not enough to sustain her interest over time. In bed, early on, when she would shake her hair across her face and moan dramatically, as if her orgasm were a performance and the mattress were a stage and a packed audience of men were watching her from the footlights with their hands down their pants, he had been jealous of those imaginary men. He had been unable to believe that the performance was meant for him alone and so he criticized her wild abandon until it turned him off. In recent months he had had to fantasize about the strangest things to keep his erections going midstream: foot rubs, cuddles on a sofa, a delicate hand pressed against his own through the window of a train. The dark studio enveloped him and Walter looked up, trying to focus on the screen. This one looked like New York, but Tom Cruise's America was the same wherever the movies took place. Even an airplane turning tricks over the Persian Gulf became a world of possibilities. Walter was already counting the days until the premiere. He spoke his lines into the microphone, perfectly in sync with the mouth on screen, and tried to conjure the famous actor in the flesh: the two of them chatting at the after-party, exchanging war stories from their shared filmography, patting each other on the back. Tom Cruise's confidence would be contagious.

In the week since the idea of returning to Los Angeles in December had suggested itself, a plan had been emerging in Walter's mind. He had checked his schedule and the balance of his bank account. He had inquired about flights. He would stay in Berlin until the premiere and leave the following day. It was far-fetched to expect guidance from a major American movie star, yet so much of his life had been the result not of hard work or canny design, but of a series of unlikely boons. Tom Cruise's acquiescence thus seemed, at the very least, plausible. Walter had made no concrete moves yet but the possibility of escape was already there, blossoming tentatively on the otherwise bleak horizon. The first time he'd left Los Angeles prematurely, he told himself. He'd taken a detour and everything had gone terribly wrong. Not this time. In Tom Cruise's America, things only went wrong if it served the script for dramatic purposes. The air trapped inside the studio was stifling and still. The structure of *Vanilla Sky* was confusing, switching between scenes in the present and the past. Walter had trouble keeping track of when the voice required distortion and when it didn't.

"Last line of the day," Orson called out. "This one's straight. Hold on to the bandana, though. You can use it again tomorrow."

Walter pulled the damp cloth quickly from his face and removed his hand from his mouth. He used the bandana to wipe off his fingers. On screen, Tom Cruise was looking at photos on the beautiful woman's fridge. The sound technician rewound the bit of film to the beginning and played the English original into Walter's headset.

"I like your life," said Tom Cruise to his date.

"Ich mag dein Leben," enunciated Walter in German.

As he mimicked the intonation exactly, he envisioned himself again at the premiere with Tom Cruise. But this time, they didn't stay in the crowd of local well-wishers, they floated out the door of the party above the winter roofs of Berlin and over the Atlantic Ocean, like two linked helium balloons. They crossed the wide, flat states in the middle of the country and kept going, over the Rockies, until they reached a full-blown sunset on the lip of the Pacific. There they were: somewhere in Malibu, toasting to success with champagne, laughing together like friends. It could happen, thought Walter, still looking up at the now black screen above his head. Because Tom Cruise's America was the place he had meant to go in the first place. He had been distracted by unfortunate circumstances last time, blown off course. This time he would get there.

8

It was the spring of 1983 and Walter was having his make-up done when a production assistant came over to tell him that his father had died. The set of *Schönes Wochenende* was in a large hangar in the Bavarian countryside, and his dressing room consisted of a chair behind a folding screen and a shared electric heater to warm his feet. The production assistant waited for a break in the conversation to make her announcement, as the actress who played Walter's mother on the show read aloud from a magazine about Priscilla Presley, who had just joined the cast of *Dallas*.

"She has her own trailer," said the actress, holding up a picture of its interior for everyone to see. "Check this out. She has her own telephone and a bed for her dog."

Although there was a small room at the back for costume changes on the *Schönes Wochenende* set, there were no trailers. The principal actors were expected to change their clothes quickly, in front of everyone else, as if on a beach in Greece. They were expected to wash their own hair and do their own nails. It was cold inside the hangar, even in the summer. The food was lousy.

"She is the wife of the King. Doesn't that make her the Queen?"

Priscilla Presley had met Elvis on an American Army base in Wiesbaden and thus occupied a special place in the collective unconscious, as if the Germans had personally set the unlikely stage for their romance.

"They got divorced in 1973."

"Still, she was his only wife. The mother of his only child."

"So she deserves a private trailer with wall-to-wall carpeting?"

There was much talk among the German television actors about the luxuries afforded their peers across the ocean. Some of them hired language coaches to work on their American accents in hopes of somehow making their way to Hollywood. Walter, who at twenty-one had never been anywhere (not even a Greek beach, let alone Los Angeles), listened but said very little. The truth was that he liked the set of *Schönes Wochenende*. Sure, it was cold and damp, dark in the winter, but he didn't know anything else. He was having his face powdered while the guys he knew in high school ran drills in the army or wiped the asses of old people for their civil service.

"There are more Germans over there than you think. Look at Schwarzenegger: he's getting into the movies and he hardly speaks English."

"He hardly speaks German."

"Hell, the first guy ever to win an Academy Award for best actor, in 1929, was German."

"I read Emil Jannings's autobiography. He was born in Brooklyn."

"He lied. He was Swiss."

"You're all wrong. He was born in Switzerland, but his mother was German and his father was American. So he was German, sort of, but he was an American citizen from the start."

"Lucky bastard."

Before the production assistant touched his shoulder and leaned down to whisper in Walter's ear, the last thing on his mind was the possibility of leaving the show. He was an American citizen from the start, like Emil Jannings, but he had never considered moving to the United States.

He left the set immediately and went back to the village where he had been raised, a place he had not visited in almost two years. The neighbor who found the body, the same woman who had cooked for Walter and his father in the years after his mother died, had organized a funeral at the local Catholic church. Very few people came; they had no relations left and his father didn't have many friends. He had died suddenly, of a heart attack, but in retrospect it seemed that he had been dying for ten years already. After his wife's death he had become increasingly reclusive, and over time had retreated even from his only son. At the funeral, Walter stayed in his pew while the others took Communion. No one was surprised. The village was small and he was its only citizen who had not been baptized or confirmed, the only one who didn't attend catechism classes in sixth grade or come to school Ash Wednesdays with a cross on his forehead. That a priest should memorialize his father at the end of his life was ironic, as he had been baptized at birth but had never returned to church after his marriage, not even after the death of his wife. But Walter had no alternative ritual to suggest. He had grown up without religion, surrounded by Catholics. This is what you do when people die, he thought, hands folded in his lap as the others crossed themselves and knelt in prayer. He would stay in town only twenty-four hours to deal with the paperwork (there was a small life insurance policy, the neighbors' daughter was going to buy the house and everything in it). He had only to clear out some personal belongings and his father's clothes.

On his way back to the house it occurred to him that he had nowhere left to call home. He looked out at the rolling hills of Bavaria, thick with green in summer, and realized that his father had been his last remaining link. He was alone in the world now, too old to think of himself as an orphan, but too young to lose his anchor all the same. In the absence of family, his career, if you could call it that, was the only thing propelling his life forward, which was a harrowing thought. Thus far he had thought of acting as a lark. He had yet to take a lesson, or cultivate future projects, but he entered his father's house now with a newfound sense of urgency, determined to get back to the *Schönes Wochenende* set as quickly as possible. There was coffee gone cold on the kitchen table and dishes from his father's breakfast in the sink. Walter retrieved a suitcase from the basement, a large, hard object his father had almost never used, and went upstairs to clear out his closet: two suits, worn at the elbows, and one good pair of shoes, a little-used pair of sneakers, and five shirts, their collars frayed, underwear, handkerchiefs, socks. In the back pocket of a pair of pants draped over a chair by the bed he found his father's wallet, which suggested that his father had not even gotten dressed the day he died, a Saturday, although the time of death was in the early afternoon. When his mother was alive his father had always dressed for work before breakfast. He had been a careful, accurate man. The picture of him keeling over in the kitchen in his pajamas in the middle of the day was so undignified that Walter had to sit down on the bed to absorb it, clutching the wallet to his chest. Then he went through it. He carefully placed his father's driver's license and identification card, twenty-three marks, nineteen pfennig and a dog-eared piece of paper on the bed. The eight-year-old picture on the license was evidence of his father's once robust appearance. In recent years his blond hair had thinned and gone gray at the edges. His face had become heavily lined from smoking cigarettes. But in his youth he had been tall and fit, pale, *typically German*, his mother used to point out, not unkindly, in contrast to their son, whose dark hair and smaller physique resembled her own. Walter placed the license in his own wallet and left the money on the bed. Folded up tightly in the otherwise empty wallet was a paper on which were written the numbers of his father's doctor, his health insurance, the switchboard at his office. Another name was scrawled at the bottom, with part of an address: *Roth, Walter and Vera. Springtime Estates. Irvine, California.* Walter stared at this information for a long time. He rubbed one finger over the name. How old was this piece of paper? His father had always worked for the same company, presumably never changed his insurance plan. Beads of sweat gathered at his temples and dripped down into the collar of his shirt. If moments earlier he had planned to return as soon as possible to the set of *Schönes Wochenende,* now another destination presented itself. The clue was flimsy, at best, but it was something. His mind raced. He had an American passport. Klara could send him his reel. Hans, his character on the show, could go into the army, or take an extended vacation; they could kill him off. Walter would work in Hollywood. It was close enough, he could check things out. Why not? Emil Jannings was born in Switzerland and he won an Academy Award! Walter refolded the piece of paper carefully and put it in his pocket.

9

The Saturday morning after Heike left, Walter threw open
the curtains and turned on the radio. AC/DC blasted into the
room as he studied the broken map still laid out on the floor.
So far he had managed to fit together four pieces of about
twenty-five, composing one small section of Wedding and
Moabit, the northern edge of Tiergarten. Because each piece
was printed on both sides it would have been impossible to
lay out the whole city flat, and he never knew which side of
each piece to try first. The fact that there were still two of
everything left over from the former division made things
particularly difficult: two zoos, two big airports, two TV towers, three opera houses. If he had two copies of each piece of
the map, he thought, it would be much easier to put the city
back together. But even then, he would have had been limited by his own bad geography.

He opened the first of the closets and pulled out a fuzzy
lavender beret, a sealskin thrift-store coat with a torn collar,

a pair of tights balled up behind his dress shoes, and two pairs of high-heeled sandals, the left heel worn down in exactly the same place. Comparing the two, Walter was confident he would recognize a shoe of Heike's if he found it lazing around by itself in the middle of a vast desert. He filled up one plastic garbage bag and then another. He searched through every cupboard, drawer, dark corner and long-forgotten crevice of his apartment: underwear that had been dyed blue in the laundry, a slip with a built-in bra, a black dress made of some synthetic, elastic material, a ruffled, high-collar blouse with flowers for buttons, a cashmere cardigan with holes in both elbows, four ashtrays and six lipsticks, all of them nearly the same bright shade of red. He danced through the apartment to the music on the radio. He bit his bottom lip, pumped his fist, banged his head in the air and let it guide him through the catharsis. First the bedroom, then the back bedroom that he used as an office, then the living room, the dining room, the master bathroom and finally the guest bathroom he never went into. Discovering a half-rusted rhinestone necklace in a basket by the toilet, he remembered that Bodo had once described Heike's carefully orchestrated look as that of a silent-film starlet after a really bad night on the town. As he said it, Bodo had even gotten up from the table to imitate her sexy, floppy walk, twisting an imaginary strand of hair with one finger and teetering on his tiptoes, as if in heels that were a bit too high. That Heike herself had laughed enthusiastically at this impersonation made Walter cringe in retrospect. Even in her private life she was always auditioning for the role of a lifetime. He released the rhinestone necklace into the third of the plastic bags and washed his hands.

• • •

On the way back from the charity collection box at the end of his street, he lingered in the lobby, hoping for a glimpse of his neighbor. He pressed the elevator button and hummed their song to himself, almost giddy, as if something far more intimate had taken place. This American blonde, with the shy, surprised look on her face, was about as different from Heike as two young women living in the same Berlin building could be, and the possibility of others like her waiting for him in California gave him hope, but when he returned to his apartment he checked the answering machine anyway. No messages. It was just like Heike to return the keys, but leave a trail of ratty, half-forgotten things in the apartment so she'd have an excuse to come back when she felt like it, he thought. No doubt she assumed her things would still be there, just as he would be, right where she left them. He walked away from the answering machine and concentrated on the comforting image of her ringing his doorbell on Christmas Eve, looking up at his dark windows and shivering away the winter evening on the doorstep without her thrift-store coat. He would be long gone by then. In his bedroom he pulled out a suitcase from under the bed and considered the season in Southern California. At night, he'd need a light sweater and jeans, but during the day the Santa Ana winds might blow in off the desert, bringing weather warm enough for T-shirts and shorts. He'd be exercising again, so he'd need running shoes. A bathing suit and sunglasses, of course. He began to take these things out of drawers.

• • •

When the doorbell rang, he almost didn't recognize the sound. It had been years since someone rang the interior bell to his apartment rather than the buzzer on the street. He left the half-packed suitcase on the bed and closed the bedroom door to conceal the mess he'd made. Still holding a dusty tube of sunscreen leftover from a trip he'd taken once to Lanzarote, he padded to the front door and stopped short behind it. There was no peephole to look through, but he knew it was Heike. One of the neighbors would have let her in. He breathed quietly, one hand on the doorknob, contemplating his housecleaning outfit. The holes in his socks, the baggy sweatpants. He looked like he'd been sulking in bed since she left. This was hardly the heroic scenario he'd hoped for. What would Tom do? Walter recalled the blowout with his wife in *The Firm*. They were outside by the swing set, the only place where bugs couldn't trace the things they said. Tom had cheated on her, he had dragged her into this terrible mess, but he didn't run away. No, he apologized. He came clean and came up with a plan to save the day and his marriage in the process. Walter rubbed his thumb against the brass doorknob without turning it. Tom Cruise never shied away from confrontation. Almost every film climaxed with a moment in which he faced his anger, his guilt, vulnerability, even shame, head-on. Walter rested his forehead against the front door.

He was preparing his reconciliation speech when a hand knocked softly on the wood a few centimeters away.

"Hel-lo-o?"

American English. A twang gave the second syllable a

long extra beat. Walter pulled his head back abruptly and opened the door to find the woman from the night before holding two paper cups of coffee-to-go in front of her hands like exercise weights.

"It's you," he said.

She had her hair pulled up and back in a ponytail.

"I wanted to introduce myself," she said. "I would have baked a pie or something but I don't have any pans. My things are still on their way over here from New York City on a boat. Or maybe they're sitting in a warehouse somewhere in Hamburg already, I'm not sure. I've been told that they're not letting anything through customs these days. So this is the best I could do."

Walter understood everything she said but watched her, dumbstruck. She handed him one of the cups.

"It's good coffee," she assured him. "Maybe we can imagine a pie to go with it."

He had been fiddling nervously with the tube of sunscreen and now he dropped it to accept the cup. When they both bent down to pick it up, coffee spilled over the plastic lid.

"I'm so sorry," she said.

The words came, finally.

"Don't worry," he said. "Please come in. Let's imagine a pie."

It was hard for Walter to remember the last time he had had a visitor in the middle of the day. His recent experiences as a host were limited to occasionally giving colleagues a ride home in his car, so he looked around his apartment as if it belonged to someone else. What to do with her? The living room furniture was still obscured by a blanket of receipts from the tax audit six months ago.

"Do you take milk?"

He led her into the kitchen.

"I should have introduced myself the other night," she said when they were sitting down at the kitchen table. "I'm Hope."

"Hope." Walter smiled. "You have a very lovely singing voice."

"I was singing."

"Humming, too."

"How embarrassing. You know, since I got here I've been alone all the time. Sometimes I go the whole day without speaking to anyone at all."

"It was nice. Really."

"Well, I need to make some friends. I thought I could start with you."

"I'm honored. I'm Walter, by the way."

"I know," she said. "Walter Baum. I described you to the super."

"The super speaks English?"

"I showed him." She used both hands to mime a smooth head, a stocky physique, a big smile. "He pointed out your door."

The shape she traced in the air was the most flattering description of himself that Walter had encountered in a long time. He wanted to step into it, conform to its outlines and live up to her good impression. He hadn't had a proper conversation in English with another person since he last lived in California. There had been short, occasional exchanges with foreign taxi drivers or the waitstaff at beach hotels, but real conversation in his mother tongue was something he experienced only in his imagination, in the elaborate dialogue with ghosts from his past that he had reworked obsessively over the years, as if he might improve the course of history if he could get the syntax right.

Hope reached back to tighten her ponytail, seemed to catch herself fidgeting and returned her hands to her lap.

"I'm taking a German class," she said. "But since the lyrics to songs playing in stores and cafés are always in English, I hear them more clearly than anything else and they get stuck in my head. Songs I haven't heard since high school."

"REO Speedwagon," said Walter, finally remembering the name. "'I Can't Fight This Feeling.' Was that 1984?"

"Exactly. You know, most days I can't remember where I put my keys but I can remember every word to every dumb song on the American Top 40 between about 1977 and 1985. I think I could come up with all the words to 'Wham! Rap' if someone held a gun to my head."

"Hopefully it won't come to that," said Walter, savoring the play on her name. "Hope."

When she smiled, the muscles in her face contracted and relaxed like an intricate origami. He did the music math. The songs she listened to in high school fell into a brief window of music sandwiched between the great, groovy rock 'n' roll of his own adolescence in the late 1970s and the mainstream revival of the Grateful Dead that preceded grunge. That brief window was exactly the period of time when Walter was living in Los Angeles. In fact, George Michael's voice still aroused in him the vaguely carsick sensation of being stuck in a morning traffic jam on the 405 South. That made her only a few years younger than he was. Thirty-five, maybe. He felt pleased with himself; he had never dated a woman old enough to remember REO Speedwagon, let alone dislike them.

He was warming up to the sound of his own English. His accent was still good and the words came more easily already. He spoke faster and louder than he normally did in German, felt looser and more dramatic. He reached over and touched her arm for emphasis, hoping that he would have the chance to go out with her in public. People overhearing their conversation would assume that they were just another American couple visiting town, he thought. He wondered if her sweet, southern-sounding twang was contagious. If he spent enough time with her, he might learn to speak English like Elvis.

"At least where you came from, everyone understood the lyrics," he said. "I grew up in a village in the Alps where everyone listened to American music but no one understood the songs. They just sang along phonetically. I was always explaining to my friends that, for example, *chew the hot dog* was actually *do the hustle*."

She nodded.

"I got in a huge fight with a friend once over the words to a Go-Go's song. I said it was *telling lies in the back of the bus.* She said it was *but that's no surprise.*"

"She was right."

"She was right."

Long before he was the only guy from his village to be on

television, Walter recalled, he was the only guy who understood all the words to the songs on the radio.

"Where are you from?"

"Kansas City, Missouri."

"I don't know anything about Kansas City."

"There isn't much to tell. Great barbecue, of course. Actually its real claim to fame is that there are more fountains there than in any other city in the world except Rome."

"That's funny. When I lived in California I spent a lot of time at a mall in Orange County that claimed to have more fountains than any other mall in the United States. Who counts these things? Tell me more about Kansas City."

"There's a Spanish plaza downtown because its sister city is Seville." She fingered the tube of sunscreen Walter had brought with him to the kitchen table. "It's in the middle of the country but it feels more like the South. It's been ages since I lived there. I went to college in New York City and I've lived there ever since."

"That must have been a change. I was nineteen when I moved from a small village in the south of Germany to Berlin. It blew my mind."

"Kansas City is spread out low to the ground. My first year in New York, the tall buildings really freaked me out. I used to lie in bed in my room on the seventh floor of the dormitory and imagine that the building was gone and I was just floating there. Then I would imagine that all the buildings were gone and all the people, all over the city, were floating in place, like I was. It seemed so strange to me that if you removed the buildings, people were lying in bed only a few feet away from their neighbors, up and down, without any contact. I would imagine the sky filled with bodies and each person alone, floating above the street in their own spot of air. After a while I forgot about it, of course. New York was home."

She put down her cup.

"To be honest," she said, "it's nice to be in a city that's low to the ground again."

"You like it here?"

"I don't know yet. But I needed to leave New York. I was relieved to have somewhere else to go."

Walter was watching her mouth as she spoke, imagining the bodies floating in the air for a long moment before he understood what she was talking about: she had been in New York in September. The way she said it, he assumed that she had only narrowly escaped, that by a monumental stroke of luck she had made it safely out of New York City and across the ocean, to sit here now at his kitchen table. The thought was exciting, as if by proxy he too had been there in the eye of the storm. (In fact, he'd been at Deutsche Synchron watching the news projected onto the playback screen overhead, replays of colorful explosions, people running, screaming, again and again up the street.) He was eager to hear a first-hand account and waited for Hope to elaborate, but she just looked down at the sunscreen, studiously reading the Spanish directions on the back of the tube: *Evite contacto con los ojos,* it said: Avoid contact with the eyes.

"Was there a Spanish section?"

"I'm sorry?"

"Of Berlin. After the war."

"Oh. No. The city was divided into four zones: Russian, American, British and French. The Russian zone became East Berlin. The other three merged together to form West Berlin."

"What was this neighborhood?"

"Charlottenburg was in the British zone. But the only thing that really mattered was East or West."

"The Wall was around East Berlin."

"Actually, the Wall was around West Berlin. But the East Germans built it. The government told the people that the Wall was to keep the capitalist fascists out, but obviously it was to keep the East Germans in."

"Then why was it around West Berlin?"

"Because West Berlin was surrounded by East Germany on all sides. Before they built the Wall, anyone wanting to defect could just walk into the West and stay there. You see what I mean?"

"Not really."

"Berlin didn't straddle the border of East Germany and West Germany, with one side in either country. It was an island in the middle of the East. West Berlin, where we are now, is, was, two hours from the closest border to what was West Germany."

Hope smiled.

"I didn't know that."

"When I was in America in the eighties, and this was during the Cold War, I noticed that a lot of people didn't know that."

"It's the same with Kansas City and no one knows that either."

"What?"

"Kansas City does actually straddle a state line, between Missouri and Kansas. But there are two separate cities named Kansas City, one in either state. Most people, most Americans, but certainly everyone else too, think there's only one."

They both laughed.

"What was it like here with the Wall up?"

"Not the way people imagine it. Actually, there was a lot contained inside West Berlin. Forests, lakes, campsites."

"Campsites?"

"It was hard to go anywhere. Three hours' drive, plus long lines at the border on either end, meant that sometimes it took eight hours to get from here to West Germany. So there were all kinds of things for people to do here, even camping. Only a little piece of real *Autobahn*, though, an old racing track that runs from Charlottenburg to Wannsee called the Avus."

"Was that important?"

"It was the only place to drive without a speed limit."

"Germans love cars."

"Of course. Without the Avus, if you had a Porsche or something, you couldn't even drive it properly. Now you can just drive right into Brandenburg if you want to."

It wasn't even hot anymore, but Hope blew at her coffee anyway. Her breath made a path through the middle of the liquid, as if she were blowing a Porsche, full speed, down the Avus.

"It's amazing how you live with history here," she said. "In New York, people only think about what's going to happen next."

Political history was everywhere in Berlin, thought Walter, but personal history was just as easily swept under the rug.

"As a kid, the worst of German history is beaten into you from every angle. When I was in high school, every year we went on a class trip to a different depressing place. One year we went to Buchenwald and spent the night."

Her eyes widened.

"Inside the concentration camp?"

No German woman would have been impressed by these stories. In Germany they were standard fare, common experience. Walter relished his own eloquence in English.

"The rooms where the Jewish prisoners slept are a museum. We slept in the former SS barracks."

"No way. That must have been really disturbing."

"It was!"

He was on a roll. He almost went on to tell her that Heike's soap was shot in a prison, in Spandau, where the British kept Rudolf Hess after the war, and where he died in 1987. The British moved out after the Wall came down, and it became a pilgrimage site for neo-Nazis, so the city converted it to a TV studio. It was a good story, but Walter stopped himself because it would have required an explanation of both Heike and the stupid soap opera. Hope's fingers picked up the tube of suntan lotion, turned it over and put it again on the table. He tried to think of something else to tell her.

"When I first moved here, someone pointed out to me that you can gauge the point of contact of each bomb dropped during World War II by tracing the radius of reconstruction around it," he said. "Have you noticed the circular patterns of buildings from the 1950s? Take our building, for example.

Where we are is still the original part, the prewar houses have long wooden windows and high ceilings, but everything extending to the corner is new, all the ugly buildings with plain façades. If you draw a circle around the corner at Schiller and Schlüter, to encompass the new buildings on either side of the street, you can be pretty sure that the bomb fell right in the middle of it."

"Why here? Was there some sort of industry nearby?"

"Berlin was the capital. Everything here was a target, even residential neighborhoods. The fanciest ones were the ones worst hit. The Hansaviertel, around Tiergarten, was completely destroyed, Grünewald, Wilmersdorf. But even here, if you walk to the corner you see that Grolmanstrasse, which used to run all the way past the Schillertheater, had to be cut off to accommodate the destruction. That's why there's a big hole in the middle."

"Wow."

"Yeah. But you know, if you just look closely at pretty much any corner of this city you'll see the same thing."

"Imagine how awful it was for the people living here at the time, I mean right here in this apartment."

Walter remembered the first day he saw Hope on the stoop, barefoot in the cold. Why was he telling her disaster stories?

"My hometown was built after the war," he backtracked. "All the houses were new and cheaply constructed. Before I came to Berlin I had never seen so many elegant prewar buildings in one place. I liked trying to imagine what the city looked like before everything was bombed, at the turn of the last century during the *Gründerzeit*. It was a good time in German history, the last really good time, actually. A big economic boom. At night when I walked down the street, I tried to recapture it."

He narrowed his eyes and looked at her through the fuzzy fringe of his eyelashes. Her blond hair was a halo, her face an Impressionist painting. She did the same, looking back at him.

"Like this?"

"That's right. But you have to do the horses too if you really want to get into the mood."

He clucked his tongue against the roof of his mouth to reproduce the sound of hooves against the cobblestones. To his relief, she laughed.

"I'm going to try that," she said.

"You'll see. This city can be very nice from the right perspective."

"I've been reading up on Christmas here."

"Christmas?"

"Do you remember celebrating the day of Sankt Nikolaus from when you were a child? Getting candy in your shoes?"

"Where I come from, Nikolaus had an evil assistant, Knecht Ruprecht. Nikolaus was ruddy-cheeked and white-bearded and cheerful, like Father Christmas, but Ruprecht was dark, the bad guy in black clothes, with a long, black beard. If you were good, you got candy from Nikolaus, but if you were bad, you got coal from Ruprecht. In our village, people used to dress up and run through the streets at night on the fifth of December making a huge racket with bells, threatening children. It was like Carnival, only scarier. In the morning, everyone was afraid to put their shoes on."

"That's amazing."

"It was awful. I hid under my bed. I hated it."

"Seriously?"

"There was nothing nice about it."

"Not even the candy?"

"There wasn't any candy," said Walter, trying to make a joke of it for her benefit. "Not at our house."

Hope's hands drifted up to her ponytail again, this time pulling it out of the elastic so that her hair fell down around her face and a few strands of her hair got caught across her cheeks. Walter just barely controlled the impulse to reach up and brush them away, to touch her skin with his fingers.

"Thank you for inviting me in," she said, standing up.

"You're not leaving?"

"I have some things to do before the shops close. If I don't go now I'll stay all day," she said. "I'm so starved for company you'll never get rid of me."

After she was gone Walter admired his kitchen, which still radiated her presence. She had been there only half an hour but it had been long enough to remind him that he could reinvent himself completely just by speaking another language, which was a relief. Because while blowing out the candles on a cake at his thirty-ninth birthday six months earlier, he'd had a strangely disheartening realization: the traditional midlife crisis was not an option for him. Although he was experiencing all the attendant frustration, dissatisfaction and ennui typical of a middle-class white man facing forty, he had no wife and children to leave behind, he already owned an expensive German car and he was already dating a much younger woman. None of this was making him happy, he realized, and yet there was forty lurking just up ahead like an unfriendly cat on the prowl. In the intervening months he had considered the range of remaining options. Weight loss, hair plugs, a sail round the world; a spiritual quest into the Eastern religions, even a doctor-sanctioned nervous breakdown at a traditional Alpine cure, with sexy nurses in starched white uniforms, a view of the Alps and chamomile tea. For a week or so at a time, he had attached himself to each one until it proved impossible: he lacked the motivation for a serious diet, and hair plugs would just make his head look like a plastic doll's. He got seasick on sailboats and couldn't get into the lotus position to save his life. The worst discovery had been that the sanatoriums described in nineteenth-century German romantic novels were a thing of the past. The nurses at Alpine cures no longer wore starched white uniforms with visible cleavage and pointy caps; in the twenty-first century, they just wore aprons over their sweatpants, and rubber clogs.

Until the evening he encountered Hope in the elevator, his most recent midlife crisis fantasy had been in danger of getting stuck in turnaround like all the others: although he had been able to see the outline of his life in Southern California, the convertible and the asphalt driveway, the suntan, the salty waves licking at his ankles, he'd stopped short when he tried to picture a domestic life across the Atlantic. Instead of seeing, for example, the sun pouring in the windows of a Richard Neutra house filled with Playboy bunnies, Walter had only been able to see himself coming home to the warm-weather equivalent of his Charlottenburg apartment and padding around, alone, in his socks. When Hope walked into Walter's kitchen, Walter walked through a newly opened door in his imagination. Suddenly he was no longer alone in the California of his mind. He envisioned their life together there in a series of future snapshots. Hope in a sundress, pulling apart a lettuce for salad behind the counter of their open kitchen. Hope asleep on the pillow next to his, holding his hand across the stick shift in the car, dancing against the backdrop of a smog-induced Technicolor sunset, her head resting on his shoulder. He deliberately kept things PG-rated. No seduction scenes or gratuitous nudity. But he did allow himself a glimpse of the two of them toasting long-stemmed glasses of champagne with Tom Cruise himself on a terrace in Malibu overlooking the beach. Why not? Even Christmas wouldn't be so bad. He could fill her shoes with candy, if that's what she wanted. They could string up electric lights around a palm tree in the yard. They would give each other handmade gift certificates, he thought dreamily: *1 Foot Massage, 1 Breakfast-in-Bed*. It would be the first time he'd ever enjoyed the holiday season.

Throughout their conversation in his kitchen, Walter had listened carefully for any mention of the man he had seen with Hope on the doorstep, even a simple reference to *we*, but none had come. He decided that the man, like Heike, was yesterday's news. A few days later, when he was coming in from the studio, he found Hope in the lobby carrying two large bags of dirty clothes.

"Where are you off to?"

"The laundromat at the corner," she said. "I don't have a machine yet."

Given the steps they had already taken toward domesticity in his mind, he automatically offered her the use of his. It was a bold move, which she accepted quite naturally, and he found himself with her again in the elevator, which had already become *the place where we met* in his mind. For years, its small dimensions had seemed to him suffocating and impractical; now they were intimate. The fluorescent light in the ceiling had been garish; now it was bright. He would have liked to take her everywhere with him. She looked him in the eye as if he made sense to her, and seemed to turn his comments over in her mind not skeptically, as Heike had done (always looking for an argument) but as if to fully absorb them. In his apartment he made a grand gesture with one arm toward the washing machine. Hope emptied the two bags on the kitchen floor.

"I'm terrible at this," she said. "I always dye everything pink."

"Let me help you."

They sorted the whites, darks and colors. When he noticed a few pairs of men's boxer shorts, colorful ones printed with polka dots and a paisley pattern, he assumed that she wore them to bed. It was when he picked up a long-legged pair of men's jeans that all the air trapped in the kitchen rushed into his lungs. He dropped them on the pile of darks and reached for a bottle of water.

"My husband will be happy," said Hope, surveying the three piles. "He doesn't like to wear pink underwear, although I'm not sure why not. No one sees it except me."

My husband. Walter's cheeks filled with air.

"He couldn't possibly wash his own underwear, of course. When I got to Berlin there was a mountain of laundry in the bathroom."

She seemed angry about it. Angry was good.

"But look at you," she said. "You're an expert."

The truth was that Walter rarely did laundry. He let it pile up in a basket until it spilled over onto the floor. But he could rise to this challenge. One of his most lucrative advertising contracts was an ongoing campaign for a line of detergents, and he had absorbed some useful information over the years. *My husband. Will be. Happy.* He put the water bottle down on the counter.

"There is a science to this," he said.

He picked up the pile of darks and stuffed them into the washing machine. Then he opened the cabinet to its right to reveal two shelves stuffed with free samples. Mango-fragrant fabric softener, bleach for sensitive skin, liquid formulated to remove wrinkles. He withdrew a bottle of soap and held it up, label forward, like a spokesperson in a supermarket.

"This one is specifically for darks," he said. "No leakage."

"No more pink underwear?"

"No."

The machine began its cycle and he put the kettle on for tea.

"German men are enlightened," said Hope.

"The laundry is nothing. We don't even leave the toilet seat up."

"What?"

"German men. We pee sitting down."

"Is that a good thing?"

"Women seem to think so."

"You do that even at home? Living alone?"

The final remains of Heike had left his apartment only an hour before Hope first came into it.

"All alone."

The clothes churned slowly through the machine. His work required an explanation since Hope had never seen a dubbed movie.

"I'll show you some of the best ones sometime, if you like. You'll like them even better in German."

"I love Tom Cruise. I especially liked *Jerry Maguire*."

Walter was ready to take requests.

"I suspect that many women actually like *Cocktail* best, but they usually don't want to admit it."

"I'm an easy target. I like it when the characters fall in love at the end."

He grinned indulgently across the table. Heike had always claimed *Interview with a Vampire* as her favorite Tom Cruise, but only to set herself apart. By contrast, Hope seemed to celebrate her mainstream movie tastes as if they, like everything else about her, were special. She rested her chin in both hands, propped up by the elbows. She had been a third-grade schoolteacher in New York, she said. She played guitar badly. She preferred red wine to beer. She was a good cook, but she could make only Mexican food.

"I'll make you salsa if I ever track down cilantro in Berlin," she said. "I make really good salsa verde."

She talked about things in an easygoing way, as if they'd known each other much longer than they had, but halfway through the evening he noticed that he had managed to gather very few concrete facts about her. She had a tendency to refer obliquely to personal things, as if they had already been discussed long ago and so required no further explanation.

"The school was only three subway stops from our apartment," she might say, without actually giving the location of either one.

Of course, he was never completely sure he hadn't missed something. Because they were speaking English, he had to concentrate to follow her, which slowed the conversation down.

The laundry reached the rinse cycle, the kitchen filled with the sound of rushing water. It was almost nine P.M. and he had almost managed to forget that Hope was married.

"Where is your husband?"

"In Poland."

Walter had been over the border an hour away only once and remembered very little about it except the sad young girls for sale by the side of country roads, dancing in their underpants in groups of two or three, waving to the German cars driving through the grim post-Soviet landscape.

"Why?"

"He's an economist. He's consulting on a project for a new business initiative here in Berlin, but spends most of his time on-site, just over the border from Frankfurt Oder."

"Have you been there?"

"Oh, no."

He decided to take this as a good sign. Let the husband stay in Poland. Hope's eyes rested on the same tube of sunscreen that had been there before.

"Are you going on a trip?" she asked.

"I might go to Los Angeles for Christmas."

"Nice."

Nice, thought Walter. *Come with me.*

"I used to live there," he said.

"That's why your English is so good."

"It was sixteen years ago."

"You must go back often."

"Never."

He gauged the temperature in the room. Where he began this story would dictate which version he told. There were many versions, developed over the years for different audiences. There was the short answer, the simple one, the sob story, the superficial explanation. There was the truth, of course, but this he almost never told anyone.

"My mother came from the United States," he said, beginning at the beginning. "From California originally, but her father was in the Army and they moved around a lot. They came to Germany in 1961, when she was seventeen. That's where she met my father, who was working in a village near the base."

"Like Priscilla Presley."

"My father was nothing like Elvis, believe me."

He looked at the clock, at the washing machine, at the smooth, square linoleum tiles that made up his kitchen floor. He pictured his hometown in winter. On a moonless night it seemed like the last village left on earth after the apocalypse, he remembered, as if the outside world had been cut off, the search teams had been called back and there was no more chance of ever being saved. He wanted to explain that to Hope. He felt that she would instinctively understand that experience of isolation, but if he pulled the loose thread here, what was to stop his life from coming completely unraveled at her feet? Quickly, he pushed his chair back and unloaded the wet laundry into a plastic basket and headed to the bedroom, but then he remembered the map.

"Hold this," he said, handing her the laundry basket.

He went into the bedroom and came out again with a drying rack. Then he steered her farther down the hallway to the spare bedroom.

"In our apartment this room was designed as a nursery," said Hope. "There are animals carved into the moldings on the ceiling. I wonder why you don't have them in here."

"Every apartment in this building has a different story. There have been so many tenants over the years. So many different renovations."

She looked down, as if trying to see through the floor into the nursery in her apartment below. He set up the drying rack by the window.

"Did children live in our apartment before we moved in?"

"I've been here for sixteen years and I can't remember ever seeing a child in this building."

"That's too bad."

She lifted a shirt out of the basket and hung it over the rungs of the rack.

"Tell me the rest of the story."

"Which one?"

"About your parents."

"After they met they started spending time together on Sundays. The premise was that my father needed to practice his English, but one thing led to another and my mother got pregnant. Her parents were pretty scandalized, I mean, it was 1961. They didn't want her to have a baby. They wanted her to go back to the States with them, go to college. But instead she left school and married my father and had me. Her parents transferred away from Germany and she never reconciled with them."

"You never met them?"

Walter glanced down at the bra he was laying over the drying rack.

"My mother used to try to reach them on the telephone, but they wouldn't speak with her."

"Wow."

"They had——" He paused. "They had what I think you would call irreconcilable differences."

They returned to the kitchen and loaded the next pile of laundry into the washing machine.

"At home we only spoke English. We listened to American music. We lived in the German part of town, but at Christmas she used to take me up to the American neighborhood, near the Army base, to see the lights. The Americans covered their houses with crazy, blinking, colored lights, with glowing displays of Santa and his reindeer on their front lawns, Jesus in the manger, the Three Kings, snowmen. All of them lit up from within. Germans considered it all a vulgar public display, of course, but we loved it."

"Did she decorate your house?"

"No, no. We didn't even have a tree. She didn't believe in that. It wasn't Christmas that she liked about the decorated houses, but the brazen waste of electricity." He laughed. "You know, people in our village were very conservative, very Catholic. My mother was always different. She just created this little bubble around the two of us."

. . .

Walter could still see his mother's pink skirt swinging in time to Otis Redding while she danced with the GI in the living room. It was a circle skirt, long outdated in places more fashion-forward in 1971. Her party skirt, she'd called it. He had loved how it swished around her legs like a fountain, defying gravity, smiling at him. Her slim legs moved in time to the music as the soldier spun her around the room. His friend cheered them on, laughing and shaking the ice cubes in his glass like maracas. Walter had laughed too, loving the music and the sudden good cheer, happy to see his mother having such a good time. He had never told this story to Heike. In the thirty years since it happened, he had told it only rarely at all, perhaps because it was not atypical. Many German–American marriages went bust in the postwar years. Had he openly complained, he would have been told to buck up. The fallout from the war was long and complicated. Everyone had paid a price.

"She died in a car accident when I was nine."

Hope inhaled and covered her mouth with one hand.

"She used to hang out with GIs from the U.S. base in the afternoons while my father was at work. She was lonely and homesick and young. My father was meticulous and method-ical about his work but he was the kind of guy who misses a lot of things happening right under his nose. The afternoon of the accident, two guys had driven over in an Army jeep. It had no hardtop, just a roll bar, and she wanted to go for a ride. All three of them were pretty drunk already. They were laughing really hard. My mother couldn't leave me alone, so one of them went with her and the other one stayed with me."

The face of the young GI left behind to babysit was fixed

forever in his mind; his broad, flat cheeks and pale skin, his droopy eyes like a hound dog across the yard as they played catch. Every detail of those last few moments remained acute: the slap of the hard baseball in his right hand when he caught it, the flip of his small elbow when he threw, the chill in the air, the purple shape of his house in the afternoon twilight.

"You know what I remember most clearly? For those few, slow-motion moments I was alone with that guy, before the police came to the house and my father came home and everything fell apart, I felt like one of those normal American kids I'd seen on television. Just playing catch in the front yard, like the Beaver or Bud Anderson. Just passing the time before dinner."

"Was there a funeral?"

"I don't think so. My father was really upset. He was heartbroken and ashamed."

"Did you still look at the Christmas lights afterward? In her honor?"

"Never. My father didn't want to do anything that reminded him of her. He never really got over her, to be honest. He died ten years later of a heart attack."

"You must have felt so lost."

Walter sat very still in his chair. He was torn between the desire to kiss her and the fear that he might cry. Instead, he got up from his chair to carry another load of finished laundry down the hallway to the spare bedroom, where he laid out her husband's damp T-shirts, paisley-patterned boxer shorts and jeans against the plastic rungs of the drying rack, as carefully as if they were his own.

10

Although they never officially made plans, since they'd met, Hope had come to expect Walter's evening visit and was already looking forward to it as she made her way to class through the dark afternoon. Along her usual route, the indistinct buildings, kebab stands, neon signs and even trees had become the landmarks she had been missing at the beginning and she no longer got lost. She had to admit to herself that her mother was right: one friend made all the difference. It was not that Walter actually showed her around the neighborhood, but the fact that Charlottenburg was his home, which made it seem less foreign by association. It grounded the unfamiliar landscape in something concrete: his memories, their conversations, the knowledge that they would see each other again at the end of the day. The night in the schnitzel restaurant only a couple of weeks earlier, when she had felt that she was clinging to Dave on a sinking raft adrift in a sea of strangers, had taken place in a different city.

Because she had the time to walk to class, she never took the subway but often stopped to watch the S-Bahn go by on the elevated tracks at Savignyplatz. On the east side of the square, beyond the barren bushes, was an old hardware store and a Russian restaurant and next to that, two women standing in front of a wide, wooden door covered in Christmas decorations. It had taken Hope a few days to understand that the women were prostitutes, but now she saw them there every day, smoking cigarettes and looking up and down the street. One was black and one was white and both were blond; the black one was wearing a Santa hat. In the windows above them, a pink neon sign said CHERRY. Hope glanced their way before a very different group of women came up the street pushing strollers; she stepped aside deferentially, letting them take over the sidewalk. Because she walked to class at the same time each day, she often saw the same people and had come to recognize in particular the many mothers, some with babies and others with older children going to and from school, meeting at the playground, hustling home for dinner. Some women had two. One had six, if Hope had counted correctly. All girls. There were so many children in the neighborhood that she would have assumed Berlin was experiencing a baby boom if Dave hadn't already complained about the declining local fertility rate. It had apparently reached an all-time low of 1.3 percent, which meant, he claimed, that the Germans were dying out.

"Who the hell do these people think is going to pay their Social Security when they're old?"

He had asked her this rhetorically, as if baby-making were simply another industry in need of critical reform, as if by resisting parenthood the Germans were putting up a dam to hold back water that might have irrigated an entire desert. He made it sound as if having a baby were the easiest thing in the world, which they both knew it was not. They had been married for five years before they ever even tried to conceive. Dave had wanted to start right away but she'd put it off because she wasn't ready. If someone had told her then that it would be so hard, she would have replied disdainfully that personal fulfillment was hard. Work was hard. Babies were a piece of cake. She had become a teacher because she couldn't decide whether or not to get a Ph.D., delayed having a baby because she wanted to keep the graduate school option open. Who could think about having a child when she had no idea what she wanted to do with her life? When she was younger, it would have never occurred to her that what she wanted to do with her life, if nothing else, was be a mother.

"The American population is still growing, Hope. Anyway, we don't have a social welfare state. Here, all they talk about is unemployment, but the real crisis is that the labor force is dwindling since they no longer have any children."

He was so angry. Why did Dave care if the Germans were dying out? If she had learned anything so far from her conversations with Walter, it was that it wasn't easy to be German in the world. Maybe they wanted to die out. Maybe they thought it was for the best.

She watched the mothers walk away under the tracks of the S-Bahn to the playground on the other side. She had resisted further argument with Dave because his anger about it was the only suggestion that somewhere inside his rational exterior he was suffering too and she wanted to believe that. In the past, she had often thought that if she were only to make one determining decision in her life, marrying Dave had been a good one. He was the eldest of three, an athlete, a National Merit scholar, his mother's favorite. He had always been the kind of person who accepted the word *no* as an invitation.

"*Nein,*" Hope said to herself out loud, thinking that in German it sounded like even more of a challenge.

His parents' objection to his choice of a non-Jewish girlfriend had only made Dave want to marry her. After he and Hope had been married at Niagara Falls and were living in the Village, about eighty blocks south of his parents, whom they rarely saw, the situation had only seemed to make him love her more. Hope waited as yet another woman walked past her toward the playground with a stroller. Six years into a barren marriage, she worried that his parents had been partially right. They had been too young. They were too different. She had to remind herself that they had once been happy together. It was only after what happened in June that she had come to resent his unrelenting personality. When he insisted on coming to Berlin in July, according to plan, she had been unable to fathom his determination in the face of grief, had turned over in bed to face the wall until he was finished packing and had wished him away. If it weren't for what happened in New York in September, she might never have joined him here at all. A gray sky was hanging over Savigny-platz like a heavy woolen blanket. She had allowed Dave to be her compass, she thought, and he had led her here.

. . .

She ducked under the S-Bahn tracks to the other side, where a couple of the mothers she had seen before sat side by side on a bench in the large playground. Beyond them, an older sister pushed a younger one on a swing, three boys jumped off a castle in the middle, and other mothers huddled together in little groups, clutching coffee. The playground was covered in graffiti and the weather was cold, but she stood close to the gate, watching a mother beckon to a little girl whose nose was running. The girl jumped off the jungle gym, presented her nose to be wiped and returned to play, her mother put the dirty tissue back in the pocket of her coat, and Hope gripped the metal gate with both hands. All summer she had jealously avoided her friends who had children. In New York, she had looked away when passing even anonymous families on the street. Since June, she had hardly seen a child at all. Now she forced herself to look out across the playground. She would have liked to go in and sit beside the mothers, but stopped herself for fear of imposing. Without child or stroller, she might seem ridiculous. For the first time in many years she did not even have a stash of emergency tissues in her own coat pocket. In the early years of her job, when none of her friends had kids yet, they used to tease her about the tissue supply and the Band-Aids, the raisins that sometimes came up with her wallet, the way she washed her hands religiously when she came indoors, or ate, or read the newspaper.

"Ms. Hope," they called her, emphasizing the *Mizz*, saying it with a midwestern accent.

Even Dave, who had often visited her at the private school where she worked, managed to imagine that she spent her days inside one of his glorified camp memories, playing kickball against the faded yellow-green landscape of a 1970s snapshot. That she hadn't been back to school since June was strange, but she didn't miss teaching. She watched a boy just about the age of her students climb up on a swing, pump his feet till he was flying, then jump off. Third-graders were eight years old, turned nine during the year, and it was a fragile age: old enough to understand what was going on but young enough to be confused by it. They asked a lot of questions. In the beginning, she had written important words and discoveries in round, clear script on the blackboard; the words listed there at the end of the day provided a kind of road map, clues to what they were thinking and where they were going.

"Why did the Beatles break up?"

"How do you know about the Beatles?"

"They're my grandma's favorite band."

"Okay. Because they were very talented people and they needed more free time."

"Why?"

"To do other things."

"What kinds of things?"

"I don't know. What would you do if you were John Lennon?"

"Sing songs."

"Like what?"

" 'Ob-La-Di.' "

"What else?"

" 'Lucy in the Sky with Diamonds.' "

After school she often studied the words on the black-board for a long time before erasing them: *talent, free time, songs, sky, diamonds.* It was hard now to remember when these conversations had started to make her uncomfortable. It wasn't clear, she thought now, if the questions themselves had changed as the years went by, or if she had just become more sensitive. Either way, she had learned that nine was not simply an age of discovery, but a loss of innocence: the age when the world came crashing through the window. At some point she started trying harder to forget her conversations with her students than to remember them.

"Why did Judy Garland kill herself?"

"How do you know about Judy Garland?"

"*The Wizard of Oz* was on last night."

"Okay. She thought her fans didn't love her anymore."

"I love her."

"Yes, but she was a drug addict. She wasn't thinking clearly."

"Is that why Kurt Cobain killed himself?"

"How do you know about that?"

"My brother told me."

"Okay, then. Yes."

"What's a drug addict?"

"It's something that happens to famous people."

"All of them?"

"A lot of them."

"The Beatles?"

"Maybe. I can't remember."

"Is that why John Lennon killed himself?"

"He didn't. Another man killed him."

"Why?"

"He was angry."

"Because the Beatles broke up?"

"No. That happened before."

"Why did the Beatles break up?"

"Because they got sick of each other."

Wizard, love, drug addict, kill, angry, famous, sick. In the years that followed, Hope stuck more diligently to the lesson plans prescribed by the school. Now she pulled herself away from the playground and toward Ku'damm, walking against the wind. Walter might have been one of her students the year his mother died, she thought, seeing him at nine: blue eyes and chubby, the sadness now written in lines across his face still fresh, cheeks trembling with the effort to contain it. She knew that look. It took far less than a mother's death to crush the face of a third-grader.

On Ku'damm, white Christmas lights decorated the trees in the middle of the avenue and the sidewalks, brightening the grand buildings on either side. In the right light, this street reminded her of the Champs-Élysées. Remembering what Walter had suggested, she narrowed her eyes and peered through the murky fringe of her lashes, to conjure an image of the avenue's illustrious past, the *Gründerzeit* boom a hundred years ago and the Roaring Twenties. She clucked her tongue against the roof of her mouth, as instructed, to make the sound of horseshoes against the cobblestones. It was easy to imagine Josephine Baker sashaying down this avenue in a flapper dress. It was easy to imagine her throwing open the French doors to one of the ornate balconies above and singing, *Evita* style, over all these sparkling lights. In fact, Hope did not find it difficult to conjure the glamorous origins of Ku'damm's architecture at all, but rather its destruction. Because Walter had explained that these buildings were completely flattened in the Allied bombings in World War II and had been rebuilt afterward.

"The entire Hitler period, including the war, lasted only twelve years," he'd said. "Isn't that amazing? In the grand scheme of history it seems like nothing, a fucked-up fairy tale. But in Berlin it is everything, even now, almost sixty years later."

Staring up through the scrim of her eyelashes, Hope tried to imagine the fancy façades ripped off to reveal furniture and wallpapered rooms, fires burning, people screaming. How did they explain any of what had happened here to children, she wondered. How did they explain even Ku'damm's history to the third grade? Walter had told her that it took years to clear the rubble. Since most of the men had been killed or imprisoned, or had to walk home from war fronts in Russia or France, the women had cleared Ku'damm themselves. *Trümmerfrauen,* they were called. They passed the chunks of stone and concrete, wood and tiles, one to the next, all the way down the avenue and another mile or so through Grünewald, where they made a massive pile. The pile was apparently a proper mountain now, grown over with grass. People liked to hike and picnic there.

"It's called Teufelsberg," Walter had said. "The Devil's Mountain. In West Berlin, it was one of the only places to go sledding in the winter."

Berlin was so flat in every direction that such a rise in the landscape would have towered over everything else. She looked around at the buildings above her head now. Children born today would match them up with historical photographs and think they had always been there, just like this. When they flew down Teufelsberg on their flying saucers they would never imagine all that rubble beneath the snow. She wondered, when they reconstructed the towers in downtown Manhattan, as they now proposed to do, would anyone believe that they had once disappeared?

She waited for the light to change in a crowd of pedestrians packed together at the corner of an otherwise unoccupied stretch of sidewalk thirty feet wide. No cars were coming up the side street, but not a single person stepped off the curb. In New York they would have flooded the street already, pushing ahead, but here they waited to move forward all at once when the light turned green. Hope controlled her own impatient impulse to cross against the signal because she was in no hurry to get to class. She kept pace with the crowd, like an animal in a pack, until they neared her German school. Then her feet dragged and she fell behind. The thought of three hours conjugating verbs in the warm classroom made her feel as if she had already fallen asleep, but skipping was out of the question, since she had never missed a class of any kind in her life. Even when her college friends had slept through morning classes after a late night out, she'd been the one to haul herself into her seat with a coffee. She was reminding herself of this when one of the other students in her German class, a middle-aged guy from Morocco, walked past her without saying hello. She raised one hand in greeting as the Vietnamese brothers came by next, but they didn't wave back. Hope watched them go up the stairs until they entered the building and the door slammed shut behind them. Then she turned and walked away from the school altogether, pace quickening, till she was running, doubling back toward Bahnhof Zoo.

The neighborhood was grittier at that end of the avenue, where no one had bothered to reconstruct the original architecture. Instead, a clutch of midcentury buildings—large, cheap, glass-and-concrete offices that might have been at home in any urban landscape—collected around a church whose steeple had been destroyed by a bomb and never repaired. Hope stopped to catch her breath in front of it. The broken steeple made it look like a soldier with his head blown off, she thought, the body still standing before it fell. She remembered that Walter had mentioned it.

"It's called the Gedächtniskirche," he said. "The Memorial Church. I think they left the steeple that way to memorialize how much the local community suffered during the war."

She craned her neck but couldn't see very well from below and so she went up the stairs to the S-Bahn, whose elevated tracks cut through the neighborhood, providing a view from above. Following the signs to find the right platform, she was surprised that no turnstiles or ticket booths blocked her entrance to the train. Every subway system she had ever used (New York, of course, London, Paris) didn't even allow the passengers to reach the platform without paying first. Here there were no conductors selling passes. There were hardly any other people. That it was free seemed impossible, but there it was. When the train going east arrived, she just got on without paying anything at all. Through the window she could see the silhouette of the crushed steeple at eye level against the darkening sky. Finally she understood what Walter had meant when he'd said that the true socialist paradise had been West Berlin, not East.

"This city is different from others because for so long it was a symbolic island," he'd said. "The last frontier of democracy, surrounded by enemies beyond the Wall. They had to make sure enough people lived here, although there was no industry and very few jobs, so everything was subsidized by the Marshall Plan. There were social benefits. Believe me, lots of people wish the Wall were still up."

The interior of the S-Bahn car was remarkably clean and comfortable, but it was the fact that it was free that made it seem like fun to her, a gift. She buzzed with the thrill of a tourist managing public transportation for the first time in a foreign city. The higher perspective revealed holes and crevices between the buildings that she had been unable to see from the ground: wide courtyards, the ragged edges of houses left standing when the ones next to them fell, ugly modern construction built right up against the shard of one original, ornate façade. Because it was getting dark out, she could peek into the lit interiors of third-floor apartments right next to the tracks (stuffed bookshelves and tables laid for supper, amber against the blue light of evening) and imagined herself sitting with Walter at her dining room table. He usually appeared around nine p.m. and always left before midnight, whether out of decorum or because he had other late-night plans, she wasn't sure. Maybe he needed his beauty sleep? Maybe he had a girlfriend or even a wife tucked away somewhere and whoever she was she came home after midnight? He never mentioned anyone, but she found it hard to imagine that he was truly single. He was too good a listener to be single, she thought. It had been a long time since someone had paid her as much attention as Walter did. She had what Dave always said was a typically midwestern way of dealing with people that confused some men in New York (she always said thank you, she always smiled, even when she was feeling like shit) and as a result, over the years there had occasionally been awkward advances from acquaintances who mistook her good manners for something more. This was different: Walter kept a respectful distance. He never made a suggestive comment of any kind. When he pulled out a chair for her to sit down, he did it carefully. But when she spoke he watched her lips move, she thought, as if imagining how to kiss her. So she moved them slowly, letting him enjoy it, because it had been a long time since someone had done that.

The train passed quickly through a park of tall naked trees, Tiergarten, the big green blob dividing the West from the East on Dave's map. On the other side was a sea of construction cranes. They looked like a herd of massive, prehistoric animals swarming, she thought, pouring forth from the park in all directions. To the south, one or two finished buildings shone brightly with fluorescent light around the Sony complex at Potsdamer Platz.

"Potsdamer Platz was destroyed so thoroughly that there

was almost nothing left to rebuild," Walter said. "During the Cold War it was a no-man's-land between East and West."

"What for?"

"It was supposed to be a buffer zone but basically functioned like a moat filled with alligators around a castle. People who tried to escape over the Wall from the East side were shot. It's only now they are building something there, a whole new city center, sixty years after it was flattened."

Hope looked out over the new Potsdamer Platz. Soon it would look like any other newly built complex of shopping malls and prefab tourist attractions like somewhere in the middle of the United States, she thought. It was a pity they couldn't leave that space as it was as a memorial, like the church, to remind people of the distance they had traveled to reconnect. She might have liked to stay longer in such a place. Speeding past Potsdamer Platz on the elevated train, she imagined the Atlantic Ocean, dark under the wings of the plane. Another no-man's-land, a moat. Her buffer zone. She imagined herself holding on to Dave's hand on one side and Walter's on the other, arms stretched so wide that they lifted her up, feet dangling like a child's, toes dipping every so often into the water.

The city flew by out the window and she thought about discussing it with Walter at the end of the day. That he spoke nearly perfect English with no regional accent made him seem familiar, yet he was unlike any American she knew. He understood the geography of the United States better than most, but had never been anywhere except Southern California. He made references to the popular culture of her youth, but his delivery of this information was oddly clinical, as if he'd been storing it up for years and examining it privately; as if this were the first time he'd actually taken it out and played with it. To the extent that he was American, he seemed to her like the result of a bizarre and not unsuccessful social experiment: the boy in the bubble, grown up in a hermetically sealed container overseas, exposed to only the bold-faced facts of the culture, not its daily reality. He held a U.S. passport but had never filed American taxes. He had never voted for president. He knew all the songs from the movie *Fame*, all the lyrics to the song "I Sing the Body Electric," and yet had never graduated from a real American high school, had not experienced the disappointment of a dry cap-and-gown graduation ceremony (no songs, no clapping, no dancing on tables). The thrill of high school was still intact for Walter, as it existed in her imagination as a child: a glamorous future fantasy culled from movies and television and the older kids on her Kansas City block. He was older than she was by about five years, she figured, but his inexperience with her world made him seem innocent. Where she had memories, not just of high school, but also of everything else (college, marriage, New York City) he still had it all to look forward to. He listened to her stories with a wide-eyed fascination that touched her. It had been a long time since someone courted her like this. It had been a long time since someone listened to her stories and remembered every detail, accepting her version of events as truth. Dave always tried to persuade her to see things differently; he always tried to cheer her up. He rationalized her emotions and bullied her with positive suggestions. But Walter didn't mind when she stared into space for too long. When her eyes filled with tears he didn't try to cheer her up, and for this she was grateful. Because in his gaze, and he gazed at her often, she was beginning to see her own reflection again. It was something she had not seen clearly in a long time.

11

The Prince Charming costume had permanent sweat stains in the purple velvet at the armpits and was threadbare on the seam where the ruffled yellow collar met the hole for his neck. Walter removed the cotton T-shirt he'd been wearing during the drive down from Los Angeles and pulled the heavy costume over his head, holding it away from his body for as long as possible, as someone knocked at the door of the windowless dressing room and opened it before he could respond.

"Can I join you? We're on in a minute."

He had met Sharon at his audition the week before. She was smaller than he was and deeply tan. She quickly removed her clothes so that Walter glimpsed her breasts before the blue polyester gown obscured her body from view, long enough to notice that, like all the American women he had known intimately in the past year, her breasts were very white. German women sunbathed topless.

"Zip me up?"

Sharon held up her long brown hair and turned the open back of her dress toward him.

"I've been playing Cinderella since 1981," she said. "At least three other guys have played Charming since then. I can't believe they haven't made you a new costume."

"It is kind of disgusting."

"Don't worry, during the performance the audience can't see it. They're too far away from the stage. But when you go into the crowd to take pictures just make sure not to lift your arms up too high. It gets pretty hot in there under the lights."

She giggled, hiking the blue dress up around her thighs and rubbing on lotion from a bottle she'd pulled out of her bag. Walter pulled on the tight bottom half of his purple costume.

"Never let 'em see you sweat," Sharon quoted the popular commercial for deodorant. "You got the slipper?"

He grabbed the clear plastic slipper sitting on the windowsill and followed her onto the outdoor stage.

At his audition, Walter had been given the script and five minutes to prepare the scene in which Charming fits the missing slipper to Cinderella's foot. He had decided to do the prince as he thought the Brothers Grimm would have imagined him, and had read the whole scene in English with a Bavarian accent. Sharon had giggled and kissed him with an open mouth during the finale.

"The Cinderella story comes from Germany, as I do," he told the casting director afterward. "I was trying to bring some authenticity to the role."

"I thought Cinderella was French."

"French?"

"The whole royalty thing seems French to me."

"Actually, all the fairy tales are German," said Walter. "This one is called 'Aschenputtel' in the original."

"'Aschenputtel,'" Sharon repeated softly.

"In the original version, one of the stepsisters cuts off her heel and the other one cuts off her toes, trying to fit their big feet into Cinderella's little shoe."

"That's gross."

"When the prince sees the blood everywhere, he knows they're lying."

"I don't think the blood would work for our audiences." The casting director tapped her clipboard thoughtfully with a pen. "But what you say is interesting, because we do have a lot of German customers at Disneyland. A little European authenticity might give our production a special edge."

When Walter signed his contract, the human resources department representative from Disneyland went over the routine with him in full. Four scheduled performances a shift, each one followed by a fifteen-minute meet-and-greet session with the audience, followed by a stroll around the grounds to socialize with the other customers. When spoken to, he was always to respond in character. If asked personal questions, he was to smile and move on. If asked for an autograph, he should sign only the name Prince Charming in a fully legible script. Any violation of these rules would result in the immediate cancellation of his contract. On stage before the curtain went up, Sharon gave him the lowdown.

"Mostly they just want to take pictures of you with their

kids. Just put your arm around them and smile and move on as quickly as you can."

"No problem," said Walter. "I'm an expert at *Knuddelbilder*."

"What?"

"Cuddle pictures with fans. I do twenty of those a day in Germany when I go out in public."

"You're famous in Germany?"

"I'm pretty huge there."

"That sounds like a joke."

"I'm not kidding."

"No, I mean like when people say that so-and-so is 'huge in Europe,' it's like they really mean he's a total flop here, you know?"

Sharon was cute, thought Walter, but not that cute.

"Seriously. I'm famous in Germany."

"For what?"

"What do you think we're doing here?"

"I'm just putting myself through school. I'm in dental hygiene at Long Beach."

"You're not an actress?"

Walter was pouring sweat under the velvet and the lights weren't even on. Sharon giggled.

"If you're so famous in Germany, what are you doing here?"

Walter brushed his hair to one side with his hand and shrugged. He pulled the yellow collar away from his neck to let some air into his costume.

"Hollywood, you know."

"In Orange County? No offense, but we're a long way

from all that down here. Bartending in L.A. is probably a better way to get into the business than working at Disneyland."

"If you must know, I have family down here."

The phrase sounded strange coming off his tongue. Although it was true, he felt nervous saying it aloud, as if someone might contradict him. But Sharon was a complete stranger; she knew nothing of his life, so new details would not surprise her.

"My grandparents live in Irvine——" he started.

Before he could continue Sharon held one hand to her mouth. On the other she counted off the seconds with her fingers until the lights came on and the curtain went up.

12

First thing in the morning, Walter arrived at the studio and turned on the lights, illuminating the wide expanse of purple carpet at his feet. He walked into the middle of it, stretched out his arms and rolled his head side to side then bent forward so that his fingers just barely touched the ground. He was teetering precariously over the carpet when Orson came in.

"*Guten Morgen.*"

Walter stood up, shook out his limbs like a rag doll.

"Try it," he said. "It feels good."

Orson raised one eyebrow over the cup of tea he was carrying.

"Who is she?"

"I just want to get in shape. I'm doing a cleanse too."

"A cleanse?"

"Boiled potatoes for a few days. At night I drink a shot of schnapps."

"Where did you get that?"

"That's what they prescribe at the cures in Bavaria."

Orson laughed.

"Only in Bavaria do potatoes and schnapps constitute diet food. You might as well just lick the pavement."

"What?"

"You've never been to India? When you're traveling there everyone tells you the story of the fat guy from England who went to India to lose weight. He traveled for eight months but he never got sick. People wasting away from dysentery all around him and this guy with the stomach of steel, eating curry and gaining more weight. He was so frustrated that the last day he was there, on his way back to England, he licked the pavement outside the New Delhi airport."

"What happened?"

"He was wrecked. I wouldn't recommend it. Lost tons of weight. But he . . ."

Walter wrinkled his nose in an attempt at a grimace but his lips collapsed into a smile that revealed all his teeth. Orson walked up the spiral staircase at the back.

"Nice shit-eating grin," he said.

"You're just too young to understand the revitalizing effects of exercise."

Orson shook his head.

"I ride my bike everywhere, man. Even in the winter. There's a woman. I can tell."

On screen, a romance bloomed. Walter grinned up at Tom Cruise like they were sharing a secret, pleased to see their lives setting a parallel course. Soon they would be drinking champagne on a terrace overlooking the Pacific. Less than a month left until the premiere and he was spending almost every evening with Hope, since her husband was almost always away. How could he just leave her alone so often? She was clearly traumatized by what had happened to her in New York. If, before they met, the war had hovered in the background of Walter's consciousness like bad interference on the radio, now it roared to the forefront. She had drawn a direct line between his daily life and the telegenic doom on the other side of the Atlantic. He hadn't felt so patriotic since he watched O. J. Simpson run the Olympic torch up the Pacific Coast Highway in the summer of 1984. He was almost ready to pin a yellow ribbon to his winter coat. My people are at war, he thought, looking up at Tom Cruise. Our people. Hope avoided the news, so Walter determined to know it all for her. How better to watch over her? He reviewed the newspaper at work and kept the significant facts in his pocket at the ready: how to differentiate anthrax from aspirin or baby powder; where to procure an emergency prescription for Cipro; how to work a short-wave radio. Although he was careful not to concern her with any of the details, he liked knowing that he could come to her rescue if necessary, that he could keep her safe.

At lunchtime he walked with Orson to a small restaurant on the corner. They bent into the wind, their shirt collars pulled up around their faces. The sun was low in the sky. It inched its way around the earth's belly two continents farther south, casting long shadows through the trees. Walter ordered a large plate of potatoes and doused them with salt.

"Did you know that there are two Kansas Cities? One in

Missouri, the other in Kansas. They're right next to each other, like East and West Berlin."

"There are a lot of double cities in the United States. Minneapolis and St. Paul, in Minnesota. Dallas and Fort Worth, in Texas."

"Dallas and Fort Worth aren't technically the same city. They just share an airport. But that's pretty good. Would you be able to name all the states that touch Missouri? Or, say, Kentucky? Do you know which city is further west, Chicago or Detroit?"

"What is this?"

"It's a geography test for American students. Most of them don't know the answers, apparently. I did pretty well."

"Cool. You pass fourth grade."

Walter smiled.

"How about history? If you had to name the five most important moments in history what would you say?"

"What—ever?"

Walter nodded.

"What is going on with you?"

"The Emancipation Proclamation tops most people's lists."

"If it isn't a woman," said Orson, "what is it?"

"I'm just brushing up on my American. You know, I'm going to Los Angeles in December."

"You have a job there?"

"It's in the works."

Orson stopped chewing and put down his fork.

"Is that why you turned down my film?"

"Sorry?"

"We might as well discuss it."

"What film?"

"The one I'm about to make! Your agent told me that it was the right vehicle you'd been waiting for, then she canceled with no explanation."

The student film Klara had offered him was Orson's. Walter studied his potatoes.

"I've made a decision to focus on Hollywood right now."

"You picked a great moment to go back."

"It's not Manhattan or Washington, D.C."

"Actually, I hear Disneyland is number six on the target list."

Walter swallowed his bite of potatoes with some difficulty.

"I will avoid Disneyland," he said. "For sure."

Orson ate without looking at his food.

"There's something funky about the whole thing. The recent attacks in America, the anthrax. You did *Mission: Impossible II,* didn't you? Do you remember the plot?"

"Of course."

"So you remember who was spreading the virus?"

"The guys who produced the cure."

"Exactly. When everyone caught the virus, they were going to make billions, right? Well, look at the lines of people stocking up on Cipro in the United States."

"Life imitates art."

"Where's Ethan Hunt when we need him?"

Walter tried to stifle a laugh. "Bayer is sending out envelopes of anthrax to boost the sales of Cipro?"

"I'm saying it's possible. They don't know where it's coming from, do they? It has been an amazing public relations campaign for the company."

"You are really cynical."

Orson shrugged. "Stranger things have happened."

Although it had been ten years since the reunification, Walter reflected, Orson was one of the only people he knew from the former GDR. When the Wall was up, he had only occasionally visited the other side, and although he knew it had since been rehabilitated, he still thought of it as the dark doppelgänger of the West, the slowly disintegrating buildings and flickering black light of the streetlamps. He still thought of East Berlin as another country.

"How old were you when the Wall came down, anyway?"

"Fifteen," Orson replied. "But that has nothing to do with this. I'm just saying that there's always someone out there ready to make money off other people's fear."

They returned to their meal in silence. Orson pointed at Walter's potatoes with his fork and spoke with his mouth full.

"You better watch out for that superficial Hollywood bullshit over there. When Franka Potente went into American films after *Run Lola Run,* everyone there said her ass was too big. Now she only eats meat and cheese."

"No potatoes?"

"Not in America."

They both laughed.

"For the record," said Orson, "you wouldn't have had to lose weight for my film."

If he were ever to sink so low as to act in a German student film, thought Walter, it would definitely be Orson's. He pushed his plate back and watched him open a small leather case of cigarillos.

"It takes place in Berlin in the early nineties," Orson began. "The main character is named Fritz. He was groomed to be an important Stasi operative in East Germany, one of the directors of the secret police. But all his methods involve illegal invasions of privacy, so after reunification his skills are obsolete. When the film opens, he's just been forced into early retirement. He moves from East Berlin into a new apartment in Charlottenburg for a fresh start and ends up getting involved with the strange old couple that lives next door. When the wife is killed, he uses all his illegal Stasi techniques to solve the crime. It's a mystery, but the kind that takes place in the daytime, like *Rosemary's Baby* or *Rear Window*."

"When do you shoot?"

"I only have the crew during the university vacation, over Christmas. We'll shoot the whole film in order from beginning to end, like a play. If I can do it in eighteen days I get the equipment from my film school for free. With the money from this gig I'll just be able to cover the catering and the tape."

"The tape?"

"I'm shooting on video."

"Really?"

"Film is dead."

Walter handed his empty plate to the waitress. Poor Orson, he thought. Most actors already had Christmas plans they wouldn't sacrifice for an unknown director making a no-budget digital film. Walter watched Orson smoke. With the leather outfit and the long ponytail, the rose-tinted sunglasses fixed onto his pale, hairless face, he looked like a high school student hoping to get into a heavy metal concert in the countryside, but maybe he was the next big thing. Walter allowed himself a rare glimpse down the road less taken: his name on a cinema marquee at Potsdamer Platz, red-carpet interviews at the Berlinale, his Academy Award acceptance speech. A surge of generosity warmed his chest. *My country is at war,* he told himself. The very phrase made him feel reckless and optimistic. He would hate to spend Christmas in Berlin, he would hate to postpone the trip with Hope, but he could change his plans to help out a friend here, couldn't he? He could push back California for a week or two.

"I was really disappointed when you turned me down," said Orson. "But I got a copy of the script to Til Schweiger."

At the sound of this name, Walter woke up abruptly, as if in the middle of a dream. Til Schweiger was the most famous German actor of Walter's generation; the actor/producer of some of Germany's only homegrown hits; the nice guy with model good looks. Say it. *The German Tom Cruise.*

"He loved Fritz," Orson continued. "He was willing to defer his salary for points on the production. He's almost too handsome so I'll have to change the character to accommodate that. But he agreed to work without makeup and gain some weight."

Walter felt dizzy. The potatoes he'd eaten congealed into a monstrous ball in his stomach; he was seeing stars, cheap Christmas lights twinkling at the corner of his vision, making the room spin. Only a month earlier he'd read that Til Schweiger was making a film in Hollywood with Sylvester Stallone, now he was coming to Berlin to play Fritz. A flood of regret quickly extinguished the fantasies Walter had allowed to blaze up on the horizon. He watched Orson crunch out the stub of his cigarillo and motion for the check.

. . .

That evening Walter left work as soon as they finished the last take. He didn't stick around to make small talk in the hallway with the actors doing *Ocean's Eleven* next door. He did not speak to Orson again. He double-parked in front of Butter Lindner to buy a marzipan stollen, a bag of sweets and three bottles of good Rioja. Normally, he went by Hope's place after dinner, taking pains to act like visiting her were an idea that had come to him spontaneously during a digestive stroll through the building. But tonight he arrived early, rang the bell and waited a few inches from the door, making a mental list of things to take care of as soon as possible: plane tickets to Los Angeles, reservations at the Beverly Hilton, a rental car. You probably had to book a car early to get a convertible, he thought, juggling his weight impatiently on the balls of his feet. Usually he had someone conveniently positioned to blame for his unhappiness: Heike, Klara, his parents, the weatherman. But it wasn't anyone else's fault that he had refused to read Orson's script. He could blame only himself for passing on the opportunity to be in a film so brilliant that Til Schweiger was willing to look bad in it for free. Walter rang the doorbell again. If before his lunch with Orson he had been looking forward to meeting Tom Cruise at the premiere, if he had been excited about going to California with Hope, now his future was pitched toward the trip like a palm tree leaning into the winter sun. Three weeks, he told himself. It was long enough. It had to be.

Hope opened the door wearing a pink sweater that made her appear flushed.

"Today is the day of Sankt Nikolaus," he said. "I come bearing gifts. Christmas cake with marzipan."

"Please make yourself at home."

He loved that. *Make yourself at home.* Her apartment was a replica of his own, cleared entirely of his personal archaeology. Each time he entered it, he remembered that before Heike his own walls had also been white. His five rooms had once been empty. Fifteen years earlier he'd moved in with one small suitcase and a few boxes. He had camped out on a mattress for months. Now his place was full of furniture and dust, videotapes he was never going to watch again, receipts collected for yearly tax returns and laid out in little piles after the audit last spring. When he allowed himself to think about the fact that he was still living with the ticket stub from almost every movie he'd ever seen, it made his palms sweat; going downstairs to Hope's apartment was a new lease on life. He liked to circle the dining room while she did her homework, idly sniffing at the corners. Since her boxes from New York were still held up in customs, there were few personal effects lying around; no wedding snapshots on the mantel, no photo albums; a large pile of Holocaust books were telling objects, but as they were always in the exact same position, he assumed they belonged to her husband. Walter walked into the kitchen to unpack the cake from its wrapper and sliced it onto a paper napkin because she didn't have any plates. Since lunch he had been counting the three weeks until the premiere, wishing that his life were a film—say, *Cocktail*—and a montage of images could flash forth on screen to speed things up. The two of them riding horses bareback on the beach, wrestling in the sand, drinking from coconuts, frolicking in a tropical waterfall, feeding each other shrimp. But since it was Berlin and nearly winter and dark most of the time, the ninety-second montage would show only two people talking together night after night in one of two nearly identical apartments.

He uncorked the Rioja and decided to forgo his cleanse prescription in favor of the wine, which set a sexier mood than showing up with a couple of shot glasses and a bottle of home-brewed cherry schnapps. Walter knew that Americans thought of schnapps as the tiny bottles of sweet poison sold at the supermarket checkout to homeless people and teenagers. In fact, the schnapps he had upstairs was very good quality, but he didn't want to risk giving Hope the wrong impression. Before he returned to the dining room, he found her shoes in the hallway and filled them with candy. Then he brought her the stollen and wine.

"You're so sweet!"

She said "sweet" as if it were a two-syllable word.

"You know, this is my first holiday in Berlin," she said. "I completely forgot about Thanksgiving. This year it just passed me by."

"We could celebrate it tomorrow if you like. There is an American section in the food hall at KaDeWe. They sell Pop-Tarts and salad dressing made by Paul Newman and brownie mix. They must have things for Thanksgiving."

"Two weeks late? It wouldn't be the same."

"Maybe you're right. Otherwise, we could just celebrate Thanksgiving every day, like that Heinrich Böll story about Christmas."

"I don't know that story."

"It's a German classic, you should add it to your reading list." Walter motioned toward the pile of books at the end of the table. "There's a crazy aunt who's only happy on Christmas Day. She gets hysterical when they tell her that it's over, so her family celebrates Christmas every day. After a while, they hire actors to play the family members. They sing all the songs and light the candles on the tree. It goes on like that for two years."

"Sounds like fun."

"Sounds like a nightmare. Christmas goes on and on here already. You'll see."

"You take it for granted. I've been reading up on the roots of Christmas, which was a pagan ritual appropriated by the Church as Jesus' birthday, by the way. Actually Sankt Nikolaus was the original figure, an old man bringing treats on December sixth. It was in America that he morphed into Santa Claus, bringing presents on Christmas Eve. He was then reimported to Germany as the *Weihnachtsmann,* which is why you have both."

We have both. This was the last conversation he wanted to have with Hope.

"The traditions seem quaint to you," he said, "but at least American materialism is democratic. Christmas here is for Christians. All the holidays in Germany are for Christians. We have nothing like Thanksgiving, for everyone."

Hope picked the raisins out of her stollen and arranged them in a neat pile on the napkin.

"I know what you mean. Since it's the only holiday uncomplicated by religion, Thanksgiving was the only one we celebrated with Dave's parents."

Walter sat down at the table.

"Why?"

"Well, I studied to convert to Judaism when I was first with Dave, but his parents didn't really approve so I dropped it. Maybe they were just using the Jewish thing as an excuse, because they didn't want him to get married young." She paused. "In any case, the Jewish holidays were awkward after that but Christmas was also a problem, obviously, so we didn't really celebrate anything. Thanksgiving was the only one we could get through without a major meltdown. We always had it at his parents' apartment, because ours was too small. I always made Brussels sprouts."

She finished her cake and wrapped the napkin around the raisins.

"Can I tell you something?"

Walter leaned forward.

"Of course."

"I haven't been to my German class in a week."

He blinked. He wanted to hear more about the problems in her marriage.

"I'm never going to learn German there," she said. "I'm the only American in my class. No one speaks to me. When we have to pair up, no one wants to be my partner. And it's boring."

"But you're a teacher."

"I was a teacher."

"The last time you showed me your homework you were doing pretty well."

"Well, there are other ways to learn a language than sitting in that classroom. How about if you and I speak German with each other?"

"No."

"I thought you would say that."

She motioned down the hall toward the back of the apartment.

"Bring your wine," she said.

In the many evenings they had spent there together, they had never left the front section of the apartment. He knew the layout of the back rooms exactly, of course, but had no idea what to expect. He followed her with his glass in one hand and the open bottle in the other. First, she took him all the way down the hallway and showed him the nursery. It was even emptier than the other rooms in the apartment, down to a loose wire hanging from the light socket in the ceiling. It was dark, but light came in through two large windows overlooking the back courtyard. She pointed at the farm scene carved into the molding on the ceiling. Trees, sheep and a horse.

"You see?"

"It's very nice."

Hope looked small standing in the middle of the empty room, looking up at the ceiling in the shadows.

"It is nice. But I have something else to show you."

She led him back into the hallway and forward to the door of her bedroom. Afraid of any evidence of conjugal passion that might be lying there, Walter dragged his feet, but the room's contents revealed very little: a mattress on the floor against the wall, some clothes piled up in a corner. She held both hands out toward a large black TV set at the foot of the bed. Other than the cardboard box the TV had come in, it was the only significant object in the room.

"Meet the television," she said.

Walter stared at the black screen, avoided looking at the unmade bed, which was positioned right beneath his own upstairs. Hope leaned down to shake out the duvet and threw the pillows against the wall.

"C'mon." She sat down with the remote control and patted the place next to her. "Let's watch some German TV."

He perched himself uncomfortably on the edge of the mattress to her right, his hands clasped around his knees. She was smiling as she pressed the Power button, but her face went blank when the news came on. A female anchor in a special report was going over the crisis since September. Over her shoulder a series of outtakes from the past few months flashed by in chronological order. A young woman sobbed on the curb outside a city skyscraper. The New York mayor did damage control in front of the ragged and now familiar mountain of Ground Zero. American troops rolled off planes into Afghanistan.

"I can't locate the world I know in any of this."

On screen the young woman was being interviewed. She was wearing the disheveled remains of what must have been a chic outfit when she left the house that morning. Her eye makeup was smeared from crying.

"All the good things are still there as you left them," Walter said, although it didn't seem real to him, either. "They only show the bad parts on TV."

"This is awful," she said.

Walter wondered again where she had been that day in September. As movies were his only frame of reference for

New York, he was tempted by images of Hope both as hero-
ine and as damsel in distress, had played the scene out in
both directions. He could as easily imagine her shepherding
a group of small children through the streaming wreckage
as collapsed over the arms of a fireman. When she dropped
the remote on the bed and brought both hands to her face,
he moved one arm to the small of her back. Her spine felt
pointy and fragile under his outstretched palm. He moved
the tips of his fingers ever so lightly against the muscles on
either side. The wine was definitely going to his head.

"Maybe we should try to take your mind off it."

She flinched and handed him the remote control, which
he accepted with disappointment. He would have been willing to envelop her in a bear hug if it came to that; he had
been expecting her to cry. He flipped through the offerings,
stopping on the dubbed version of *Smokey and the Bandit*.

"Burt Reynolds speaks German better than I do," said
Hope.

She watched in silence and Walter watched her watching, still trying to read the meaning of her flinch, like war
code. Maybe he had moved a little too fast? The voice of Burt
Reynolds had retired midway through his career and had
been replaced by a younger actor. Walter listened reflexively
for a moment, trying to ascertain which one had been responsible for this particular movie, and as he concentrated on
the voice, he began to feel better.

"We sync the movement of the lips very carefully to the
languages so that it's almost imperceptible," he said, like a
tour guide showing off his favorite corners of the city.

"You think?"

"What?"

"I find it hard to follow either language when the lips move in English and German comes out."

He stiffened.

"That's because you don't really understand German yet. If you did, you would follow the audio unconsciously. Most people focus on the eyes when they watch movies. They've done studies about that."

"It must be me then." She reached for the bottle of wine on the floor. "I always watch the lips."

Walter resisted the urge to argue with her.

"Let's watch something made originally in German," she said.

He looked at the remote control as if it were the dash-board of his car and he were holding the wheel halfway through a badly organized date, unsure where to take her next. His saddest stories usually elicited the warmest response from Hope, but to start in now would have been awk-ward, even vulgar, he thought, on the heels of the New York coverage. Smokey was sauntering through a backyard some-where in the South when Walter made a decision. She wanted to see a German original? Fine. Klara had said that it was always on at night; it had to be showing on one of these channels, somewhere. The few times he'd caught a glimpse of it in recent years he'd been so unsettled to see his own baby face and the thick bush of dark, moussed-up hair that he'd slid right past without registering where and when it was playing. If his true potential wasn't clear to Hope under its current layers of neglect and malaise, he would show it to her. He would find his former self on television and offer the image up to her as collateral; he didn't have time for her to discover him slowly, like the heart of an artichoke.

He took a gulp from his glass of wine and picked up the remote. She settled back against the pillows and watched indeterminate flashes of the German-speaking world go by until there it was, unmistakable. A wide shot of the Alps in the distance was followed by a quick cut to the interior of a stable, a zoom in on a young man feeding a large brown horse. Walter stopped flipping and held his breath. Hans walked the horse into a stableyard ringed by snow-capped mountains. Julia, the pretty city girl, was coquettishly perched on a picket fence and dressed up for church. They exchanged a shy greeting. Hope's face didn't indicate recognition immediately, but she seemed interested, so Walter tried to relax. Hans filled a bucket with water and lathered up the horse slowly, sneaking fleeting blue-eyed looks Julia's way. He was short and compact. His upper body muscles rippled visibly as he moved the brush in circles against the horse's flank. Walter glanced back and forth between Hope and the TV. He had spent almost every day on the *Schönes Wochenende* set for three years, but it struck him now that it didn't seem any more real to him than New York City. He couldn't even place this particular episode in the show's chronology (he'd washed an awful lot of horses during that time). Maybe his hair was never coming back, but his body could look like that again. He'd lost two kilos already this week. A pleased expression had settled across Hope's face, but he couldn't tell what she was thinking. Had she recognized him yet? She sipped her wine. Hans spilled his bucket of water all over his flannel shirt and Julia laughed on the picket fence. Hope laughed too. Walter held his breath as on screen Hans shook his head and grinned at them both, then pulled off the shirt to reveal a toned brown chest. A voice called to Julia from somewhere off camera. As she hopped off the fence, the camera went in for Hans's handsome, symmetrical face. This is it, Walter thought. He was waiting.

"Tschüss," said Hans with a wink. Bye-bye.

His blue eyes sparkled intensely, reflecting a room full of blazing television lights. The camera lingered for a moment before the credits rolled.

"That one was really good," said Hope.

Walter waited for more but nothing came. At first he thought she was being coy, but she just hadn't recognized him. He was that far gone.

He stared at the black box where his young, buff self had been. In place of Hans, now a cartoon tube of toothpaste promoted a new striped formula. Hope leaned over to pick up the bottle of wine, filled his glass and her own without saying anything at all. Walter was still focused on the toothpaste, when she picked up the remote between them and cut off its singsong monologue midsentence. He drank everything she'd just poured into his glass.

"There isn't a lot on," he said.

One after the other, she flipped through channels showing talk shows or the late-night news. One had a series of quick commercials for phone sex, women in black leather and red lipstick making eyes at the camera. Their breasts were exposed and enormous. Neon pink phone numbers flashed across the screen. He rubbed his temples and closed his eyes. When he opened them, a blond girl was undressing slowly in a park while a muscular man watched from behind a tree. Hope had stopped changing channels. The woman walked over and slowly started to pull down his shorts.

"I can't believe they just show porn on TV," said Hope. "It's like that brothel right on Savignyplatz. What about the children?"

"The children?" He felt weary. "The children are asleep."

Her eyes were open wide in simultaneous disgust and fascination, but she only pressed the remote when the blond woman bent her head. The next scenario was different from the others: no phone number, no makeup, no romantic surroundings or mood lighting, whips or chains; no leather. Two girls were wrestling on a plain gym mat. They were naked, but they weren't doing anything sexual, per se. There was no mud or Jell-O. There was no disco music either, just the sounds of panting. Pink circles formed high on Hope's cheeks. Less than three weeks till the premiere. Walter needed some kind of confirmation from her. A chaste kiss would be great, he thought. Holding hands would be enough. Plan B: When he reached the middle of the bed, he would let his arm rub lightly against hers. As long as she didn't scream or slap him, he would move one hand to cover hers. When she turned her face in response to this touch, he would kiss her. He started inching his way across the bed. On TV, the wrestling girls went at it. One had short brown hair and the other's was long, bleached blond. They got into headlocks and leg twists. The brunette was stronger. She had a determined expression that looked familiar but he couldn't recall seeing this one before. Hope's body was tilted at a slight angle toward the middle of the bed; he could feel the heat of it only centimeters from his own.

"You two look like you're having a good time."

Walter jumped away from Hope so quickly that he spilled wine on the duvet and almost fell off the bed. In silhouette against the bright back light of the hallway, the man he recognized as her husband ambled into the dimly lit bedroom. He was carrying Hope's shoes.

"I'm Dave," he said. "You must be Walter. Please don't get up."

He shook Walter's hand and then held up the shoes for Hope.

"Look what Santa brought you."

When he set them down on the bed, some of the candy spilled over onto the duvet by her feet. She unwrapped one, put it in her mouth.

"Nikolaus!" She smiled at Walter. "I must have been good this year."

Walter had half a hard-on in his pants and pools of perspiration gathering on the palms of his hands. Since he'd seen him a month earlier on the stoop, another mental image of Dave had developed in Walter's mind. He had become smaller, colorless, slumped at the shoulders, fuzzy at the edges, so that the full force of his presence now was shocking. The loud voice. The full head of hair. He had perfect teeth.

"I went to the most incredible restaurant tonight," he said. "The customers cook their own food. There's a chef who gives general directions then you decide among yourselves how to prepare the meal. I took my team from work because it's an amazing exercise in cooperation. I mean, you'd be surprised how challenging it is to coordinate a meal for ten people cooked by ten people. You can really learn a lot about people's strengths and weaknesses. In the end we found a really good synergy."

Walter looked up at him as if he were speaking Chinese.

"Ignore the management-speak," said Hope.

"How you doing, kiddo?"

"I bought a television."

He sat down and leaned across the bottom of the mattress to wrap his fingers around Hope's slim left ankle.

"I see that."

"I quit my German class. I'm just going to learn from the TV from now on."

He removed his hand from her ankle.

"I thought we agreed that it was a good thing for you to get out of the house every day."

Walter thought of the scene he'd first witnessed on the doorstep, and silently encouraged them. *Fight, fight, fight.*

"The people in my class were so unfriendly. Here, at least I have Walter."

Dave reached over to pat Walter's knee.

"Good man."

What was wrong with this guy? Behind his head the wrestling match continued. The brunette pinned the blonde's legs and arms to the gym mat. The blonde squirmed for a few moments and finally gave up.

"She won," said Hope.

Suddenly, Walter recognized her as the girl on the poster out front.

"Time for Action," said Hope. "It took me a second to get it. It's not obvious like the other posters all over town. The naked woman wearing stars on her nipples?"

"Sexyland."

"That's it. What's Sexyland?"

"A sex shop," said Walter.

"On the corner of Leibniz and Kant?"

"This one's on Martin-Luther Strasse. They've been using the same poster forever. There was an article about the model once in the People of Yesterday section of the paper. It's a sort of chronicle of famous has-beens."

"Germany loves the famous has-beens," said Dave. "I heard that Bryan Adams is starting up a fashion magazine here. And how about David Hasselhoff singing on the Berlin Wall, New Year's Eve 1989, wearing that electric leather jacket?"

He laughed and Hope shot him a dirty look. David Hasselhoff was at the peak of his fame in 1989, thought Walter. To be fair, he had only more recently qualified as a has-been.

"What happened to the girl on the poster?"

"She was paid twenty marks to pose in the early 1980s as a one-time thing. But everyone loved the picture, so Sexyland kept it up. In the end she had to move to Majorca because everybody recognized her here. She couldn't get away from it. They say she calls her family once in a while to check if she can come back to Berlin yet, but the posters never go away."

"That's an awful story."

It was kind of awful, he thought. The winner of the wrestling match raised her fists in the air like she did on the poster. *Time for Action* came up in red with the phone number beneath it.

"I still can't believe they show porn on TV here," said Hope.

"These are just commercials," said Dave. "To watch the whole thing, you have to pay. You have to call that number and order the video. But I think the wrestling series is better than the others. The women are more natural without makeup. They're naked, sure, but the sex is implied, not explicit. I think it strikes a good balance by being less exploitative to the women involved. But it's still a turn-on for the potential customer. Don't you agree, Walter?"

Walter, who was thinking that Dave had been spending way too many nights alone in hotel rooms in Poland, blushed. He couldn't remember beating off to the porn ads for years although he and Heike had occasionally left them on in the background during sex. Still, he was determined to set himself apart here.

"I'm not into this kind of thing," he said.

Dave winked at him.

"I see."

Walter shrugged. Dave now assumed that he was gay, which, he figured, wasn't such a bad thing. It meant that he would leave them alone. Walter reached for his shoes. Hope's husband had turned out to be the kind of guy who almost certainly kept his watch on during sex; who winked and chuckled and called his own wife *kiddo*. But his confidence

was enviable. Whether it derived from arrogance or ignorance was not yet clear. Perhaps it was just something American, something they put in the water over there, like
fluoride, to give the men an unfair advantage from the start.
Time for Action, Walter decided, standing up. This guy deserves whatever he gets.

13

On the fourth stage of the Disneyland theater, Walter looked around the side of the curtain. The theater was packed: adults holding children on their laps; preteen girls clustered together in groups, standing in the aisles. The audience seemed to have increased exponentially every weekend since Thanksgiving.

"It's official," he said to Sharon when he came back behind the curtain. "Every school in the world is out for Christmas vacation. And every single family decided that this was the year to take that trip to Disneyland."

She was applying lip gloss with one finger from a little plastic pot and he admired the shiny bow of her mouth. He liked the way her body felt in his hands. He wasn't in love with her, but he liked her a lot.

"Work that accent, Charming," she said. "Give the girls a little European fantasy to take home with them to Boise."

She blew him a kiss. He had been sleeping with her since the beginning, but it was a couple of months before he'd realized that he'd stopped sleeping with anyone else. Possibly because his previous sexual experiences in America had been quick, and rarely twice with the same person, or simply because she was a dental student and noticed physical details, Sharon had been the first woman to comment directly on his foreskin. She had inspected it like a scientific specimen, tested its elasticity and asked questions as if it were, like E.T., a strange, cute animal descended on Southern California from another planet.

"It's like the difference between a normal sweatshirt and a hooded one," she said finally. "No more, no less."

Walter had never seen a circumcised penis. Everyone in Germany had foreskins. That all American men were circumcised made him uncomfortable (setting him, in his nascent Americanness, even further apart) but Sharon seemed to like it. Unlike the majority of Americans he'd encountered, she seemed to think the fact that he came from Germany was interesting. A plus, not a minus. She even asked him to talk dirty to her in German sometimes, although she didn't understand a word of it.

"I could be saying anything," he protested. "*Looks like rain on Tuesday.* It just sounds dirty to you because you don't understand it."

"No, no. I can tell. The words have meaning. I can feel it without understanding the language."

They were eating breakfast. He spent most nights at the house she shared with friends near work now and went back to Los Angeles only a couple times a week. She held up a piece of pineapple from her fruit salad.

"You're saying that pineapple isn't pineapple anymore when you call it by a different name."

Walter laughed.

"Seriously. What do you call this in German?"

"Ananas."

"Ananas," Sharon repeated, eating the fruit. "It's still pineapple, baby. I know what you like in any language."

Walter ran his fingers through his hair and took a deep breath before the curtain went up. Normally he didn't look directly into the audience during a performance. The lights were so bright that it was impossible to see anything beyond the first few rows. When he was taking a bow with the others and he heard the voice call out from the middle of the theater, he thought he was imagining things.

"Hans! Guck mal hier!"

Walter looked out off the edge of the stage, but all he could see were hands clapping, until he walked down the stairs from the stage and found himself engulfed in a sea of young girls. They were all screaming in German now, they were all calling him Hans. Judging from their accents, they came from the south of Germany, as he did, where *Schönes Wochenende* had been especially popular. They pulled at his arms and kissed his cheeks. Some of them cried. The Disneyland guards watched Walter suspiciously from the edges. Nothing like this had ever happened. The girls usually went for Cinderella with their kisses and their snapshot cameras. The Prince was second choice! Walter tried to stay in character, a smile plastered to his face as he peeled back their fingers and pressed through the crowd.

"My sweet ladies," he shouted, "Prince Charming only speaks English."

The girl standing closest to him seemed tall for her age; she was able to look him directly in the eye.

"We know it's you, Hans," she said in German. "Just because you're wearing a different costume doesn't mean you're someone else."

They were standing near the back wall of the theater and over her shoulder he could see the entrance to the dressing rooms behind the stage. Walter met her gaze. He wondered, Is *Ananas* still *Ananas* when you call it a pineapple? He broke free of his fans and made for the door.

14

Most days, Hope waited until rush hour was over to set out on her trips around the city. Compared to what she had been used to in Manhattan, rush hour in Berlin wasn't even that bad. On the occasions that she set out too early or came home too late, she still almost always got a seat on the subway. During the past ten days, as she'd been switching tracks in stations scattered all over the city, from U-Bahn to S-Bahn, she had quickly established certain preferences: the right side of the car not the left, the back, four seats to herself if possible. On long stretches above ground, she put up her feet. Every morning she planned out a different route before she left the house. She did not choose her destinations for the areas around the subway stations but rather for the stations' names. Weissensee to Spandau, Frohnau to Lichterfelde to Wannsee. Sometimes she picked a series of stops that rhymed, or began with the same letter, or sounded funny, like Blankenberg, or nice, like Paradestrasse. Sometimes she got off at the end and looked around, but mostly she just rode. She liked to think of the city out the window as a person, clocking its schedule by the ebb and flow of students getting out of school, the older women with their midmorning groceries, strollers at the elevator stations in the afternoon, the general flow of citizens from east to west, north to south. Although she never set out without a plan, she knew that another person (Dave, for example) might have said that her traveling lacked an organizing principle, might have suggested that instead she make a list of important attractions or at least pick a theme: graveyards, museums, modern architecture, flea markets, parks designed by someone famous, World War II battle sites, Cold War battle sites, soccer stadiums. But he would be missing the point. The point was to figure out where she was. The point, she thought, was to let the city unfold on its own.

The train drove through Stadtmitte station, walking distance from Checkpoint Charlie and Libeskind's empty Jewish Museum, but Hope did not get out. Walter had already pointed out that all big-name tourist attractions were pretty depressing.

"Here in Germany we only celebrate guilt," he'd said. "Our greatest national monuments honor the suffering of our victims. It's the opposite of the United States, where you come away from battle sites in California feeling proud to be American, regardless of what happened to the Mexicans. You know what I mean?"

Hope figured the museums could wait until she had formed her own opinion. The only other person in the subway car at that moment was an old woman with a red wool hat and a dog in her lap. That the dog was allowed on the train at all was a novelty, but the woman just rubbed behind his ears as if it were the most normal thing in the world. When Dave told his parents they were moving to Berlin, Hope's mother-in-law had retorted that the Germans loved dogs more than people.

"The SS guards always had their little dogs with them," she said. "Feeding them steak while the Jews starved."

Dave's mother had spent the war years happily ensconced in Forest Hills, Queens, so it was unclear how she knew this; it was the kind of thing people in New York often said about Germans, thought Hope. Random, but incriminating. She was wondering if the woman was old enough to have been one of the *Trümmerfrauen* who cleaned up Ku'damm, when she got up at the next stop and dropped her dog to the ground. The dog wasn't on a leash, but he didn't leave her side. They sauntered through the open doors of the train together as if heading out for a night on the town.

As the U-Bahn pulled up above ground, Hope blinked into the daylight thinking that it was possible to see every layer of the city's history at once in any direction. A drive through Berlin was like visiting a grand archaeological site, but unlike that of a civilization from thousands of years ago—already dug up and dusted off, set aside at a clinical distance—this one was fully in use; it was up to visitors to excavate the remains, to make sense of it for themselves. In New York, as soon as one building came down, another went up so quickly as to completely obliterate the memory of what had been there before. In the other European cities, the past was glorified, the architecture spruced up for tourists to the point of caricature. But here, nobody seemed to be in any hurry one way or the other. Buildings had been bombed and the city had been ripped apart, but years later holes remained all over the place without explanation or apparent concern. The city moved forward with a lack of vanity that she found relaxing. As the days got shorter, speeding toward the winter solstice, she was beginning to feel at home. Hope leaned back in her seat and looked out the window, thinking about her first year in college, when with a boyfriend she had ridden each New York train to the end of the line just to see where they went. One afternoon they had ended up in Far Rockaway, a windswept neighborhood of dilapidated Victorian houses and a long, white beach where they'd come upon a tree, barren of leaves, but decorated all over with dirty old stuffed animals. Dingy rabbits and teddies of all shapes and sizes and the occasional filthy zebra and a very large, blue, one-eyed bear. The tree was outside a bar and the bartender there told them that around the corner was the parking lot for all the garbage trucks in New York and that the bar was where the men hung out after their shifts. He said that the tree was a time-honored tradition (regularly maintained and updated with new decorations), a reminder to everyone at the end of the day to keep their sense of humor when handling other people's trash.

It was during one of the few crowded moments in the afternoon when the police came onto the train. Hope was standing up at the time, holding on, when she noticed a plainclothes man and woman, with official-looking badges hanging around their necks, making their way through from the other end of the car. The man was middle-aged and the woman was younger. As they addressed the passengers, each one nervously but obediently produced a little piece of paper for their inspection. One by one they looked closely at the papers, then passed them back. They appeared to be tickets of some kind, although unlike any other subway ticket or pass Hope had seen before. Most apparently passed muster, but those passengers in possession of the wrong kind of paper were rounded up by the door. After a while the man stayed back to guard the prisoners and only the woman continued up the aisle. The train, which had been loud with conversation at the previous stop, had fallen silent. People waited with their hands in their laps, little papers in their hands. Hope fished around in her pockets automatically, though she knew she didn't have a ticket because she didn't even know she needed a ticket. The understanding that the subway was free wasn't the only reason she had been riding it every day, but the sheer generosity of it had been very appealing. It had made her feel welcome, and the sudden realization that she had been wrong about this made her feel queasy. She backed herself into the closed doors at the other end of the car.

"Fahrkarte," said the female cop when she reached Hope.

Her eyes were a grayish-blue and small, her thin lips pursed. When Hope failed either to produce a ticket or to explain herself, she took her arm as if to pull her toward the other prisoners, but just then the doors opened and the crowd pushed past them in both directions. Hope pulled her arm free and backed onto the platform at Friedrichstrasse station, turned at the top of the stairs and ran down them.

It was drizzling outside the station. She ran up the sidewalk without looking back, intoxicated by the flight forward. She ran past the traffic that marked the northern end of

Friedrichstrasse, past the construction sites and empty spaces, through puddles cast the murky yellow of streetlights at dusk, feeling the distance left behind by each footstep. But at the first corner past the station a hand, then two, landed on her back; then an arm around her waist. The cop, who had been chasing her, now hugged her from behind and Hope, no longer able to move forward, collapsed against her, panting.

"Where is your ticket?" She spoke basic, if heavily accented, English. "No good to run."

She released Hope from the hug but held on to one wrist.

"I didn't know I needed a ticket."

"There machines in every station."

"But no turnstiles." Her cheeks were wet. "Nobody checks."

"I check."

"Now? I've been riding the subway every day for ten days."

"Lucky for you, then. You should have paid. We have honor system here. Please show me your passport."

"An honor system for the subway," said Hope. "That's just a trap."

She was crying now. The rain came down harder.

"I don't have my passport with me."

"It is illegal to go out without identification."

"Illegal?"

Hope stared at the policewoman through a thick lens of tears, thinking that if they took her to jail and she were allowed one phone call, she would call Walter to bail her out, not Dave. It wasn't that Dave couldn't successfully negotiate with the German police; actually, he would relish the opportunity. It was that afterward he would ask her too many questions that she couldn't answer, while Walter would ask her none at all. He would bring a towel to dry her hair. He would take her home and make her tea.

"Then you pay sixty marks now." The policewoman pulled an official-looking pad of paper out of her pocket, rounding her body over it to protect from the rain. "Fare is four. Penalty is sixty. Since you have not identification I cannot send you a bill. You must pay now."

"That's fifteen times the fare."

"You ride for long time already free. Penalty sixty."

"That's too much."

"This is a free country now. Be lucky. We have honor system now. Next time you buy ticket or worse."

She reached deftly for Hope's handbag and pulled out a pack of gum, a pen, Dave's copy of *Weimar Culture*. It was a small, attractive, yellow book; raindrops stained the cover immediately.

"You can't just go through my bag like that."

The policewoman removed a brown leather wallet from the bag, opened it, took out sixty marks and handed it back to Hope, along with the bag itself. Then she leaned over her pad and wrote out a receipt.

"I am the police," she said. "I do whatever I want."

15

The last day of work on *Vanilla Sky*, the trees gave up their last few leaves. Construction sites all over the city came to a standstill, kilometers of scaffolding forsaken until spring. On the way to work, Walter watched December descend over Berlin through the windshield of his car with affection he could feel only for a lover he had already decided to abandon: her cracked lips never to be kissed again, the uneven sighs in her sleep. He could appreciate the winter now knowing he didn't have to live through it. He would miss the fresh air most of all, he thought. When he lived in Los Angeles in the 1980s, the city had been in an almost permanent state of smog alert. He remembered constant warnings to keep your windows closed in the heat against the heavy, orange-pink haze. There was no industry in Berlin, he reflected, and thus no money, but as a result it did have good air. Out the window a group of people waited at the crosswalk behind a scrim of frozen breath. At the Christmas Market by the Gedächtniskirche, vendors were already heating up their grills. The greasy smell of bratwurst came into the car. Tourists were eating kale and bacon for breakfast. The working stiffs at the Europa Center hurried into work in beige overcoats. The mothers soldiered up the sidewalk in groups of two or three, while tucked deep into their strollers, the next generation watched the storm clouds gathering overhead, breathing in Berlin's fresh winter air like a drug.

Wrapping up the latest Tom Cruise usually left Walter with postpartum melancholy, but not today. He would treat his last days as a farewell tour, do all the best things one last time, this time with Hope: ice-skating on Wannsee, a winter stroll through the gardens at Schloss Charlottenburg. He had not told her yet about his plans for the two of them in California, but there would be time for that now too. Dave had returned to Poland, leaving them alone again in peace.

"You free for dinner?" He called up the stairs when he arrived at the studio.

"Me?"

Orson's voice came over the loudspeaker. He stuck his head out of the cabin door above and said it again in a normal voice. They hadn't spoken much all week.

"You inviting me to dinner?"

If there were two of them it would be natural to invite Hope along. Just a casual outing among friends. The perfect first date.

"It's our last day. We should celebrate."

"Sounds good."

Orson closed the door to the cabin and Walter turned to the screen overhead where a clip from the end of the film played in slow motion. Tom Cruise took a flying leap off the top of a tall building in downtown Manhattan, his arms out-stretched like a diver. It looked as though the wind might catch his body and bring him up, giving him wings, but instead he just fell to the ground. It wasn't until the clip was over that Walter realized he'd been holding his breath.

Outside Deutsche Synchron, a cold rain hovered at one or two degrees above freezing, resisting snow. Orson unlocked his bike and pulled it up alongside Walter's car.

"Don't you want a ride?"

He tapped the hardtop of the Mercedes convertible.

"How many days a year can you actually take that thing off?"

"In the summer I keep it off all the time."

"In the summer it rains every other day."

"So I put it back up between trips."

Orson laughed, loudly, pulled a waterproof poncho over his parka. "You should get one of these," he said.

"You sure you don't want a ride?"

"No, thanks. I need my bike to get home later."

They agreed to meet at The Wild West in half an hour, leaving Walter alone in his car with the radio. Marvin Gaye came through like California on the pitch-perfect sound system. *Let's get it on.* He leaned back against the headrest above the driver's seat, moving his head in time to the music. In almost every Tom Cruise movie he could think of, *Rain Man, Jerry Maguire, Days of Thunder, The Firm,* you name it, somewhere in the second act his character danced and sang along to a pop song on the radio to illustrate a sudden flash of optimism. He closed his eyes, imagining himself dancing with Hope on that terrace overlooking the Pacific. Champagne and the sunset, Tom Cruise smiling somewhere in the background, Marvin Gaye on the radio. He moved his shoulders and tapped his feet against the floor of the car. It was more than a month already since Heike walked out on him and although he still checked his messages regularly to see if she'd called, he only did so out of habit. Things were looking up. He loved this song. He felt so good tonight. But he had seen enough Tom Cruise movies to know that a sudden flash of optimism was usually just a harbinger of further disaster. He grooved in place against the smooth leather interior of his car, but for fear of further plot twists he controlled the urge to sing.

He found Hope standing in the lobby in her raincoat.

"Are you going out?"

"No. I just got in."

She squeezed the water from her hair onto the floor.

"Why don't you come to dinner with Orson and me? We finished the job today and we're celebrating."

"Like this?" She looked down at herself. "I don't know."

"You look great. Come on, my treat."

He hurried her into his car and drove around the corner. He had no time to appreciate the novelty of having her out in the world. He didn't get to clock her reaction to his beautiful car because he knew that if Orson arrived first at The Wild West, Bodo wouldn't give him a table. Walter found a parking place and steered Hope into the restaurant just as Orson was locking up his bike at the curb. It was not until the three of them were sitting at a nice corner table at the restaurant basking in the warm light of its yellow walls that he saw what a terrible idea it had been to bring together these two people to this restaurant for dinner. He and Orson had never spoken English to each other; Hope had never heard Walter speak German at all. Trapped between two selves at the table, he said nothing for fear of alienating one or both of them. Orson's long hair was wet from the ride over; his leather pants gave off a meaty smell as they dried. Among the moneyed, elegant patrons of The Wild West, his personal style screamed for the wrong kind of attention. People at surrounding tables looked at them, sniffed, looked away. Walter searched the restaurant for Bodo while Orson smoked and Hope drank her wine. She had removed her raincoat to reveal an equally wet sweater, and every few seconds, both men glanced at her nipples poking through the tight green wool. She was already well into her second glass when she started talking.

"I was caught today riding the U-Bahn without a ticket."

Orson took off his pink sunglasses.

"Inside the train or on the platform?"

His English was good.

"On the train, but then I made it about a block up Friedrichstrasse before she caught me."

He leaned forward as if to get a better look at her face.

"Who?"

"The policewoman."

"The people who check you on the subway aren't really the police. They're just security guards."

"Whatever. She chased me down. She went through my things."

"She ran after you?"

"Yes. It was terrifying. I mean, being grabbed by a German policefrau in Berlin obviously conjures up pretty terrible images."

"Technically she wasn't a policefrau."

"She said she was."

"In English? I am sure she didn't know the difference."

"Regardless. You can't help but consider the historical context."

Orson laughed. "Please. Why didn't you pay the fare?"

"Because I thought the subway was free."

"Free?"

"Walter said that Berlin was a socialist paradise."

"What?"

"I was talking about West Berlin in the eighties," said Walter, clearing his throat. "But even then we paid for the subway."

"Even in the East we paid," said Orson. "Anyway, how could all the transportation in Berlin be free? The city is totally broke."

Hope looked tired. "I don't know. Maybe that's why the city's broke."

"It's broke because when the Western world no longer needed Berlin to be their island behind the Iron Curtain, they pulled out all the subsidies and there was nothing left here. No industry, no business, no money——"

"Orson," said Walter, cutting him off, "the East was already broke when the Wall came down. The West went broke rebuilding it."

He turned to Hope.

"East Germany was one-third the size of West Germany, both in population and size, and everything there was in terrible condition in 1989. But we just absorbed it."

"You could have let us continue to be our own country," said Orson.

"Since the early nineties, every German citizen has been paying solidarity tax every month to rebuild the East."

"Even if they live in Munich?"

"Everyone. Imagine if the United States annexed all of Mexico and said that in ten years they were going to have the same quality infrastructure as we do and that we were going to pay for it. The *Autobahn* in Brandenburg is gorgeous now but it leads nowhere."

Orson exhaled impatiently through his nostrils.

"You didn't pay on the subway today because you thought you could get out of it by playing the dumb American," he said to Hope. "You thought the rules didn't apply to you. I spent a year in America on a high school exchange——"

"Where?"

"In Montgomery, Alabama."

Hope ran her left hand through her hair. Her gold wedding ring caught the candlelight on the table. Walter hoped Orson hadn't seen it.

"You Americans are always complaining that someone is infringing on your rights. I mean, what really happened to you today? You skipped the fare, you had to pay a sixty marks penalty and so you cried?"

"I felt trapped."

"Orson, stop," said Walter. "She's been through a lot."

"It felt good to make a break for it, actually. I mean, in New York——"

Orson cut her off.

"Where?"

"Just leave it alone," Walter said to Orson in German, so that Hope would not understand. "She's been through a lot. She was in New York in September, understand?"

Orson replied in German too. "Do you realize the social capital it has to suggest that she was in New York on 9/11?"

"She isn't just suggesting. It's true."

"But to refer to it like that, in public like that, in the middle of an argument, is a trump card. It is the present-day equivalent to rolling up your sleeve to show us her number."

"What?"

Orson slapped the inside of his forearm.

"Her identity number? You mean a tattoo from a concentration camp?" Walter shook his head. "Where are you going with this?"

Orson turned to Hope and switched into English.

"I might disagree with you, but I'm not going to argue with you now. You personally suffered through the seminal tragedy of our generation."

"A lot of other people suffered more than I did."

"Well, you aren't going to run into any of them here. You were there and we just watched it on TV. You win."

"Win what?"

"For the rest of your life you'll be sitting around with groups of people and everyone else will describe where they were when the planes hit. At work, on the toilet, on the phone. People will cherish the telling of their insignificant stories and then you'll shut them down. *I was there,* you'll say. And people will look at you differently."

"Is it so different from being in Berlin when the Wall came down? That used to be the seminal moment of our generation."

Walter reflected that he had been in exactly the same place—Deutsche Synchron—when both events occurred. In 1989, he had eventually left the studio in Wedding to walk into Mitte, against the flow of people rushing into West Berlin.

"It was an amazing moment," said Orson. "But it was not a tragedy. Tell us what you were doing when the planes hit."

"Why should I?"

"Because you're going to tell this story many times and this is your chance to practice it with an excellent director."

Hope held her wineglass with both hands and looked into it. Walter imagined her covered in white soot, running up the street like the people on TV. Maybe she was trapped in one of the towers herself, on a class trip with all of her students. He had read stories in the paper about heroines like her, teachers escorting their children down a hundred flights of stairs in the dark.

"I was asleep," she said quietly.

"Asleep?"

Walter almost yelled the word, so that the people at the next table turned to look at him. At least she might have saved a cat abandoned in an apartment building. Asleep is where Heike would have been had she been there that day, not Hope. Walter stared at her profile in the candlelight, and corrected himself. Heike would have been right in the thick of it, her face smeared with soot and camera-ready, working the publicity for all it was worth. It was he who would have been asleep. That's right. Other people jumping out of windows to save their own lives while he slept; the most significant public tragedy of his generation and Walter in bed while it all passed him by. *Asleep*. Maybe it was something he and Hope had in common. He tried now but was unable to remember the last time he felt truly, completely awake.

"By the time I went outside, both towers had already come down."

"But you felt trapped," said Orson.

"We were all trapped. You can't imagine."

"I grew up in East Berlin."

"That's different. In Berlin it was a permanent situation. It must have seemed normal."

Walter was picturing himself asleep with Hope, their arms wrapped around each other in a bed floating over a war-torn city.

"Americans," said Orson. "Your own experience is always so much more important than other people's. Your own defense is always worth a struggle, regardless of consequence. *Angriff ist die beste Verteidigung.*"

"What does that mean?"

"Attack is the best defense," Walter translated.

Orson leaned toward Hope over the table and spoke quietly.

"It means that the security chick on the subway was just doing her job, but rather than take responsibility for your own actions you fought with her, got her wet and upset, ruined her afternoon."

"Better to go down fighting."

Orson shook his head and whistled a few bars of "Dixie"; it happened to be a popular ring on German cell phones that year and everybody knew the tune. Hope fiddled nervously with her wedding ring. suddenly the shiniest object in the restaurant, flashing like the emergency lights on a double-parked car. He looked back and forth between Orson's eyes and the ring. Where the hell was Bodo? Orson definitely assumed that Walter was already sleeping with Hope. When he saw the ring he would tease her about it, Walter was sure of it; Orson couldn't keep his mouth shut about anything. Her hands rested on the table in front of her. She pulled the gold band up to the knuckle, swiveled it, and pushed it down the bottom of her finger.

"You know what?" said Orson. "The thing I admire most about Americans is the same thing that most disgusts me. Your obstinate self-determination."

Hope twisted her ring.

"But it's the same with Germans. That is, our best quality is also our worst. Apologetic cautiousness. Fewer mistakes, but a lot less progress. Case in point: when an American director wants the actors to begin, do you know what he says to them?"

"Action."

"Exactly. Do you know what German directors say?"

"Achtung?"

"We say *Bitte*," Orson told her. "It means 'please.'"

Hope watched Orson's face carefully over the edge of her glass.

"You are amazing, Orson Welles," she said. "You just sit back and tell me that Americans are so awful, but you name yourself after one of our most famous filmmakers and make money dubbing our movies into your language so that more of your people will watch them. You can't have it both ways."

Orson shrugged. "Last I checked there was still a fine line between appreciating American fiction films and agreeing with the government's foreign policy."

"Look, we have a right to defend ourselves. They started it, remember?"

"That's one way of looking at it."

"We also happen to be defending the rights of very weak people. You know how women are treated over there, don't you? If nothing else, you must agree that we have a responsibility to liberate them."

"I just don't think that's what this war is about. Even so, I don't think liberating anyone else is the responsibility of the United States."

Hope smoothed two fingers across each of her eyebrows toward her temples and sighed. "You grew up in a totalitarian regime."

"And I don't remember the United States coming to our rescue. As I remember it, we liberated ourselves."

Walter motioned to the waiter for another bottle of wine. So much for the celebration dinner, he thought, so much for his first date with Hope.

"I thought you weren't going to argue with me anymore. I thought I was beyond reproach."

"*Touché.*"

Orson watched the waiter uncork the new bottle and, as she held up her glass to be filled, finally caught sight of the gold band on the fourth finger of her left hand.

"Are you married?"

Hope looked down at the ring as if she'd just discovered it. Walter inhaled slowly through his teeth.

"Yes."

"For a long time?"

"Six years."

"Is your husband American?"

"Why?"

Orson glanced at Walter, licked one finger and touched it to the burning end of his cigarillo so that its flame slowly sizzled to a stop. Walter held his breath, pleading silently, the weight of his immediate future hanging on the delicacy of Orson's response.

"We wear wedding rings on the right hand here in Germany. Not on the left. I always forget that Americans do it the other way around."

Bodo arrived at the table and Walter let the air out of his stomach.

"Just in time," he said under his breath.

"Did I hear correctly? We have a convict in the restaurant?"

Hope held out her hand to be shaken.

"I was myself once arrested at Friedrichstrasse," said Bodo.

He rolled his r's in English as if speaking with an Irish brogue. He formed his sentences as if still speaking German. A yellow ribbon was still fastened to the collar of his shirt.

"I was coming back to West Berlin from a day in the East

with another actor friend. We were separated and questioned for hours in little rooms. Good cop, bad cop. Finally, we tell them everything."

"What did you do?"

"We bought the complete works of William Shakespeare. One set for each."

"It was illegal to buy books?"

"No. But the books cost more money than was legal to exchange in one day. We had exchanged ours with a street guy, black market, instead of at the official place. We got a much higher rate."

"How did you get out of it?"

"We told the police we were poor actors, which was true, that we could not pay to buy such important literature in our own terrible, capitalist country, which, by the way, was also true. Eventually they let us go."

Orson laughed. Walter, relieved, laughed too.

"Nice ribbon," said Orson.

Bodo looked down at his shirt collar.

"Born and raised in West Berlin, my man. We always remember the airlift."

Their eyes met and in the slow moment that followed, Orson seemed to be swallowing his words. Bodo smiled.

"Have you already heard the specials?"

When the food came, they were well into their third bottle of wine. Hope listened intently to the plot of Orson's movie.

"I want to say things about my country that people never say out loud," he said. "But the film is going to be funny. I want to draw people in by making them laugh and then make them think."

"It's a cool idea to have this guy reinvent himself by putting his skills to good use. When I was teaching, I always tried to use humor to communicate the difficult concepts."

"Well, I tried to sell this script to all the public funding agencies and no one would touch it. They said it would offend people in the East. *The GDR wasn't just ironic furniture, young man*, they told me. But I think if it's done right, humor will heal people, not offend them. So I am funding it myself. At least this way I can stay true to my vision."

"You know what, if you need an apartment to film in for free, you're welcome to use mine. It's completely empty. My stuff still hasn't arrived from New York."

The only thing worse than losing the role was the idea of passing Til Schweiger every day in the lobby during the shoot, thought Walter. Thankfully he wouldn't even be here. He would be drinking piña coladas by the pool at the Beverly Hilton.

"I might take you up on that," said Orson, taking down her phone number in a notebook. "We're still scouting for locations."

She lifted her glass.

"To your first Academy Award," she said.

They clinked their glasses together and turned to Walter, who lifted his own reluctantly.

"I wanted him to be the star but he turned me down," said Orson.

"Really? I didn't know you were an actor," she said, turning to look at Walter. "I mean, I thought the dubbing thing was something different."

"He's an icon!"

"Don't exaggerate."

All evening he had been unsuccessful in trying to influence the conversation's direction.

"You have to see *Schönes Wochenende*," said Orson. "It's a TV show from the early eighties about people in the Alps. It's a classic and Walter was the star. His character was named Hans. Everybody loved Hans. When I was a child, we could pick up West German TV signals over the Wall. We never missed *Schönes Wochenende*. My sister even had a black-market poster of Hans up behind her bedroom door."

Hope clapped her hands together, looking at Walter in delighted disbelief.

"You have to show it to me!"

He cleared his throat, scanning the soft surface of her face.

"Remember the guy washing the horse? The German show with the beautiful landscape?"

Her lips opened up in a circle that exposed all her teeth.

"That was me."

"You look so different now."

He could feel the blood pumping through his heart.

"It was years ago."

"Have you been in other things since then?"

"No."

"That's a pity."

Orson nodded enthusiastically.

"He looks even better now, don't you think?"

"Please—"

"He does. Hans had a baby face."

"That's right. Now it's weathered into something more interesting."

Walter rubbed one hand over the face they described. His thumb and forefinger pressed into the sharp, day-old stubble on either side of his mouth as Orson went on.

"He walked out on his contract at the height of the show's popularity. Hans went off to the army. The whole thing was something of a local industry mystery."

A mystery! Walter laughed. Better than a cautionary tale. In the years since then, he had nervously gauged how much of his history to reveal to each new person that came into his life.

"Where did you go?"

"Los Angeles. I told you that."

"Why?"

"My father died——" He stopped himself: He would tell Hope everything but not now, not here. "It was complicated."

"Must have been tough to get work again when you came back," said Orson.

"I never planned to come back."

"Will you stay for good this time?"

"You're going back to L.A.?"

"I told you——"

"That's why he turned down my film."

"I told you. I'm going to L.A. for Christmas. After the premiere."

"To stay?"

"Maybe."

"No," she said.

Walter gazed at Hope in the candlelight, unclear what she meant. *Come with me*, he asked her silently. He couldn't bring himself to say it here.

"He was great as Hans but he would have been even better as Fritz," said Orson.

Hope put one hand on Walter's arm and squeezed it.

"You would have been perfect."

16

Sharon shared a small house in Irvine with roommates from Disney. It was a pinkish bungalow in a development of pinkish bungalows laid out like checkers across a board. In the mornings Walter liked to sit on her front step with his cereal and look down the street, which was perfectly straight. He would close one eye and then the other, checking for a slight curve in the pavement, waiting for someone to appear on the concrete horizon. People in Irvine never walked anywhere, not to dinner with the neighbors, not for exercise. They drove their cars somewhere, went for a jog, got back in their cars and drove home. But he waited there anyway, because he could imagine it so clearly: an old couple, just taking a morning stroll through the neighborhood, would come up the sidewalk and there he would be, eating cereal on the front step of a pink bungalow in Irvine as if random coincidence had brought them together. In his mind the scene that followed played out different ways. Sometimes they recognized each other immediately and fell tearfully into an embrace. Sometimes they stopped to stare at him, since he looked just like his mother, and he played it cool.

"I didn't know I had grandparents," he'd say. "What a surprise."

After she died, he had waited for them to come for him. Every day he had expected to find them after school, waiting for him on the low wall that lined the front yard of his house, calling out to him with the familiar English words that had all but disappeared overnight: *honey, breakfast, night night, love-you, baby.* They never came and he had never seen a picture of them, and so he examined the face of every American tourist who appeared in his Alpine village, just in case. As a teenager, when he traveled by train and found himself sitting next to an American couple of a certain age, he always wondered. They might have been anyone then, he thought, but now they were only a few miles away. He had located Springtime Estates on the map soon after he got the Disney job and had been driving past it for months now, had even idled once in the car at the front gate, next to the sign advertising "Independent Living with Friendly Assistance." After twenty minutes, he'd chickened out and driven away.

At first he did not register the beige Star of David that decorated the sign. That his grandparents chose to live in a Jewish community struck Walter as no more or less of a surprise than that they lived in Irvine at all, or in California. He didn't know if they were short or tall, elderly or just getting on, if they were friendly, busy, sick; he knew nothing about them. The day he finally went inside the gates of Springtime

Estates was a January Monday blessed with the kind of weather that makes people who moved west from colder climates want to kiss the ground with gratitude. He drove slowly through the front gates and up the flat, flower-named avenues until he found 53 Bougainvillea. The house was a bungalow not unlike Sharon's. It was light blue with small front windows and one car parked in the driveway, a powder blue Buick sedan that almost matched the color of the house. Walter pulled over to the other side of the street. Only crickets punctuated the silence, chirping in time with the rapid staccato of his heartbeat. The house shimmered in the sunshine, ripe with promise and half unreal. Walter turned on the radio and Lionel Richie crooned. He watched the dark blue front door for signs of life, thinking that by being here now he had veered off the linear trajectory of his life. Worse, that he was breaking an unspoken rule that bound him to his father. In the ten years between their deaths, his father had only mentioned his mother's parents once, drunk on schnapps their first Christmas Eve alone.

"They killed her," he'd said, raising his voice, tears in his eyes. "They made her choose between us. No one should have to make that choice, especially not a seventeen-year-old girl. Do you understand me? They killed her with neglect."

Walter nodded, although he had not understood. He'd been shocked to see his usually taciturn father fall apart.

Not a leaf stirred that warm day in Irvine, but the fear that he was betraying his father made Walter shiver in his car. If it was nine A.M. in California, it was nine hours later in Germany: six P.M. If his father were still alive (and Walter had to remind himself that he wasn't), he would have just arrived home from work. He'd had the same job for twenty years, the same routine. Walter was picturing him with a glass of beer, alone at his kitchen table, when an old man came out of the blue house wearing tennis whites and got into the Buick. He was nearly bald and at least eighty years old, if not older, but for his age appeared to be quite fit. Even from where Walter was parked ten meters away the resemblance was immediately obvious. The square jaw, the round eyes, the quick-paced, short-legged gait. Walter pulled his car around at the end of the street and followed his grandfather from half-a-block's distance away. The streets of Irvine were wide and free of cars. When his grandfather pulled into the parking lot at Fashion Island, Walter followed him, parked his own car and, maintaining his distance, walked into a small restaurant by the entrance to the mall.

Inside, an icy blast of air-conditioning. The wet film of sweat that covered Walter's body froze instantly. He rubbed his bare arms and looked around. Simple booths and Formica tabletops lined the walls of the all-purpose diner. Senior citizens and housewives chattered together in small groups over coffee and eggs. Walter's grandfather sat down alone in a booth near the back and pulled out the newspaper. Walter sat down just past him, where like a gangster he had the whole restaurant in view. He ordered a cup of coffee while his grandfather read the sports section and ordered eggs with toast, no bacon. A waitress made the rounds, stopping at his table. They seemed to know each other.

"Playing tennis again today?"

Walter's grandfather looked up from his paper.

"Every Tuesday and Thursday. Aren't you from Chicago?"

"I am."

"Bears fan?"

"Of course!"

She smiled and held up her pot of coffee with the other hand on her hip.

"Think they can beat Boston?"

She laughed. "I sure do. You wanna bet?"

Walter's grandfather turned to Walter, who was so surprised he spilled the contents of his coffee cup into its saucer.

"You want to take her up on this?"

The waitress leaned down to wipe up the mess.

"I don't—"

"You're not from back East too, are you? I'm surrounded!"

Walter's grandfather leaned back in his seat and faced Walter squarely. He grinned.

"No," said Walter carefully. "But I don't know anything about the Super Bowl. I'm from Germany."

He waited for the grin to either expand with recognition or fade in shock, for a cloud to cross his grandfather's lined, brown face. Nothing happened. The waitress refilled Walter's cup and moved on to other tables. His grandfather kept his chair tilted toward him.

"You know you've got some good tennis players coming out of Germany," he said. "These young kids from that town near Heidelberg, what's it called again?"

The training ground of both Boris Becker and Steffi Graf was one of the only places in Germany ever mentioned in the *L.A. Times*.

"Leimen."

"That's right! You know, I was in the service over there years ago. The winters were damn cold."

"Yes."

"I'm Walter," said his grandfather. "By the way."

He extended his hand. Walter looked down at the swollen veins that lined five thick fingers just like his own. What to say? He had never imagined it this way. He had never allowed for the possibility that they wouldn't know him: he had his mother's eyes, his grandfather's hands. He was German. He was twenty-three years old. *Do the goddamn math*, is what he wanted to say, but it choked in his throat.

"I'm Hans," he said.

The name came out easily, so he said it again as he shook his grandfather's hand. It was the only time they ever touched.

"I'm Hans," he said again. "It's nice to meet you."

17

Hope waited in the living room, standing up by the window. They had agreed on eleven and it was five minutes past and she was irritated that Orson was late. This morning she had woken up exhausted and now paced the empty living room, unsure what to do with her day. Since the incident two days earlier she had not returned to the subway. The magic was lost. From where she was standing in her apartment, she could see a clean sweep of Berlin's flat, unremarkable skyline to the south. But from afar, it did not have the immediacy she experienced from the train. She couldn't see any of the details, into apartments or the courtyards of buildings or people's faces. She was unable to grasp the sense of mystery about the city that had kept her coming back to the subway day after day. She had treated her daily investigations like a job, and the loss of its imperative left her aimless and restless. Hope turned from the view to watch the pattern a rare ray of sunshine was making on the parquet floor. She was startled when the doorbell rang.

"I'm late," said Orson. "I'm sorry. Normally I ride my bike, but today it's just too damn cold."

She stepped aside to let him in.

"At least it's sunny."

"Sun is overrated. I hate high-contrast lighting. The shadows just get in the way of the shot. Let's pray for gray skies over Christmas. I'm shooting video, remember."

She followed him down the hallway into the living room.

"Nice," he said, taking in the white space, the intricate floorboards, the view.

"I told you it was empty. Our container is stuck in customs in Hamburg. Even if they deliver it before Christmas, which is unlikely at this rate, we can just put everything in one of the bedrooms until you're finished shooting."

Orson walked the length of the room, counting off his steps in German, under his breath. When he was finished making a calculation, he looked at Hope.

"This might work really well. Of course it's much fancier than the place my character is living in, but we can dress it down."

"It's all yours. The space is kind of wasted on us."

"Can I look around?"

She held out her hand. Orson removed a small camera from his pocket, took a few pictures of the living room and they walked into the dining room and then the kitchen.

"Walter lives in this building too?"

"Upstairs."

"In an apartment like this?"

"It's the same layout, but it's not renovated. You know, he's lived there for a long time. I think he pays a lot less rent."

Orson opened the dishwasher, examined the three dirty glasses inside, closed it and left the kitchen. They headed into the back down a long corridor, where she opened the door to the master bedroom. The TV stood at the foot of the mattress, the dust on its screen now illuminated by sunshine. At least she'd made the bed. The comforter was thrown flat over the mattress and the pillows against the wall.

"I recently directed the voice-over for a TV commercial about fabric softener," said Orson. "In the film, a family was making a bed, you know, beautiful shots of clean sheets and all that. It sounds simple enough, but they had to shoot the bed made nine different ways, one for each of the other European countries where the commercial was going to air, because no one could agree on how to make a bed."

"I don't even have a real bed yet. Excuse the mess."

"It looks fine to me. I just had never given any thought to this question before. Apparently the English tuck in their sheets and blankets. The Swedes use separate comforters for each person, overlapping in the middle. The Austrians fold back their duvets into little poufs at the bottom of the bed that look like meringue. It's a good metaphor for the chaos of the European Union, isn't it?"

"You don't think the European Union is a good idea?"

"It's a good idea, but the reality is that people do not give up their national identities so easily. The Germans are the most enthusiastic members of the EU only because they want to be linked to something other than the Holocaust."

"What about the euro?"

"It goes into effect on January first."

"Are you sad to lose the deutschmark?"

"I don't care what money we use. I am already living in the afterlife. The money I knew as a child disappeared when East Germany was absorbed into the West in 1990. The country I come from no longer exists. I never expected any of that to happen, could never have imagined it, but it did. So whatever happens next is a surprise, you know? I try to embrace it."

"Do you miss the way things used to be?"

"Even if I did, it would be impossible to go back for a visit. I still live in the neighborhood where I grew up, but everything is different there now. The people, the products, the politics, the value system. It's a whole new world."

Hope pictured the scenes from New York that she watched on the news every day: people rendered speechless with pain, sick from the contaminated air, terrified to open their mail. She wondered if she would ever be able to go back to the place she had known as home there.

"Have you ever seen that movie from the eighties, *Buckaroo Banzai*?" Orson asked her.

"The time-traveling superhero."

"Remember his motto?"

She shook her head.

"Wherever you go, there you are." He smiled. "I consider myself a citizen of the world."

Hope led him down the hallway and held open the door to the bathroom. Its glorious expanse of white tiles looked especially bright.

"You can definitely fit your crew in here," she said.

"Amazing. I'll have to write in a bathtub scene. How did you find this place, through a broker?"

"My husband found it. I think there was a broker."

"He must have wet his pants."

"My husband or the broker?"

"The broker. The real estate market here is totally depressed. I mean, this is a city built for five million people that currently has a population of only three and a half because so many people left for the West after the Wall came down. They can't give places away. Germans know that, so they haggle and bitch, but when someone from New York shows up, it's their big chance to cash in. Any price he quoted would have seemed cheap to your husband, compared to what a place like this would cost there, right?"

"That's true."

"The funny thing is that every Berlin real estate agent carries a Louis Vuitton briefcase and drives a nice car," he said. "It's absurd. They probably make two sales a year, but they act so superior. It's as if they all read the same self-help book."

He had on something of a uniform himself, thought Hope. Textbook renegade filmmaker. His leather pants were molded to his legs as if he hadn't taken them off in six months. The look was universal, in no way distinctly German or even European, and she was struck by how he might easily be an American if she didn't hear his accent. Walter was fifteen years older, and yet for all his interest in the United States he was utterly German in style and effect. His cleanliness, the hovering length and tighter cut of his pants, the confidence with which he ordered wine in a restaurant. The summer she traveled around Europe with her parents she had found the local teenagers completely exotic hothouse flowers cultivated on a strange and careful planet. On and off hot trains all over the continent, Hope and her parents came apart at the seams while their European counterparts suffered the heat gracefully, not a hair out of place. With Orson's generation you could hardly tell the difference, she thought. Everyone was American, more or less. It was too bad.

"Maybe it helps," she said sympathetically. "Maybe carrying a Louis Vuitton briefcase helps them believe in themselves despite the odds."

He turned around in the hallway and looked at her.

"You're too nice."

She shrugged. "I used to teach third grade."

"But you don't get it. They're shooting themselves in the foot. They carry the briefcase as if to say, *I don't need your business.* In other words, *I don't care about your needs.* It's a defensive measure designed to preempt the customer's rejection. Typically German. Germans can't sell anything. It has to do with our history, of course."

He brought both hands to his face and framed the hallway through a rectangle of thumbs and forefingers.

"One of my friends recently went to see a house with his wife," he said. "It was old-fashioned, built before the war and restored after the Wall came down; a nice place with a garden. But when they tried to negotiate the rent, the broker said that the previous inhabitants had been a mother and her adult son, and that the son had shot the mother with a hunting rifle while he was cleaning it. The charges were dropped, the broker said, but the fact remained that a murder had taken place there and he just wanted to make sure they knew that in advance, before they rented it."

They entered the empty nursery at the back of the apartment. It was cold in there. Hope wrapped both hands around her body and held her elbows to warm herself up. She looked up at the sweet animals in the ceiling.

"Did they take the house?"

"Nope."

"I can understand that. I wouldn't want to live in a house where somebody died."

Orson laughed. "This is Berlin, Hope. If you start worrying about the ghosts around here, you'll never sleep again. I mean, who do you think lived in this apartment before the war? A beautiful apartment like this, in Charlottenburg? Where do you think they are now? All the real estate is haunted."

The sheep on the ceiling grazed near the light socket. The horse stared back at her. Hope was no more able to conjure an image of children playing in this blank white room than the unbearable possibility of what had happened to them.

"It's hard to imagine anything bad ever happening here."

"Because bad things don't happen to rich people?"

"Maybe. Maybe because I can't imagine that anyone even lived here before me. I know this is an old apartment, but the walls are so white and perfect. It seems completely new."

"Americans are the greatest customers in the world. You're so easily sold."

He had been facing her, standing in the middle of the room, and now he walked to the nearest wall by the window and ran his hand over it as if feeling for the latch of a secret door.

"What are you doing?"

She took a step toward him. His finger moved vertically and then across the wall from side to side, as if drawing boxes on the plaster.

"I'm just trying to prove a point. Come here."

His finger was pink and slim, the nail bitten ragged. At the point in the wall where it rested was a nearly invisible seam, where one sheet of paper appeared to have been glued against another. The seam ran from the ceiling to the floor.

"White *Rauhfasertapete*," said Orson. "It means rough, textured wallpaper. It's a special German invention. Looks like plaster at a distance. It's a faster and much cheaper way to cover things up."

"Is it all over my apartment?"

"Of course. It's all over the walls of every apartment in Berlin. When one tenant leaves, the owner just wallpapers over his mistakes and starts again with the next one. Check this out."

With what was left of the nail on his finger, he picked at the seam until he was able to lift the edge, then quickly pulled away a chunk of it about the size of a quarter to reveal a glimpse of bright orange wallpaper underneath it.

"What is that?"

"The good taste of the people who lived here before you did, obviously."

"They left up the old wallpaper?"

"God knows how many layers there are underneath. That's my point."

"That's disgusting,"

Up close, it smelled of old smoke, she thought. She could practically hear it exhaling through the hole in the white top layer. Long, sour breaths held in for years. Then she realized it was Orson she smelled. His arm was almost touching hers, as if they were trapped together in a telephone booth at a bar. Did they still have telephone booths in bars, or anywhere else anymore? She stepped back trying to remember the last time she had actually been in a proper bar in any city.

"Don't worry, the crew can fix the hole when we're finished," said Orson. "Along with everything else we move around. We'll leave the place looking exactly as we found it."

When he turned to make a phone call, Hope stared at the orange spot. From a few feet away it was hard to tell if it lay on top of the white wallpaper, like a stain, or was actually a hole, sucking the brightness of the room in toward it. But when she touched it, she could feel its depth against her fingers, and was struck by the sense of reaching through a portal, as if, when her finger pushed into the orange wallpaper, it might pull her hand with it, her arm, the rest of her. She looked up at the white wall, stretching to the ceiling, that only moments earlier had seemed flat and lifeless, but now rippled with the possibility of layers beneath it. When she was a child, her family had moved into a house that had previously belonged to visiting professors from France. The house had a big backyard, in which she found a bathtub, buried under a beech tree. Actually, she found only the lip of a bathtub, a round of white porcelain rough with age, peeking through the undergrowth. She had begged to dig up the rest of it. Her parents had made a lot of jokes about the dead body that might be buried in it (*Those crazy French people, ha ha ha*), but had insisted that she leave it where it was. In the end they planted a flower bed, and as the years passed, the bathtub was no longer visible at all. With her fingernail Hope picked at one side of the hole in the wallpaper, then another, lifting the edge. Suddenly she knew what she wanted to do with the rest of her day: if she could no longer ride the subway, she would stay right here in this room and see where it went.

18

Saturday morning Walter awoke early to surprise Hope with a real American breakfast. The cold spreads of sliced ham, cheese and bread served in Germany couldn't compete with the pancakes and scrambled eggs his mother had made when he was a child. He was the only person in the dark morning on Goethestrasse, but when he reached the market at Karl-August-Platz, it was crowded. Bare lightbulbs illuminated piles of vegetables and fruit, whole wheat bread and pastries, meat, eggs and seasonal arrangements of holly, mistletoe and myrrh. The Christmas people had colonized the western edge of the square selling trees, wreaths, handmade wooden ornaments and boiling vats of *Glühwein*, the telltale stench of cinnamon in the air. Customers were already drinking it for breakfast. Walter stayed on the opposite side of the market, making his way slowly between the stalls. He bought eggs from a Brandenburg farm and juicing oranges from Central America. Holding his shopping bag above his head to protect the eggs, he searched for real maple syrup. He thought he heard someone calling his name, but it had been a long time since a fan chased him down. When he heard it again, he looked back over his shoulder.

"Walter! How're you doing?"

Stuffed into a dark blue parka, Dave was panting like a dog.

"Can you believe this many people get up early on Saturday morning? I came over to pick up a Christmas tree for Hope. I want to decorate it and everything before she wakes up."

Walter stared at him. "I thought you were in Poland."

"I came home to surprise her for the weekend. I got in late last night. Thanks for taking such good care of her this week. Sounds like you've been showing her a good time. She said Orson, you know, your friend, is really nice too."

Dave winked as he had the last time they'd met. Like Bodo, he had a small yellow ribbon attached to the left breast of his jacket.

"Are you done with your shopping?"

Walter looked down at the precious ingredients packed into his bag. His Saturday with Hope had just walked away from him.

"I guess so."

"Could you help me carry the Christmas tree home?"

On the other side of the church, a forest of pine trees had been cut down, tied up and stacked ten deep against the wall.

"What is the ribbon for?"

"Oh, that, yeah. It's a symbol to support the American troops. The Poles love the United States. They're big supporters of the war so the ribbon's good for business. I just wear it when I'm over there. I forgot to take it off."

Dave's hands struggled with the tiny safety pin.

"Smells great here, doesn't it?" He inhaled deeply. "I love the smell of pine. Christmas really feels like Christmas in Germany."

Surprised, Walter started to ask him a question then re-phrased it as a statement.

"Hope said you were Jewish."

"I am. This is all folklore to me. But Hope seems really interested in it, so tonight I'm going to take her over to the *Weihnachtsmarkt* on Alexanderplatz. Help her get into the culture."

"That's not culture, it's business."

Dave chuckled. "Where we come from culture is busi-ness. Anyway I'm hoping it'll cheer her up. She's been through a lot this year. I don't know how much she told you."

Walter hated the thought of Hope being subjected to the hell of the Alexanderplatz Christmas market: drunk teen-agers, fried food, the stench of old beer; but the suggestion that he didn't know what she was going through made him furious. Dave was the one who was out of the loop.

"I know about what happened in New York."

"Really?"

"Of course."

"She told you about the baby?"

Walter set down the bag of groceries he'd been carrying at his feet.

"The baby?"

"We lost a baby last summer, right before I started this job. The plan was for Hope take a few years off from work while it was little. We thought Berlin was a good place to do that. But there were complications."

Walter nodded his head automatically. He could see shapes and colors, the idea of a baby.

"Complications. She didn't tell me."

"That doesn't surprise me. After it happened, she just went to bed and didn't get up. She refused to come with me in July when I started this job. In fact, if it weren't for what happened in September, I don't think she would have come here at all."

He rubbed his hands together. Asleep, thought Walter. Hope had been asleep when the buildings were hit, asleep when they fell, asleep all summer, afraid to wake up. He looked up at the red brick church steeple. Neither of them spoke for a moment.

"It's a relief to be back in Berlin," said Dave. "Things can get pretty bleak over on the other side of the border."

"Especially for—" Walter paused. "For you. I mean, living in West Berlin in the eighties we felt like anti-Semitism had been banished more or less completely. Then the Wall came down, and a whole new world of it opened up a hundred fifty kilometers away from here."

"But I have the opportunity to make a different impression. I'm working in the middle of nowhere and there is certainly a lot of ignorance there, but we have to start somewhere. Has Hope told you about my work? Probably not, huh? She doesn't know a lot about it."

Asleep. Walter thought he might cry. Dave pulled a tree out from the thicket and paid for it. They moved slowly, Dave with the trunk in hand, Walter bringing up the rear.

"I'm doing a sustainable development project in an agricultural area about an hour east of Frankfurt Oder. I was in the Peace Corps in Ecuador in the early nineties; we set up weaving cooperatives among women in communities where farming was no longer profitable. We're applying the same model here."

Walter vaguely remembered Ecuadorians selling colorful sweaters in the subway. He had had one; it smelled like sheep. He pictured a group of doe-eyed Polish women, cigarettes balanced between the slim fingers that held their knitting needles, bare legs crossed under skeins of thick, itchy wool.

"Christmas is awesome in Ecuador," said Dave. "By the way."

"Weaving cooperatives."

"Not here. Not exactly. But something like that. I'm trying out a pretty radical new idea of mine, actually."

"Great."

"The truth is that I'm dying to talk about it, but it's top secret."

"That's fine."

"Not top secret, really, it's just that I don't want Hope to know yet. It might upset her."

They came to a standstill in the middle of the sidewalk. The tree was heavy.

"You don't have to tell me anything. Really."

"No, no. It's okay. Here's the scoop. Instead of knitting sweaters, they make videos."

"Who watches Polish videos? No one even watches German movies."

"They're porn videos."

Dave put down his end of the tree and held up one hand.

"I know what you're thinking, but it's all totally kosher, believe me. The videos have no sex in them, just naked women wrestling. You watched one of our ads the other night."

"Time for Action?"

"Yes! You have to remember that the women were prostitutes before. They were regularly exposed to AIDS and other venereal diseases, violence. They had abusive pimps, German johns who harassed them. Now they're off the street. They act in and direct the videos themselves. It's an all-female operation. We provide the seed money and equipment. We launched the original ad campaign. But the rest is up to them and the initial response has been great. I think the project will be self-sustaining by next summer. We're planning franchises all over the Eastern bloc." Dave raised his eyebrows, his chest inflated with self-importance, and sighed. "We're saving people's lives here, Walter. It's important stuff."

For years Bodo's favorite game had been casting the movie version of their lives. He and Walter played it late nights at The Wild West, arguing about which Hollywood stars should play the various important characters (Heike, Bodo's wife and kids, Klara, the waiters, the Polish chef in the kitchen, the bartender and his girlfriend). There was a certain satisfaction in finding exactly the right fit; as their roster of favorite actors changed, so did their all-star line-up. One night Heike was played by Michelle Pfeiffer circa *The Fabulous Baker Boys*, another night by Veronica Lake, another by Jennifer Love Hewitt. The chef was always played by Harvey Keitel. The game had only two unspoken rules. One, Bodo and Walter never cast themselves. Two, River Phoenix and Tom Cruise never played anyone else. But a painful realization now passed sharply through Walter's mind. Tom Cruise would play Dave in the movie. They didn't look alike and there was something morally questionable about his project, but his enthusiasm about it, his blind faith in himself, was all Tom Cruise, much as it frustrated Walter to admit that.

They moved toward Leibnizstrasse in silence and set the tree down again at the stoplight, panting as they waited for it to change. For a Saturday morning, the road was busy with cars, people rushing out to do their Christmas shopping. Only two weekends left. Dave pointed to the *Time for Action* poster up on the wall across the street. They were everywhere now. The young woman eyed them back, fierce as ever. *I Love NY*, written with a heart, was scrawled across her cleavage with black spray paint.

"One of ours," he said. "Nice, huh?"

Walter removed his gloves and rubbed his hands together, relieved to be only about sixty meters from home.

"Hope said you just finished a new Tom Cruise movie. Is it a good one?"

"It's okay."

"She wants to see the German version to hear your voice. But I saw some dubbed films myself last summer and I have to say the dialogue sounded weird to me. If I closed my eyes, I could tell immediately that it wasn't recorded on location. What do you call that?"

"Reverb."

"The people I work with always tell me that they think American actors sound better in German. Like, *Robert De*

Niro has such a great German voice. That's kind of funny, don't you think?"

"Christian Bruckner is a pro," said Walter. "The best."

"Who's that?"

"De Niro."

"De Niro's voice, you mean? That is funny. But Woody Allen is the most absurd."

"Why?"

"A German Woody Allen? I mean, come on. It's an oxymoron. It isn't possible to be Jewish and German at the same time. Not anymore."

Dave's proprietary claim on everything that crossed his path (America, Christmas, Woody Allen, Hope) made Walter feel like a drifter, untethered in a dangerous sea.

"How did they choose you, anyway?" Dave asked. "What criteria are involved in becoming the voice of a famous Hollywood star? Is the woman who does Julia Roberts beautiful? Does Jack Nicholson smoke cigars? Is a resemblance even important or is it just a question of good diction?"

"There are many factors. It's like casting any other role."

"But in this case you aren't playing a role, are you? You're just feeding the lines into a mike somewhere."

The hair on the back of Walter's neck bristled.

"It's a challenge to hit those notes, believe me. I'm not just a glorified translator." He was raising his voice. "Your culture is encrypted in the language of the movies. Think of me as a diplomat."

Dave was paying attention, so he continued.

"Woody Allen might be Jewish but he's an artist. He's an entertainer. If he doesn't communicate, he dies. Sixteen percent of American box office comes from German audiences alone, and I am willing to bet that Woody Allen, specifically, sells more tickets here than he does in America. We are the second-biggest market in the world for Hollywood films. You're a businessman. Do the math."

"I'm an economist, not a businessman."

"Have a little respect."

"Okay, okay. So show me the money."

"What?"

"Do Tom Cruise for me now. Just a line or two. Something famous."

"I don't think so."

"Come on! *Show me the money!* I'd love to hear that in German."

"Uh."

"I love black people!" Dave shouted.

People on the street looked over.

"I just speak like myself when I do him."

"What? No special accent? Not even a different pitch?"

"No."

"So everyone you meet recognizes your voice as his? They think, Hey, that's Tom Cruise's voice in another guy's body? That must be weird for you."

Walter coughed.

"People don't recognize my voice as Tom Cruise when they see me in person," he said. "Only when I'm speaking on the phone."

"Do you ever do voice-overs?"

Dave pulled one arm across his chest with the other and stretched his shoulder.

"Ad campaigns. Once I did a documentary about Formula One racing, just after *Days of Thunder* came out."

"Ever thought about getting into the porn thing?"

"The porn thing?"

"You know, Tom Cruise narrating the action," said Dave. "I'm thinking out loud here, but there could be a real market in that. You could get some of your colleagues into it, too. Your friend Christian, like you said."

"Who?"

"The pro. De Niro? And how about Julia Roberts, or George Clooney? Hell, Woody Allen. Why not? You must know the other voices, right?"

Walter slowly pulled his gloves back on.

"You're kidding."

"I'm totally serious. Listen, you know what the all-time favorite American movie is in Poland? The one that everybody mentions when I say I'm American? And I am not exaggerating."

"No idea."

"*Pretty Woman.* No joke. A movie about a prostitute."

"Actually, it's a movie about shopping."

"Look, you wouldn't have to watch the videos yourself. You could just record the voice-over in a studio. The idea has huge potential."

"Right."

"Think of it as doing a good deed. You'd be helping people out."

Finally, the light changed.

"Just think about it."

Walter grabbed the bottom of the Christmas tree's trunk and pushed toward home.

. . .

Hope opened the door as they came up to the third floor and Dave tripped on the top step so that the tree fell at her feet. She looked down at it without comment for a long time. She was wearing a flannel nightgown that was buttoned up to her neck, a flowing sack that appeared to have swallowed her whole. Walter waited a few steps down from the landing. He could hardly look at her. He could not tell her he had learned about the baby, at least not now, right here, but the information had changed her anyway. He peeked through the pine needles thinking that he could see a glow around the shape of her that gave her small frame depth against the open doorway. When she spoke to Dave she was cold.

"A Christmas tree? What would your parents say?"

Dave dusted off his pants.

"I thought it would be fun to have one this year. I got some decorations too, at the market. We can get some more tonight at Alexanderplatz."

He reached into his coat pocket and withdrew a white paper bag. Walter wanted to keep going on up to the fourth floor, but he was trapped behind the tree.

"How did you get roped into this?"

When she looked at him, he found it difficult to speak. He lifted one shoulder, motioning to the bag of groceries hanging from it.

"I was there."

"Walter really helped me out," said Dave, turning to him. "You want to join us for breakfast?"

Hope and Walter both stared at him as if the mere suggestion were absurd.

"Or you could come with us to the Christmas market

tonight. I'm sure Hope would love it if you came. I've heard it's a lot of fun."

"Walter lives here, Dave. He's been to the Christmas market at Alexanderplatz."

"I have plans tonight."

"How about breakfast?"

"I really should be getting back to my place," said Walter.

His eyes met Hope's for the first time that morning and he tried to smile. *Asleep,* he thought. He could hardly bear to be standing so far away from her.

When Dave went back to Poland, he would tell her about California immediately. They would start over together there. They could make a new baby together. He would save her from this. He tried to communicate that silently as he placed his end of the tree down on the landing and disentangled himself from its branches. Then he ran up the stairs to his own apartment and lay down on the cool linoleum in his kitchen, to still the rapid beating of his heart.

For the next thirty-six hours he did everything he could to avoid running into her while Dave was in town. He went out early, stayed out late, took the stairs. When he was home, he worked on the map. He had finished more than half of it already, had taped the center back together with invisible tape, but the remaining pink and yellow ragged pieces represented more mysterious sections of the city. He'd had more luck coming up with the eight American states contiguous to Missouri than he did figuring out which section of the city connected to Frohnau, or to Adlershof. Walter moved the whole operation into his living room so as to escape the thought of the couple sleeping right beneath his bed, but found himself pacing the blueprint of Hope's apartment anyway, tracking her movements in vain. Was that the front door opening? Was that the shower? Why was it so quiet? He had only half listened to Orson's daily rants about the clash of nations, but he had picked up the gist of it: knowledge was power. His own battles were personal, but still: Dave had given him a secret weapon and Walter intended to use it. He walked from room to room like a sniper plotting his shots. He had already decided to tell Hope all the details of the business in Poland, had mentally prepared a complex presentation for her benefit, complete with florid embellishments (drunk girls running around naked in the countryside, her husband in his underwear with the camera). She would be horrified. She would beg to come with him to California. He could think of nothing else. When he tried to concentrate instead on the image of himself alone, fit and tan, jogging along a sunny Malibu beach with Tom Cruise, he couldn't do it. He made it to Sunday evening before giving in to the urge to press one ear against floor. Finally he kneeled in his bedroom, but heard only the sound of his own breathing and the muffled crunch of carpet against his cheek.

By the time he woke up late on Monday morning, Walter's head hurt. He made a strong pot of coffee, sat down at the kitchen table and dropped his face into his hands. *Vanilla Sky* was finished. Only a week until the premiere. He should have been rehearsing his plaintive but professional pitch for the crucial party afterward, but he could only focus on the next few hours. He waited nervously for Hope to call, and the empty morning gathered around him. When Heike had lived with him, mornings had been his favorite time of day. He didn't smoke but he had always enjoyed her first cigarette. Her enthusiasm for daily rituals was contagious. Long morning showers, long breakfasts, coffee over the tabloids. In her hands even his emptiest days had taken shape, transformed into a series of significant moments from that first cigarette to sex before bed and three meals in between. Now a Heike-shaped negative space sliced into the trapped air of his kitchen. He fished around in the refrigerator for the ingredients to make himself a Toast Hawaii, her favorite guilty pleasure. He layered a ring of pineapple over ham and the butter and bread, topped off with a slice of cheese. As the cheese melted over all of it in the oven, he eyed the day's gossip in the tabloids, imagined her reading it aloud, one knee up against the table in an old silk dressing gown, her hair still wet. People of Today: Tom Cruise met with the CIA to see how *Mission: Impossible III* could help cast the government agency in a positive light.

"A lot of stars have been coming to us," said the CIA representative. "Post 9/11, we've gone from being an agency of bogeymen in Hollywood to a force of good." Goldie Hawn was leading a mission to stop America from gossiping in the aftermath of the September 11 atrocities, it said, with a new campaign called "Words Can Heal."

"People should not just return to normal now," said Goldie, "but to a better normal. They should recognize how hurtful unkind words can be."

Heike would love that one. She took particular glee in pieces about the unlikely political righteousness of Hollywood stars. People of Yesterday had a profile of Anthony

Michael Hall, Brat Pack star of *The Breakfast Club,* now living in suburban Chicago. He was pictured coming out of a supermarket, looking like a beleaguered accountant; he was also losing his hair. When the usual relief passed, Walter felt a stab of pity for him and ran one hand over the smooth spot on his own head, thinking he could just hear Heike's throaty laugh. Somewhere out there, she was probably reading this article aloud to somebody else. He got up to open a window and turned on the radio for a glimpse of the world. He ate the sweet, sticky toast and wondered when his downtime started feeling so much like work. When he returned abruptly from Los Angeles in 1985, he had meant to take a break from acting, not abandon it altogether. The announcement of his hiatus had been greeted in the German industry by rumors of addiction, depression and rejection. They were all way off, but the saying went in German that *to excuse yourself is to accuse yourself,* so he'd said nothing, had let the stink of failure linger around him like a cloud of stale smoke, accepting *Top Gun* as a one-time thing, but then Tom Cruise's career had just snowballed, carrying Walter's voice along with it. One after the other, the films were hits. Walter didn't even try to get the advertising work, he didn't do anything; money just fell into his lap. He had been lulled into exile, he thought now. Tom Cruise was the kind of gig starving actors only dreamed about. Financial security plus nine months off each year to do other things. The problem was that he never did other things. Orson was probably going over his action-packed schedule of rehearsals with Til Schweiger right at this moment; maybe he really would make it on the outside after all. Bodo had, but only because his American died. The evening they'd learned that River

Phoenix overdosed, drinks were on the house at The Wild West and Bodo had insisted the patrons observe a collective moment of silence. Only Walter had noticed the relief that washed across his face, that of a man in a miserable marriage whose wife suddenly leaves him for somebody else.

Walter went into his bedroom to look at the Berlin map again and contemplated the possibility of Tom Cruise's sudden death. He would most certainly be hungrier. He couldn't sell detergent to housewives as a ghost. But even with Tom Cruise dead and gone, he would never be free of Hans, with the thick, curly hair and his shit-eating grin, popping up at odd hours of the night, dragging him down like dead weight. Walter moved a stray piece of the city around on the carpet. Marienfelde looked nice, he thought: a lake, a green park, small streets. Where did it belong? Giving in to the steep downward slope on the other side of the caffeine high, he was about to climb under the covers when the suitcase in the corner, still half-packed with summer clothes for winter in Los Angeles, caught his attention. He dropped his underwear and pulled on a tight blue swimsuit that was lying on top. He didn't own a full-length mirror but he didn't need one to know that he wasn't Malibu material; he could hardly see the tight blue of the suit for his stomach. His skin was pale under a light film of chest hair that extended down to his navel over the pregnant swell. A single gray, curly hair poked out near his left nipple. Just as he yanked it out, the doorbell rang. Hope! He pulled on a T-shirt and rushed across the apartment.

"What are you wearing?"

Those were the first words out of Heike's mouth. The light from his foyer shined on her, so that through the doorway she was illuminated against the dark backdrop of the landing. She was wearing a black leather coat and jeans. Her long brown hair hung straight around pronounced cheekbones, like the exaggerated female beauty in a Japanese cartoon.

"It's December."

Her light blue eyes looked him up and down. Walter pulled down the edge of his T-shirt.

"Are you going somewhere?" she demanded.

"Maybe."

"Where? Why haven't you called me? You could have asked my parents. Or Klara."

When he didn't respond, she pushed past him down the hallway into the bedroom. Walter had conjured Heike's image so many times since she left that her sudden three-dimensional reality took his breath away. If she wanted to see him again, he thought, why had she returned his keys? He looked down at the floor, fighting the desire to folllow her, reach out to her, wrap his arms around her, sniff desperately at the private recesses of her body, lick her face. He couldn't answer her question because the truth was pitiful. It had never occurred to him to call her; it had never occurred to him to do anything but wait. She came back.

"Where are my clothes?"

"I gave them away."

"Seriously?"

He shuffled his feet.

"It's winter, Walter. I need my winter clothes."

"You should have thought of that when you left."

She shook her head and looked over at the half-finished city on the floor of the living room.

"What is that?"

"It's nothing."

She walked over to examine it.

"Walter Baum's view of the world," she said, rolling one hand into a tube, looking up at him through it with one eye. "This big."

Walter pulled at the bottom of his T-shirt.

"Marienfelde is in the southeast," she said, picking up the piece he'd been trying to place before she came. "It's a beautiful neighborhood, actually. Almost like the countryside and only twenty minutes from here. But you wouldn't know that, would you? Because you never leave this apartment."

When the doorbell rang again Heike beat him to the front door and opened it. Hope stopped short on the doormat and leaned against the wall.

"Oh. I'm sorry. I'll come back later."

"*Wer ist das?*"

"Are you okay?" Walter asked Hope over Heike's shoulder.

"I'm fine. Am I interrupting something?"

"Yes." Heike switched into broken English. "Who are you?"

She pulled Hope into the foyer of Walter's apartment.

"Why wears he a swimming costume? What's going on?"

"Why don't you tell her?"

"California," Walter mumbled. "I'm going to California."

"What?"

Heike paused to light a cigarette she'd pulled out of a small purse hanging from her wrist. A cloud of smoke enveloped Hope, who waved one hand quickly in front of her face.

"I'd appreciate it if you'd put that out," she said.

Heike rolled her eyes.

"Americans."

"That has nothing to do with it."

"Yeah."

"Seriously. I'm pregnant."

Heike pulled hard on her cigarette before tapping its long ash onto the hardwood floor. Walter stared at Hope as if she had slapped him.

"I just took the test this morning," she said. "I was coming up now to tell you."

Heike pulled on her cigarette. "Why?"

"What?"

"This is Walter's baby?"

"No."

"Then who?"

He cleared his throat.

"Did you ever meet the American guy who moved in downstairs last summer? Hope is his wife."

"American Dave? He has a wife?"

"I was in New York till October."

"Funny," said Heike. "I always think he's with that Polish girl from the wrestling movie."

"Who?"

"You know that girl on the posters. They always come in and out of the building together."

Walter recalled acutely the sensation of Heike's tongue

buried in the crease behind his ear. She dropped her cigarette into a cup of cold tea sitting on a table by the door where it went out like an exhausted fuse. Hope's eyes filled with tears.

"Oh, please," said Heike.

"I just don't understand what you mean."

"Time for Action," said Heike. "You know, Dave's project. You're his wife."

"No."

She checked the clock on her mobile phone impatiently.

"He explained to me once in the lobby. Just like what he is doing in Ecuador but better, because pornography is big business."

"I thought it was a secret," said Walter indignantly. "Why did he tell you?"

It felt strange to speak English to Heike. He wondered if Dave had been coming on to her. Bastard.

"I tell him I'm an actress. He ask some questions about makeup. So I ask questions too. He said the pornography is bigger industry than Hollywood because language is not important. Totally international. Of course I am interested."

Heike shrugged.

"Instead of knitting sweaters, the Polish girls make the videos and sell all over the world," she said. "Progress because they were prostitutes before. *Sure beats selling blow jobs at the side of the road,* he said. I remember because it sounds funny."

Walter pictured Heike on the poster: arms in the air like a champion, her sly look following him from eyes pasted up on walls all over town.

"I don't believe you," said Hope.

"I make this up? Look. It's not a bad idea. Very modern, actually. He is helping people."

Hope glared at her.

"It's a horrible idea."

Walter reached out for Heike's arm.

"Americans," she said again, flinching him off. "You are so uptight."

She turned to Walter and spoke in German.

"I'm leaving now. You know how to reach me."

He lingered at the front door after she left, silently dividing up the female leads in Tom Cruise movies into two groups. There were only a few Heikes, he realized. The girlfriend in *The Color of Money*, the first fiancée in *Jerry Maguire*, random women in the *Mission: Impossible*s. Most of them were Hopes. Nicole Kidman always played Hopes; Renée Zellweger, the wives in *The Firm* and *Cocktail*; all Hopes. The brunette in the new film was definitely a Hope. Walter was almost surprised to find the real one still standing in his foyer, staring miserably at the floor. When he tried to read her mind, he caught only a fleeting image of the Polish girl with Dave in a headlock, his big body flaccid against the gym mat while the girl's champion ass lorded triumphantly over his chest.

"You knew about this?"

"The girl? No."

"I mean the project."

He nodded.

"Why didn't you tell me?"

"I assumed Dave had told you."

"Yeah. Well, he didn't," she sniffed loudly.

"Where is he now?"

"He left early this morning. I tried to call him earlier, to tell him about the baby, but I didn't get through. I guess his phone's out of range."

She wiped one cheek with the back of her hand.

"What am I going to do?"

"Let's get out of here," Walter said.

The weather outside was cold but clear. Berlin's distance from the Gulf Stream stripped it of Western Europe's humidity, and its citizens suffered symptoms of the desert: rough skin, cracked fingernails, dry tonsils, chapped lips. Walter put one hand on Hope's back, steering her north toward the university campus and the park beyond. Students streamed past them in both directions, shouting to one another, lit cigarettes hanging from their mouths.

"Why do they all wear black coats?" she asked. "It's the same in New York. You'd think in cold climates everyone would wear bright colors to cheer themselves up."

Walter looked down at his own black coat and around at the black-clad students' bulky bodies, dreary silhouettes against the cityscape.

"People only wear yellow and turquoise in sunny places. Why is that?"

He took her arm, leading her past the train station toward the entrance to the zoo. A tour group was assembled in front of the large stone elephants at the gates. One of them came up with a digital camera.

"Can you take a picture of us?"

He had a British accent. Hope peeled away silently, as if resigned to perform a regular duty. The camera in hand she waved the group closer together.

"You ready?"

"Cheese!"

When she handed the camera back, they asked her where to get a bite to eat.

"Walk that way for about ten minutes," she told them. "Then take a left at the light. On the opposite corner you'll see a café with big windows and comfortable chairs. The menu is in English."

Walter felt proud. Most people in Berlin would never take the time, even on a good day.

"Should we see the giraffes and zebras?" he asked her.

"Isn't it too cold for them?"

"They take good care of them. They have lots of African animals here. Elephants and gorillas and everything. There's a panda. The hyenas even had babies this spring."

"In captivity?"

"Well, yes."

"That's so depressing."

There was no one else in line to buy tickets and the guard at the front booth was clearly impatient to get back to his newspaper.

"There are all different kinds of parrots," said Walter.

Hope looked through the gates as if the parrots were flying right there in front of them, a few steps away.

"They're really colorful. None are black. One of them can repeat anything you say exactly, in any language. Once I heard him mimicking an Italian tourist."

"We could train him to say *bitch* in Polish," she said, "or *asshole.* Do you know the word for *asshole* in Polish? He could repeat it for me till I remember it, then I could repeat it into Dave's answering machine."

Forget the zoo. Walter looked over her shoulder at what was once the center of West Berlin. The neighborhood had been a symbol of capitalist power in the 1960s and 1970s, but now the buildings were shabby, and many appeared to be empty. It was three in the afternoon and already getting dark.

"It's getting cold. Let's go to Café Keese."

Hope sighed.

"You'll like it," he said. "You'll see. They play music in the afternoon and people dance. It's a real Berlin establishment, just around the corner. It'll cheer you up."

Inside the club the light was dim, punctuated by the reflection of colored spots off a disco ball. Walter hadn't been inside in years but it was exactly as he had remembered it. Velvet-cushioned seats and small tables lined a round dance floor, each one equipped with its own old-fashioned telephone.

"Why the telephone?"

"So people can ask each other to dance."

He waved to the waiter.

"I think the average age here is about seventy-two," said Hope.

"It's Monday afternoon. Germany has mandatory retirement at sixty-five. That's a lot of old people with nothing to do. In the summer they go walking, in the winter they come here."

Nat King Cole sang his heart out over the loudspeakers, working his way through an album of greatest hits. They watched the dancers move together slowly in pairs.

"The women are dancing with other women."

"There aren't enough men. We die off early."

"That's the problem, isn't it? So many women, so little time."

She ran her hands across her stomach. He leaned forward to make sure she could hear him.

"That isn't my problem."

The waiter brought them Cokes and pretzel sticks. Hope stared like they were the tools of an exotic tribe and she had no idea what to do with them. Walter ate a pretzel, grabbed his Coke and stood up.

"Where are you going?"

He walked a few paces to the left and sat down three tables away, picked up the phone and dialed her number. She let it ring twice before picking it up.

"Hello?"

The phone volume had been adjusted for people of a certain age. Even with the dance music, he could hear her clearly.

"Hello."

They looked at each other through the flashing light.

"Dave told me that when you speak German on the phone, people think you're Tom Cruise."

"When I speak on the phone, my voice sounds more similar to the way it sounds recorded, in movies. That is, people recognize it then as the one they know for Tom Cruise."

"Speak to me like that."

"In German?"

Walter tried to recall some relevant dialogue.

"Was machst du hier allein?" he said. "What are you doing here alone?"

He ran through some of the better pick-up lines from *Cocktail.* Once he got going, the German dialogue rolled off his tongue.

"It must be great to be someone else for a while," she said. "I wish I could do that."

"Be someone else?"

"Get away from yourself."

Walter took a deep breath.

"Dann, komm mit mir nach Kalifornien."

"Come with you?"

"Yes."

"Where?"

"Nach Kalifornien."

"Kalifornien."

She didn't understand the translation. Walter cleared his throat and said it in English.

"California."

She was leaning forward over the telephone.

"Wann?"

"Nächste Woche."

"Next week."

"After the premiere of my new movie."

The disco ball sprayed blobs of color across the room. Red, yellow and green across her forehead. An eternity passed.

"Christmastime is nice in Los Angeles," he offered.

"Okay."

"Okay?"

"Yes."

Before she could have a chance to take it back, Walter hung up the phone. *Yes*. None of the fireworks he had expected went off. Maybe she was just kidding, but when he stared at her across the room, she looked totally serious. She was playing with a pretzel, breaking it into smaller and smaller pieces, arranging the pieces into a pattern by the phone. It was an unlikely escape plan. The chances of meeting Tom Cruise were slim. The chances of Hope coming halfway across the world with him were possibly slimmer. But the image of the three of them together on the beach at the distant rim of continental America was so seductive, so palpably real in that moment, that despite all suggestions to the contrary, he believed it was going to happen. Sometimes, he thought, sometimes it was just a question of having a plan, however unlikely, for everything to fall into place. He wanted to hold her in his arms. He wanted to feel her breasts pressed into his chest. He stood up and walked to her table.

"Should we dance?"

When they met at the edge of the dance floor, her body collapsed against his like a rag doll. They moved slowly in circles without speaking and did not stop dancing when the song changed. Walter held her in his arms but he could not feel the warmth of her body through her sweater or see her face, which was buried into his neck. When the band behind Nat King Cole kicked into high gear, he felt her crying; first the piano, then the strings, then the horn section, muffling her sobs. He just kept moving as her tears soaked into the collar of his shirt. Old women looked at them and smiled sweetly. From the outside, he thought, we look like a couple in love. It was a beginning. Hope was coming with him to California! He would take the role being offered him and run with it: a family man. Tom Cruise had children, didn't he? Walter saw them all on a Malibu terrace overlooking the Pacific. The golden pink sunset, the sound of waves in the background, kids running around on the beach below. Let this be my midlife crisis, he thought, pulling Hope tightly into him and closing his eyes.

19

From January to June 1985, Walter ate scrambled eggs every Tuesday and Thursday morning at the diner with his grandfather. They had fallen into an easy routine. They sat at separate tables but shared the newspaper. They swapped stories like two strangers on neighboring bar stools night after night. His grandfather was friendly but his warmth had distance built into it, a chalk line drawn firmly through the playing field. He said he was a doctor, long retired, that he played a lot of tennis. He never mentioned his family, preferring to talk about sports and the weather. Walter was careful not to kick the conversation out-of-bounds.

"After World War II, I stayed in the service," his grandfather told him early on. "We moved around a lot. Eventually we settled here and I went into private practice, but at the end, in the early sixties, I was stationed in Germany for two years."

"Did you like it?"

"No, to be honest. Too cold in the winter." He snorted one

breath of laughter through his nose. "Didn't much mix with locals."

"Nobody?"

"The war was still a recent memory for us, Hans. We did our work on the base and kept a distance. Your family and friends sound very nice, but believe me, the people in the village we were in were nothing like you."

He finished his eggs and pushed his plate away. He never ate bacon and so Walter didn't either. He copied other things too, after a while: tucking in his shirt, pulling up his socks, rubbing one hand across his head, then still thick with hair, in exactly the way his grandfather rubbed his own bald pate.

"In fact, you don't seem German to me at all," said his grandfather. "I mean that as a compliment."

After almost two years in the United States, Walter was used to this particular compliment. Casting directors, even other actors, often said it in an effort to be comforting. With the exception of Sharon, almost everyone he'd gotten to know in California had said it at some point, as if to be German, even to seem German, would be shameful, which he accepted. Everyone of his generation in Germany had been trained to enter the conversation with head bowed, to apologize for the sins of their forefathers as a matter of course and principle. They knew never to wave a flag, or promote their own agendas too aggressively. In Hollywood, when he occasionally came across other Germans, he ignored them and they ignored him, too. No one wanted to call attention to themselves or to be seen as a group on foreign soil. By the time he started having breakfast with his grandfather on a regular basis, Walter hadn't even spoken German aloud in more than a year. Still, he knew he retained a minimal accent in English, because people always asked where he came from.

He was used to receiving this particular compliment, but when his grandfather said it, he could not help but wonder if he meant it as some kind of bait. *Actually, my mother was American*, he might have replied. But he believed that the moment of recognition would come about naturally if they could just get close enough. He was careful not to say anything that might betray his true identity prematurely. We have time, he told himself. So he stayed in character as Hans, drawing freely from the scenarios cooked up by television writers for *Schönes Wochenende*'s faithful audience. Hans had been a character on the show for three seasons. A lifetime, thought Walter as he replaced his own biography with Hans's fictitious one. Sixty-six episodes complete with a family, location names, background details, funny anecdotes, a first love, childhood friends, even pets; he never ran out of things to talk about. Since his grandfather hadn't been back to Germany since the early sixties, the anachronistic world of *Schönes Wochenende*, contrived to tap into the German audience's nostalgia for simpler times, rang true: milkmaids in lace-up dresses with their cleavage spilling out, red-nosed men drunk on *Weissbier*, hilly fields dotted picturesquely with bales of hay. His grandfather listened attentively, he seemed to enjoy it, so Walter ran with it. The more Hans stories that he told, the more he took them for his own; the more he believed them, the more he wanted to tell. Walter told his grandfather everything. At the time, the fact that none of it was true seemed insignificant.

Craving more than two breakfasts a week with his grandfather, after a few months Walter starting following him when he went to play tennis. He became good at keeping a stealth distance behind, a few cars between them on the road, parking in the shade (his car was a common brand, the color an undistinguished brown). Sometimes he waited outside the tennis club, listening to the radio and years later, when he remembered those mornings sitting in the car, it would seem to him that the Madonna song "Holiday" had been playing in a loop the whole time. Its early electronic beat and her high-pitched voice reverberated in the midday heat, waves of energetic enthusiasm dancing across the hot pavement like a mirage. Sometimes he stayed long enough to pick up the chase again two hours later and follow his grandfather around on his errands (the drugstore, the bank). He was tempted to arrange a spontaneous encounter, to roll up with his own basket at the supermarket and say hello, as if by coincidence, but he wasn't sure he could pull it off. He was tempted to follow him into Springtime Estates but he bided his time. When he noticed that the beige Star of David on the sign at Springtime Estates was replicated on the sign outside the tennis club, he absorbed it as any other logo. The club was clearly an extension of the housing development. But in the hours he spent looking at it he began eventually to wonder if the whole organization was a Jewish one and if his grandfather too, then, was Jewish. The idea was unexpected and thrilling. Walter had had no contact with Jews growing up (there were only a few in Berlin when he lived there, and perhaps none at all in rural Bavaria) but the cultural void left behind by the Holocaust had loomed large. If only because the majority of German émigrés who had come to Hollywood before him were Jewish, he had already felt a private kinship. That his mother's parents and thus his mother, and thus he, too, might be Jewish offered not only a connection to famous luminaries in his profession, but an explanation for his lifelong sense of dislocation and therefore, finally, the possibility of a home. If his people were out there, then he could find them; if he had been adrift all his life, he had now been thrown a rope. It wasn't a question of God, but kinship. He never asked his grandfather directly, but the clues added up, and after a while Walter accepted the possibility as fact. A new identity began, proudly, to crystallize.

On a high school trip Walter had once visited Regensburg, a medieval city in Bavaria not bombed during the war. All the architecture was intact. In the *Rathaus* there, the huge town hall, there was an original prison in the basement, including a whole room devoted to violent and primitive torture devices that left a particularly strong impression on the teenage boys in the group, who took turns trying to stick each other into them. There were many levels, for each kind of prisoner, descending into an isolation chamber at the bottom for the worst of the worst. It could be reached only through a small opening in the ceiling. There was no light and nowhere to sleep but the floor. There was only a makeshift toilet in the corner, a hole in the ground covered by a stone that served as a seat. The tour guide had been very thorough and perhaps because his audience was so attentive, went into great detail. He told them how each of the torture devices worked and what the prisoners were fed (in descending order) and pointed out, finally, that the stone surface of the toilet in the dungeon at the bottom was actually a tombstone stolen from a Jewish cemetery during the pogrom of 1509. The entire class had leaned in to peer down at the Hebrew letters inscribed in the stone.

"The scum of the earth sat on a stolen Jewish tombstone to take a shit?"

Someone else had asked the question, but the heartbreaking thought had crossed Walter's mind too. Now sitting in his car outside the tennis club, bare legs plastered to the hot plastic seats, the thought of that tombstone made him sick. He was twenty-three that year in California. High school was a recent memory, even his childhood was relatively fresh. He stared at the Star of David and found himself sifting through the details of class trips and history lessons, his own father's family stories from World War II. And when Walter imagined his very young mother; when he imagined his mother, his Jewish mother, alone in that small town and surrounded by its incomprehensible history, the image took his breath away.

20

The store reminded Hope of the hardware store she had grown up with in Kansas City, in business since the beginning of time. As she opened the door, a bell hanging over it chimed. Every step she took now already felt like a step for two. She took in the thick patina of daily use on the store's walls, the display of plastic buckets, arranged by size, gathering dust in the window. She examined a pile of real candles for Christmas trees. The tree Dave brought home had just been sitting in a corner, so she picked up three boxes of candles and two of the little gold clips and gathered her thoughts before approaching the counter. If her project in the nursery had initially been driven by curiosity, it was personal now. It was taking too long. Her German wasn't good enough to describe what she needed in detail, but she had collected a few key words from the dictionary and had written them down on a piece of paper.

"Was kann ich für Sie tun?" asked the shop clerk.

He had on thick glasses that made his eyes expand behind their black plastic frames. Hope laid the small piece of paper down on the counter and he removed his glasses to get a better look at it. The eyes underneath were human-sized, brown and kind. He read her list and looked up at her, replacing the glasses on his nose.

"*Rauhfasertapete,*" he said, at least this was the one word she could identify from what came out of his mouth.

She nodded. He left the counter and went into the back. While she waited, she examined the hundreds of drawers lining the walls, from the floor to the ceiling, each one with a sample of its contents on the front: screws, nails, hooks, handles, knobs. She hadn't had a shower in two days and had her hair pulled back in a knot held in place by a pencil, which felt loose as she bent her neck. Behind her, a line of other customers gathered, agitating silently as the wait went on. She reknotted her hair and stuck the pencil in as deep as she could, so that it felt like even sides of her face were pulled back into the bun. When the man emerged from the back, he was carrying a square-shaped, old-fashioned machine and a collection of other objects: a paper mask, a flat, sharp metal tool, garbage bags and an X-acto knife. He placed the machine on the front counter.

"*Wasser,*" he said slowly, pointing into the hole in the top. "*Fünf Minuten.*" He held up one hand with five fingers spread.

Hope nodded quickly. She made a deposit for the rental, paid for the other supplies and the Christmas candles, which she threw in her shoulder bag, and left the store carrying the machine carefully with both hands.

The drunks on the bench at Savignyplatz were already well into their morning despite the cold, and they hackled when she approached them, so she walked the other way around the square. As she came up on the southeast corner, she had to force herself to continue past the clothing store and the Russian restaurant separating her from the brothel's entrance. Only one woman was standing there today, the black one with blond hair, no Santa hat. She had on moon boots that went up past her knees and thick stockings and a very short white down jacket over a bright red leotard, hips and breasts swelling impossibly from the tight belt at her waist. The outfit made her look like some punk Wonder Woman, thought Hope, putting down the machine. She pulled her trench coat protectively around her stomach thinking that this woman would not be standing outside in the cold at ten A.M. if it were not worth her while. Apparently, Dave had been right about the local market for a quick morning fuck.

"Three businesses boom during a recession," he'd told her not that long ago. "Liquor, movies and prostitution."

"How cynical," she'd replied.

She already knew how his affair would play out. She was certain that he had placed limits on how far he'd go with someone else (oral sex, no penetration; fingers, hands; no kissing), that he had managed to circumscribe the experience in his mind, keep it separate from their marriage. Meat and milk. Eventually he would come back, if she wanted him (of this she was certain, but she was no longer certain that she did). She shook out her arms and as she did so, the prostitute looked over. Her makeup was garish, bright and metallic against her dark skin, and when their eyes met she licked her lips. The lick was lazy, provocative, a pink tongue run slowly over red lipstick; Hope realized only halfway through that it was meant as an invitation. She shook her head. The woman shrugged. *I'm sorry*, Hope wanted to say. *It isn't you.* She quickly picked up the machine and hurried under the S-Bahn tracks to avoid the posters, which she knew were wrapped around a wall by the entrance to the train. They would be rain-soaked and peeling off the walls by now, she thought, but the image was still there: the hooded smile, the arms still lifted victoriously, the stupid headline in red. At the playground on the other side of the tracks, the mothers sat together on a bench while their children played, bundled up in handmade-looking woolens and snow boots. Hope couldn't hear them, or see their lips move, but she knew they were talking from the breath that rose up from their heads in the cold.

She pushed open the gate. As it slammed shut behind her, the view of the playground seemed to both retract and expand, as if filtered through a fish-eye lens. The jungle gym bloated in the middle, the line of women pulled off to one side and the strollers to the other, and the whole picture warped around her, sucking her inextricably inward. She considered the possibility that she might be jinxing everything by entering hallowed ground so early in her pregnancy, but last time, she had not eaten sushi, had not had a single sip of alcohol or flown in a transatlantic plane. Last time, she had told no one that she was pregnant until twelve weeks had passed, which was no comfort when the baby died at thirty weeks. By then, she already had told everyone and quit her job. Hope put down the machine and approached the bench. The mothers looked up and moved to one side to make space for her without asking why she was there without a child. If they had noticed that she had entered the playground with a humidifier instead of a stroller, they did not say so. They made space for her and spoke to her in English.

"I've seen you at Balzac," said one with short gray hair and an American accent. "You must be new in town, because there are way better places to get a cup of coffee."

"If you saw her there, then you were there too," pointed out the woman to her left. "And you've been here for years."

"I go there all the time because the menu is in English," said Hope.

They nodded. There were three of them, each very different in style. The one with short hair and the American accent was the eldest. She had a serious, slightly defeated expression and wore clogs. The one to her left was wearing a proper winter coat with a wide collar and buttons made of tortoiseshell; she had long, polished black hair and an accent. The third one had not spoken yet. She had her blond hair fixed in a bob and clasped her hands in her lap over a pale blue parka that matched the color of her eyes. Hope sat down next to the dark-haired woman closest to her side of the bench.

"When I first came, there wasn't even coffee-to-go in this city," continued the American. "You couldn't get anything to go in Berlin."

"When was that?"

"Late eighties, right before the Wall came down."

The blond woman yelled something to one of her children in German. The child, a girl about six years old, pulled her hat down over her ears.

"What was it like here then?"

"Very left-wing, very laid-back. None of these business types you see around here now, running the world."

"She always complains that the Ties have ruined Charlottenburg," said the blonde. "But my husband is a Tie."

"A Suit," the American woman corrected her. "Your husband is a Suit. In English we don't call them Ties."

Hope laughed.

"The Wall came down and the Suits came charging over from the East?"

"No, the Suits came from Munich to make money in the New Berlin. The people who came over from the East just wanted to eat bananas. That was the thing they had craved most. For weeks you had to kill someone in the supermarket to get a banana. Anyway, it wasn't until the official reunification that the change really sank in."

"In 1990."

"I remember going down to Unter den Linden to see the celebration, and I'm telling you, it was like the Germans won the war after all. They won the World Cup that summer with a reunited team. They even got all their land back in the end. They were dancing in the streets. It was scary."

"We didn't get everything back," said the blonde. "It isn't fair to say that. My family had been living for five hundred years near Königsberg. They had a castle there."

"You always bring this up. The aristocrats supported Hitler, so in the end they lost their castles to the Russians. Please."

"They survived only by foraging for mushrooms."

"At least they survived," said the American woman.

No one said anything for a moment.

"It's insensitive."

"Because you're Jewish?"

All three women looked at Hope, surprised.

"Because she is," the American woman indicated the dark-haired woman sitting next to Hope. "Because she lost more than a castle, if you know what I mean."

The dark-haired woman shrugged.

"My family is Jewish and German, but I was born in Colombia. I decided to come back. I have been living here for three years now."

"Why?"

"Because it is a good place for a family and those"—she pointed to two children on the jungle gym, a boy and a girl—"those are my children."

"Is this a good place for children?"

"Of course. Berlin is a city of the future."

"But what about the past?"

"You have to make peace with the past to get on with the future." She smiled. "I live with my ghosts here. I keep them company. They like that."

Hope watched the children playing on the jungle gym. For the first time she noticed that this playground had been built in a bombed-out lot. On either side were the ragged edges of other buildings, leaning up against the air.

"What about you?"

"Me? No, but—" She paused. "My child."

The Colombian woman placed one warm hand on Hope's cold one.

"*Felicidades*," she said. "A summer baby. The summer is beautiful in Berlin."

"That's hard to believe."

"You'll see."

Hope squinted into the dim daylight and tried to imagine the city in summer. The winter here was like being locked in a room with nothing but a low-burning lightbulb overhead, she thought. In college, she had once taken a film history class and remembered the German Expressionist period. Rain pouring against windows while, inside, the actress despaired.

"I think the problem with Berlin is that the winter weather so perfectly reflects the mood of its international reputation that it's almost vulgar to imagine it otherwise. I mean, people taken from their homes on a green summer afternoon? Bombs falling from a bright blue sky? The sun shining over a population in captivity?"

"I wasn't there," said the American woman. "But everyone says that September eleventh was a perfect autumn day."

Hope looked down the bench at the other mothers but said nothing more.

"You know, in Bogotá," said the Colombian woman, "the weather is always the same. The sun rises at seven and sets at seven the whole year. Nobody ever talks about it. We take the sunshine totally for granted. But here it's like a gift every time the spring comes back. Just when you think you can't take it anymore, everything blooms at once. The trees are green and the cafés are full and the children are running around in their underpants."

Hope laughed. "I have totally lost touch with the spin of the earth," she said. "I just don't believe that it will ever be warm here."

"Not just warm," said the Colombian woman. "Light!

This week it will be the shortest day of the year. Already it is so dark that you walk around feeling half asleep. But the payoff comes around on the other side in Berlin. You'll see, in June it is sunny until eleven in the evening."

Hope had never considered this: the payoff on the other side, the yin-yang of the seasons. She could not picture Berlin in summer any more than she could actually imagine going to California for Christmas, but suddenly found herself trying. A sunset at midnight, a green view from her apartment, the children unwrapped from their layers, and people, everywhere, spilling out onto the sidewalk. She found herself wondering what it would be like to stay and find out.

At her apartment one hour later, she dropped her coat by the door and headed straight for the nursery in the back with the machine. Paper hung off the walls onto the floorboards, stinking of glue. Where she had already pulled the white paper free it revealed wide stripes of the orange wallpaper beneath it. She had begun with the small hole Orson had made and worked outward, picking at the glue with a kitchen knife. She had managed to pull off almost all the white layer of paper on that wall, revealing the orange paper beneath it. There were three walls left, and then the orange layer and whatever she found below that. She filled the machine with water and plugged it in, pulling it into the middle of the room and paced around it for the five minutes it took the water to boil, as the man at the hardware store had instructed. When steam billowed from the machine in gusts, rising to the ceiling and filling out to the sides, she sat down on the floor and watched until perspiration poured down the walls.

When the wallpaper swelled up in ripples and bumps, she put on the paper mask and pulled with both hands. The top layer came off easily now that it was wet. After an hour, her hair and clothes were soaked with steam and her fingertips bloody with paper cuts. When she pushed back the orange layer underneath the white, she found another paper there: a textured disco pattern, sparkles blended into a background yellow and sticky with age. She reached for the X-acto knife and cut a square, one foot wide, into the orange paper and pulled up the edge. The disco paper was deep beneath it, followed by a layer of pink flowers, and beyond that a big pattern from the 1950s, in white and avocado green. When Hope scraped at that layer with the knife, she found a thinner paper beneath it, simple newspaper. She took a step back now and examined the open edges of the square through the steam, layers of wallpaper snuggled up against each other like generations of sediment in an archaeological dig.

She liked the idea that each layer had been chosen by a different mother to decorate the nursery of a different child, and pictured the women she had met in Berlin so far laid out along a timeline, populating the history of the room. The black prostitute on Savignyplatz would have looked good next to orange paisley. The American from the playground might have picked the sparkle in her disco days. Had she lived here in the sixties, the policewoman at Friedrichstrasse might have chosen bright pink flowers to distract her children from the bewildering fact that this room was just a tiny island floating above another island, surrounded by a hostile nation full of people who looked just like them. And the big avocado-green print? The blonde in the light blue coat had a certain 1950s vibe. Beneath the newspaper was the original wall, plaster wet and warm at the surface but solid. Hope hooked her fingers underneath the free edge of the square and with one strong pull tore the whole thing from the wall at once, leaving a hole one foot wide and one foot high and sixty years deep. The years came apart in her hands: white, orange, pink and disco, avocado green. The original walls were beige and blue, a pattern painted by hand. Hope pushed the top edge of the square. Another wet handful came off and she stood back again: a blue cat in black boots was staring at her. His face was crooked, but delighted, with long whiskers and a black nose, jodhpurs and a buttoned jacket. In her mind's eye she saw the Colombian mother from the playground holding a paintbrush and palette, painting a whole world for her children right here in this room. Hope wrapped both arms around her stomach, touched her forehead to Puss in Boots and closed her eyes.

21

All week, when Walter called downstairs, Hope begged off further excursions. She was sick to her stomach, she told him, she had a cold. But she sounded just fine.

"I'm not even getting out of bed today," she said.

He offered to bring her chicken soup, bananas, yogurt, aspirin, a VCR and videotapes, but she declined. He called downstairs throughout the day to discuss their California plans, each time struggling to come up with new details that required her input: the hotel, the rental car, dinner reservations, day trips. If she agreed to the details she couldn't possibly back out. They were planning this trip together, he told himself. It was only fair to run things by her.

"Hello?"

"It's me again."

"Walter. Hi."

"I'm just wondering. Can you drive a stick shift?"

"Yes."

"Do you have a valid U.S. driver's license?"

"Yes."

"Is there something special you'd like to eat for dinner Christmas Day?"

"Nothing I can think of."

"Goose?"

"That would be nice."

"Or roast beef, perhaps?"

"That would be nice too."

On the phone she was friendly but distracted. Sometimes she was out of breath. He always hung up feeling worse than he had before he called, but then the empty hours would pass and he'd find himself back in his bedroom, imagining her lying there, silently and separately, only meters below, asking himself what was wrong with this picture. Since they'd met, they'd seen each other almost every day, and now she was slipping through his fingers. He'd pace his bedroom with the phone in one hand until he couldn't control himself and call again.

After a few days had passed, the sound of champagne toasts made on that imaginary California terrace had faded out; the sun had set, the children had gone home; the whole plan was threatening to ship out to sea. Walter tried to focus on the premiere (Tom Cruise patting him on the back like a buddy, telling him jokes) but it didn't stick. He spent the day drinking coffee, wandering around his apartment, unpacking and repacking his suitcase. He flipped through the first trimester in a guide to pregnancy that Heike bought when her soap character got knocked up by a security guard (she had really gotten into it, method acting her way through a bottle of folic acid pills). In the living room, he taped the last few pieces of the map together. Where it had been damp it was now wrinkled, so he laid it out under the biggest books he could find. He retrieved the newspaper from his doormat but couldn't sit still long enough to read it. He returned to the living room and looked out over the dusty carpet of invoices and paper receipts that covered the furniture. What a mess. It reminded him of a story Bodo had told him years ago, about a trip he'd once made to a remote part of China. There had been no special accommodations for foreigners, so he'd slept in a large monastery where instead of toilets there were just rooms with holes in the floor. When he squatted over one of the holes, his shit had just dropped down into the room below.

"When the room downstairs filled up with shit," he'd told Walter, "they just locked the door and moved on to the next one. It stank worse than anything I ever smelled. But I was impressed. I mean, that's true detachment for you. They just left their shit in a room and forgot about it."

Walter walked around the apartment he'd lived in for the past sixteen years and made a decision. When he left Berlin he would take nothing with him; not the old bathing suit he had tried on the other day or the sunscreen on the kitchen table or any of the other clothes he'd packed and repacked into his suitcase. He would not clean up the piles of paper from his tax audit or empty his closets or give things away; he would leave the interior of his apartment exactly as it was. Let his landlord have his stereo and his security deposit. Hope was coming with him to California. He would start over there from scratch.

. . .

In the kitchen he ate four Toasts Hawaii in a row without sitting down. He prepared each one carefully, taking as long as possible, biding his time. Thirty seconds to open the can of pineapple and three to slice the bread, ten to cut a piece of cheese, seven for the butter, five for the ham, six minutes in the toaster. He was slicing off bread for a fifth when the phone rang.

"*Hallo?*"

"Walter?"

Hope's voice materialized like a miracle on the other end of the line. He removed his hand from the bread.

"Do you have a very sharp knife up there?"

She was polite, as if she were asking an enormous favor of him, as if they hadn't spoken three times the day before. He ran his thumb along the serrated edge of the knife he'd been using.

"I'm working on a little project," she said. "A sharp scissors will do if that's all you've got."

"Are you cooking something?"

"No, no. Nothing like that."

"Can I help you?"

"Oh no, I can do it alone. Just the knife if you've got one. The sharpest one you have. I'll come up and get it."

"I'll bring it down."

He wrapped the knife in a dishtowel and fifteen seconds later he was ringing her bell. When she opened the door, the first thought that crossed his mind was that he hardly knew her. A few days apart was a long time and he'd already forgotten many things: the color of her eyes, the sound of her voice, even the shape of her face was different from how he'd remembered it. She was wearing a large I LOVE NY T-shirt and shorts and, although it was the middle of December, appeared to be sweating. If he didn't know better, he might have thought that she had been working out, but there was something off-kilter about all of it. The hair down her back was tangled. The clothes looked as though she'd been wearing them for days.

"Did you get that T-shirt from Orson?"

"Orson? No, I bought it years ago in New York."

He nodded. Even her legs glistened, but she was barefoot. There were flecks of colored paper across her forehead. Stranger still, she seemed happy. She held out one hand for the knife and grinned. There was no way he was leaving her alone like this.

"When was the last time you ate something?"

"Oh, I'm not very hungry."

"What about the baby?"

She tapped one foot impatiently against the floor.

"In the first trimester it's really important to eat a lot of iron," he said. "You have to keep your energy up. You should eat a steak or something."

She wiped her hands directly on the breast of her shirt like a worker at a construction site and sniffed, eyeing the knife.

"Maybe you're right."

"Let me take you to dinner at Bodo's. The fresh air will do you good. Think of the baby."

Hope pulled her hair up out of her face.

"You don't mind?"

"Mind?"

"You don't have anything else you want to do tonight? It's one of your last free nights in Berlin. Tomorrow night is your premiere, isn't it?"

He leaned stiffly into the doorjamb.

"I don't mind."

They walked toward the restaurant in silence. At the Schillertheater, a rehearsal for the musical *Hair* was going on inside, men and women's voices poured out through the window, singing together in German-accented English: *Let the sun shine in!* A short, thin man coming down the steps of the theater called out to them but they kept going until he called out again. Only then did Walter recognize him as Jens Kossendrup, the actor who had played his brother on *Schönes Wochenende.* He ran up to meet them on the sidewalk. His face was ruddy and his eyes exhausted, but he had kept both his figure and his hair.

"How you doing, man?"

Jens slapped one palm against Walter's and patted the other against his back in a half-hug.

"Good, good."

"Tom Cruise?"

"Yeah."

"What a cash cow. Lucky you."

Walter was relieved that Hope couldn't follow the conversation in German.

"What are you up to?"

"It's been tough, man. But now I got a gig, here, in *Joseph and the Amazing Technicolor Dreamcoat.* Weekday evenings and Sunday matinee."

Walter never went to musicals; the overacting and heavy makeup reminded him of Disneyland. The most popular show at this particular theater was a Korean extravaganza called *Cookin'*, in which actors danced enthusiastically with knives. But he was relieved that Jens had a job.

"You playing Joseph?"

Jens laughed, slowly at first and then big, as if he'd suddenly realized that Walter was joking.

"Yeah, right."

"No?"

"Joseph? C'mon, man. They always have a name for the main roles."

"You're a name."

"I *was* a name, my friend. That was years ago. Now I'm just one of the brothers."

Walter glanced at Hope to make absolutely sure she couldn't follow the conversation, but she was just staring at the theater, lost in her own thoughts.

"One of the brothers?"

"Joseph has eleven brothers."

"Right."

"You should come see the show sometime. We can get a beer after."

When he finally got to California, thought Walter, he was never, ever coming back.

They said goodbye to Jens and headed north toward Savignyplatz. As they followed the familiar route, he tried to picture their exact location on the globe, the curvature of the earth beneath their feet treading steadily across the neighborhood;

Pestalozzi to Bleibtreu to Kant, toward Savignyplatz. He saw Charlottenburg laid out against the shapes of countries and oceans, the small, square grid of his daily ritual like one of those warped maps drawn from a particular provincial perspective. *Walter Baum's View of the World:* their beautiful yellow building on Schillerstrasse in the foreground, the various nearby shops, Deutsche Synchron outlined in red, The Wild West swollen to the size of an important country, and off in the distance a sliver of Atlantic Ocean, a tiny New York City skyline and a single cartoon palm tree bobbing hopefully at the far western edge. When they passed the cop patrolling the synagogue on Pestalozzistrasse, Hope spoke for the first time.

"Why is the synagogue a secret?"

"It isn't. There are other synagogues in the city that you can see from the street."

"There are policemen in front of all of them?"

"Since September, there's been a tank all the time in front of the big one in Mitte."

"This one seems so mysterious, though, since they built it behind closed doors. Maybe they knew they would have to protect themselves."

"I don't know."

"Did you know that this neighborhood was very Jewish? Do you know anything about our building?"

"Yes," said Walter. "There is evidence that most the residents before the war were Jewish."

"Evidence?"

He looked up the street.

"The super was born in the building in 1944. In fact, the day before a bomb dropped and destroyed the rest of it."

"How did they survive?"

"By hiding in the basement. Have you ever been to our basement?"

"No."

"Well, the super's mother told him that they were the only non-Jewish family before the war. She said that the people who couldn't get out of Germany hid in the basement, but that eventually they were discovered, rounded up in the courtyard and taken away."

"No."

"They left their furniture and everything inside their apartments. They were fancy apartments, you know, so eventually other people just moved into them, dusted them off and used all their things."

Hope stopped walking.

"Non-Jews."

"Of course. By the time the super's mother went down into the basement to hide from the bombing, she had a whole new group of German—I mean non-Jewish—neighbors. None of the original people were left."

He put one hand behind Hope's back to push her gently forward, steering her past the *Time for Action* poster without comment. It was frayed and wrinkled from the rain.

"The sad truth is that if you ask almost anyone in Charlottenburg about their building, they'll tell you something similar."

"You think that a Jewish family lived in my apartment?"

"*Kristallnacht* was in November 1938. It is likely that a Jewish family lived in your apartment before that, but not much later."

"So they were killed."

"This is Berlin, Hope."

"Why do you say it like that?"

"Like what?"

"Like it's old news."

"It is old news."

"But it's horrible."

"You're right." He paused. "Honestly, if I thought about this all the time I wouldn't be able to get up in the morning."

"What about the children?"

"Which children?"

"In my apartment. Do you think they killed the children, too?"

They reached the restaurant, saving Walter from a response, and he pulled open the front doors.

Velvet curtains hung in a half-circle around the front door that made it impossible to see into the restaurant until you had passed through into the sea of guests. Hope went first and Walter followed her into the dining room, like walking out onto a stage. *I'd like to thank* ... He scanned the crowd automatically. It was early but it was already dark outside and packed inside, and loud; it took him a moment to focus and another to realize that Heike was sitting at a table in the middle of the restaurant with a group of people. Some he recognized, some he didn't, one of them was Klara. Heike was wearing her hair pulled up and red lipstick. She was holding a glass of red wine and laughing dramatically, head back, eyes closed, one shoulder thrown forward like a pinup. He watched until she stopped laughing, dabbed the tears at the corner of her eyes with a napkin and noticed him. The other people at her table looked up too and fell silent. It seemed to Walter then that the noise level in the whole restaurant dropped. Conversations paused midsentence. People whispered. The soft background music rose up to the surface: Sade. Klara got up from her seat and walked toward him.

"Sometimes things just have to get worse before they get better," she said, taking him by the shoulders.

He hadn't seen her in ages. She was wearing a dark blue suit and funky red glasses. Her hair was frosted and blown straight to her shoulders.

"I should have called this morning as soon as I saw it."

"What?"

"The phone works both ways, Walter. You could have called me, too."

"Walter!"

Bodo pushed Klara aside to get to him.

"Don't worry about a thing," he whispered in Walter's ear. "I'll take care of this."

He turned to Hope.

"Maybe you can settle a debate raging in the kitchen. There are only a few really tall skyscrapers left in New York now, right? Which one is tallest? The Empire State or the Daimler-Chrysler?"

"The Daimler-Chrysler?"

"Of course not. I knew it was the Empire State."

"No," said Hope. "I mean, yes, the Empire State building is taller. But the Chrysler Building is still called the Chrysler Building."

Bodo steered them toward a table near the window. He

pulled out a chair for Hope, who sat down. Klara had followed them and sat down next to her. Walter stayed on his feet.

"I saw her," he told Bodo. "I can handle it."

"You saw the paper?"

"She's sitting in the middle of the restaurant."

"She's celebrating, of course. I couldn't just turn her away."

Klara leaned into Hope, who was reading the menu.

"Ich empfehle den Zander."

"I don't speak German very well," said Hope.

Klara observed her face more closely. "I recommend the fish," she said in English.

Bodo glanced at Heike's table and back at Walter, who still had not sat down.

"Just hold your head up and ignore them. You know how people are. It's a big deal today but it'll be forgotten by tomorrow."

"What are you talking about?"

"Don't tell me you haven't seen it."

"What?"

Bodo sighed.

"Leute von Heute ran a profile of Heike today."

Walter looked down at the place setting beneath him. To his left, Klara was translating the menu for Hope. He reached for a glass of water and brought it to his lips but didn't drink. Out the corner of one eye he saw that a man waiting for a table by the entrance was reading the local paper, today's issue with the profile inside it; the very issue sitting unread on Walter's kitchen table at home.

"I see."

"That's not the worst of it."

"How'd she look?"

"What do you think? It was a fluff piece."

"Nice."

"Look, nobody reads this shit——"

"Everybody reads it."

"Well, nobody cares."

"Of course they do——"

Walter looked over at Heike, who turned away. The other people at her table were laughing. Regulars all over the restaurant were watching him under heavy lids, over wineglasses, holding their collective breath, waiting for him to make a scene. Wasn't this why they read the tabloids in the first place? Why they ate at an industry restaurant instead of staying at home? *Fight, fight, fight.* Even Bodo and Klara, babysitting him so carefully. He imagined pulling the white tablecloth out from underneath the drinks at Heike's table, the sound of glasses crashing to the floor, the smell of liquor, a stricken look on faces all over the restaurant. He could have silenced the room instantly by raising his voice. It was a strangely powerful realization. How would he begin? *We live in a cynical, cynical world.* Walter looked over again and this time Heike languidly returned his stare.

"Let's get out of here," he said to Hope, who put down her menu.

He moved quickly toward the door, leaving Klara and Bodo at the table. A tall man with a black cap was waving at Hope, trying to get her attention; he appeared to have only one ear. The eyes of fifty other curious diners were following them. As he reached the front of the restaurant, Heike called out Walter's name, drawing on the first syllable so that it sounded worn out. He pretended not to hear her.

"Walter," she called again, this time sharper, like a pout.

When still he didn't stop, the man who had been reading the newspaper by the door blocked his path.

"She's talking to you."

Walter tried to shake him off without looking at him. He focused on the velvet curtain ahead, the sanctuary beyond it. Keep moving, he told himself. Make it to the sidewalk without turning around.

"Walter," said Heike. "Stop."

"She said stop."

The man grasped Walter's shoulder. He was maybe thirty, blond, red cheeks and a wide chest, nondescript; a tourist from Bremen or Hanover from the sound of his accent, clearly come to the capital, to The Wild West itself, looking for exactly this sort of brush with national celebrity. He was holding the newspaper in the hand that wasn't on Walter's shoulder. It was folded open in half, so that the profile of Heike was turned outward and Walter came face to face with the glamorous shot that took up the top right corner of the page. Three-quarter turn, glossy hair, come-hither smile.

"Let's go," he said again to Hope.

But the tourist from Bremen was still in his way. He glanced down at the side of the newspaper he was holding and back at Walter.

"What are you going to do about it, Santa Claus?"

He said Santa Claus as if it were a four-letter word. Walter could feel the heat from the eyes of the restaurant crowd, Klara, Bodo, Heike and her friends. Hope came up behind him.

"Please," said Walter, so that only the man could hardly hear him.

"What was that?"

"Please."

"Walter," called Heike again.

"It's Christmastime, Santa. Be nice to the lady."

He wanted to rip the man's hand from his shoulder and spit in his face, but in front of this rapt audience he would not give Heike the satisfaction.

"Santa?" The man grinned. "Isn't that you?"

He turned the paper around so that the other side of the fold was now visible. Under the headline "People from Yesterday" were two pictures. A production still from *Schönes Wochenende* taken twenty years earlier and a paparazzi shot taken on the terrace of The Wild West in the summer. In the first one, Walter's thick hair was gelled back and he was grinning like a playboy. In the second one, his bald spot shone like a light over the grimace on his face. He was wearing a loose red T-shirt that made his belly hang over his belt. The caption read: *Santa Claus came early this year.*

After the planes flew into the World Trade Center in September, Walter had spent all night transfixed in front of the television at the studio drinking coffee with his colleagues who comforted each other with stories of near-death experiences they had personally survived.

"I thought my world was coming to an end," said one editor, describing the day he discovered that his first wife was having an affair. "But then I met my second wife."

"I felt something cool at the back of my neck and in that split second everything changed," said an actor, about being held up at gunpoint on a bus in Brazil. "But the real surprise came afterward, when the thieves got off the bus with my money and left me alive. It was almost as if it never happened."

"This too will pass," they told each other. "Life goes on."

Only Walter had said nothing. They were wrong. Life might go on, but things would be different. These experiences, however distant, altered the course of your life. It might be imperceptible at first, but eventually their force gained momentum, until you had veered so far off in the wrong direction that you were undeniably lost. Standing by the front door at The Wild West in December of 2001, the man holding up the newspaper removed his hand from Walter's shoulder, but it didn't matter. The restaurant around him had already disappeared. Walter saw only the photographs in the paper, and in the distance traveled between them he counted backward, sixteen years, to that last day in California in June of 1985. His grandparents in their dark living room. Hot congestion on the 405. Tears streaming down his face.

"Walter."

Hope said it this time, not Heike. She was next to him but he heard his name as if she were whispering it through plastic cups drawn taut with string.

"Walter."

She wrapped her arm around his waist. Her small body was surprisingly strong, he thought, but she couldn't stop the palm trees speeding past out the window on the freeway, the candy-colored houses gone by in a blur, the smell of fuel and sweat and the ocean. She couldn't stop the tears streaming down his face because he was actually crying now, sobbing like a baby in the middle of the restaurant. Hope couldn't stop him and she didn't try. She propped him up gently, led him out through the velvet curtains and took him home.

22

By the spring of 1985, Walter had stopped going to auditions or reading *Variety* or sending out his show reel. He stayed at Sharon's all the time, now that there was no reason to go back to Los Angeles. By March, they were no longer having sex; by April, he was sleeping on the couch. He moved through his daily Prince Charming shows in an automatic daze. Line here, flick of cape, line, worried expression, line, thrilled surprise, bend on knee, final line, kiss.

"You're not yourself, Walter," said Sharon.

"No," he replied. "I'm not."

The two mornings a week with his grandfather was the only thing that mattered. In between, when he wasn't working, Walter drove aimlessly around Orange County. Sometimes he went all the way to the beach and looked out at the ocean and practiced Hans's stories aloud until they came out like spontaneous memories. In the shower he reviewed the chronology of Hans's life so that he wouldn't get anything backward during a performance (because that's what it was, he realized, the best performance of his short career). He had played Hans already for three years on television, but this time he absorbed the character completely; he took the outline of himself, like a cartoon on the page of a comic book, and filled it in with Hans until the space inside was solid color. If the first time he'd played him for the teenage girls in the boondocks, for the cuddle pictures and the free drinks and the mob scenes in shopping malls, now he played him for the one bright face in the audience, standing out from the anonymous throng. And if he played him differently, better, it was not because he'd learned new techniques. In the intervening two years, he hadn't taken any classes or done research. He had not acquired a method, a guru or a teacher; he was simply motivated. For the first time in his life, at twenty-three, Walter wanted something passionately: to reel his grandfather in, make him comfortable, make him laugh, make him come back again every Tuesday and Thursday. He wanted to make his grandfather love him and so he entertained him.

One morning late in May, a Tuesday, Walter arrived to find other people sitting at his grandfather's regular table. In six months he had never been late. He looked around the restaurant at the breakfast crowd. The icy wind of the air conditioner traveled down his neck to his fingertips. Customers went in and out; the parking lot filled and emptied. His grandfather never showed up. Two days later, on Thursday, his table was simply empty. Walter ordered coffee by himself in hopes of conjuring the usual routine, but an hour later the coffee was cold and the table beside him remained empty. Over the weekend he didn't sleep, he hardly ate, he sat on the steps in front of Sharon's house and watched the yellow line up the middle of the street until it bent to the left and then to the right, until it zigzagged across the flat pavement baking beneath it and not a soul walked up the sidewalk. When on the following Tuesday morning his grandfather still didn't show, Walter returned to his car and put his head down on the steering wheel in despair. Old men died, he thought, even the ones who played tennis. His grandfather was dead. Walter should have told him when he had the chance but he didn't. Now he was gone and with him the possibility of reunion. Walter pressed his forehead into the vinyl. *The most successful performance of my life,* he thought, looking through the windshield at cars pulling in and out of the parking lot, unsure whether to laugh or cry. He turned the key in the ignition and pulled into midmorning traffic, blinking quickly into the sunshine. He could feel his kidneys throbbing softly in his back, the flow of his blood. REO Speedwagon played on the radio.

"*Even as I wander I'm keeping you in sight,*" he sang along.

When he came to the entrance to Springtime Estates, he paused.

"*You're a candle in the window on a cold, dark winter's night.*"

He crept through the community at twenty mph, its blue bungalows and evenly spaced young trees. When he hit the high notes, he closed his eyes.

"*I'm getting closer than I ever thought I might.*"

His grandfather's car was sitting in the driveway of his house. Walter got out of the car and walked slowly toward the house.

"Hans."

His grandfather greeted him at the door. He was wearing chinos and a button-down shirt, street clothes, not the usual tennis gear. He had a cast on his leg but otherwise appeared to be very much alive. Walter's voice cracked.

"You're okay?"

"I broke my ankle playing tennis."

"That's great."

"Great?"

"I mean. I mean—"

His grandfather's eyes narrowed.

"How did you find me here?"

"I asked the waitress."

"She doesn't know where I live."

"She looked it up in the phone book for me."

The screen door stood between them like a scrim in the theater, dividing the light: his grandfather in the cool darkness of the house and Walter in the sunshine on the doorstep.

"I was worried when you didn't show up for a week. I thought—"

"You thought I was dead!"

"No. Yes."

"Almost," he said. "But not quite."

Almost reluctantly, he pushed open the screen.

"Since you're here you might as well come in."

"Walter?"

Both men turned in response to the high voice that preceded a woman moving slowly toward him in a pale green housecoat. If his grandfather was old, his grandmother was ancient. Her white hair was pulled back tightly into a bun.

"Who's this?"

"Hans," said Walter's grandfather, "this is my wife, Vera. Vera, this is Hans from the diner. I told you about him."

She turned to Walter and looked him up and down.

"From Germany."

Walter nodded.

"You came here to work at Disneyland."

He nodded.

"What part?"

He smiled at her.

"What part, dear?"

"I play Prince Charming in the Cinderella panorama."

"I meant which part of Germany."

The same answer was true of Hans and himself, but still he had to think about it.

"Bavaria."

"We lived in Bavaria," she said. "When Walter was in the service. Did he tell you?"

"He did."

"It was a long time ago. Before you were born, probably."

"Probably."

"We have pictures."

"Really?" He took a step toward her. "I'd like to see them."

His grandparents looked at each other. She clasped her hands together and released them.

"I feel homesick sometimes," said Walter, as if to explain his interest.

"It does sound nice there," said his grandfather to his wife. "A lot nicer than what we remember. He's told me some great stories."

He was nervous, thought Walter. He was speaking more

quickly than usual, as if trying to convince his wife that what he said was true.

"Tell her about the horse, Hans. About the time you found it in the neighbors' living room. Tell her about it."

They were still standing in the dark foyer, where lamps were on despite the midday sun outside. There were thick curtains on the windows and wall-to-wall carpeting. Walter listened to the purr of a fan. His grandmother looked at him, seeming to consider the fabric of his T-shirt, the shape of its sleeves, the width of his neck.

"Let me see if I can find the album," she said finally. "Come into the living room. I'll get some lemonade."

She was shaking almost imperceptibly when she served the drinks. Walter's grandfather seemed to concentrate on a sliver of sunlight struggling to push in through the curtains, uncrossing and recrossing his legs. Walter's palms were wet. He switched hands so the glass wouldn't slip from his fingers while his grandmother searched through a cabinet at the back of the room. When she found a large leather photo album, she sat down next to him and balanced it between their laps. They touched; her skin felt like tissue paper against the muscular curve of his arm. She smelled like apricots and soap, he thought, a clean but thoroughly indoor smell. He could get used to it. She reached across him and opened the album's cover.

Walter's mother had been a teenager when the pictures were taken. She was wearing ice skates in one of them, standing in front of a house with her schoolbooks in another. In the background, the landscape of his childhood. The snow-capped peaks whose jagged outlines he could trace in his sleep; the ugly brown houses and grazing meadows behind them; the thick pine forests of the foothills.

"We were in the Alps," said his grandmother. "Do you come from that area? I know there are flatter parts of Bavaria. It's probably changed a great deal since we were there."

"The mountains haven't changed."

"Of course not."

"They still look familiar."

"The mountains *were* beautiful."

She emphasized the verb, as if to say that nothing else was.

"You didn't like it very much."

"We are religious people," she said, looking up at her husband. "To you it seems like ancient history, I'm sure, but we lived through the Second World War. It was very difficult for us."

"Of course."

"Germany was very difficult for us."

"And for your daughter?"

"I'm sorry?"

Walter pointed to a picture on the page. His mother was smiling in a snowsuit. She was holding up a set of skis.

"This is your daughter?"

"Our only child. A miracle. We thought we couldn't have any children at all and then she came to us late in life. I was forty-one years old. My husband was forty-four."

Walter ran one finger over the yellowing photograph, his mother's face still softened by lingering baby fat. She had been beautiful when he was a child, but thinner than the girl in these pictures, as he remembered her, sadder, wearier.

Now, he told himself. Say it now. It was a simple line; he had said it a million times before: *I am Walter Baum*. Walter could feel the shape of the words on his tongue, but his grandmother spoke first.

"She died the year this picture was taken," she said.

"When?"

"1961."

His mother had become pregnant in 1961. Walter was born in 1962. His mother died in 1971. She had been twenty-seven at the time.

"When?"

"1961."

"No."

"I'm afraid so. She was seventeen. Much too young."

"1961."

His grandmother told the lie with calm conviction, as if she believed it to be the indisputable truth, as if the past could be actually changed by describing it differently often enough.

"It was a long time ago."

"Twenty-four years ago," Walter whispered.

"That's right."

He pulled the photo album gently into his lap and stared into his mother's smiling face.

"We say Kaddish for her every year."

"What?"

"It's a Jewish prayer."

Across the room, his grandfather shrugged.

"Not a lot of Jews where you come from."

He said it kindly, as if to explain Walter's ignorance to the room, but Walter was still staring in awe at the photograph of his mother. How many times had his grandmother told this story? How many people had she told that her daughter died in 1961? How long had she been telling herself that, because her daughter died in 1961, she had never had a grandson born in 1962? Her version of events was much simpler than the truth, and if it had not eradicated the very fact of his existence, Walter might have liked to accept it himself. Because the truth was so much harder to handle. Because the truth was that his mother was Jewish and had married a German, which meant that she was as good as dead to her parents in 1961, ten years before her time.

"I'm Walter Baum," he said, clutching the sides of the photo album with both hands.

His grandfather cleared his throat.

"I'm her son," said Walter.

"That's impossible."

"Hans," said his grandfather. "Please don't."

Walter turned to him.

"Not Hans. My name is Walter. Your name. She named me after you."

"*Walter*," said his grandfather, whispering the name but no longer contesting the fact of it, as if to admit that he had known all along.

"Yes," said Walter.

"It's impossible," said his grandmother. "No."

The veins in her temples stood out, pale blue rivers running into her eyes. When Walter's grandfather moved to comfort his wife, he did not try to convince her. He looked plaintively at Walter, who was gripping the photo album against him like a breastplate of armor, and the look on his face said everything. That it had been easier to feel each other out through a smooth curtain of artifice. That Hans and his happy stories, his flower-topped hillsides and big-breasted Bavarian milkmaids and a horse in the neighbors' living room were preferable to the truth, because the truth was too painful to imagine: his own grandchild, grown up motherless in a godforsaken land.

Walter ran from the dark house into the sunshine as if into the blast of paparazzi flashbulbs and held up one hand to block the light from his eyes. When he'd first moved to Los Angeles two years earlier, he had mapped out a tour to pay homage to German émigrés who preceded him. He went by the small room on Vine that Peter Lorre shared with Billy Wilder when they first fled Germany in 1933; had a drink at the Chateau Marmont Hotel on Sunset where Hedy Lamarr lived in 1937; and sniffed perfume at the Beverly Hills department store where she was arrested for shoplifting in 1965. He visited the studio lots where Johnny Weissmuller played Tarzan in twelve films and Jungle Jim ("Tarzan with clothes on") in an additional sixteen. He peeked through the front gates at the villa on Roxbury Drive that had once belonged to Marlene Dietrich. But his last afternoon in California, he just drove. Out the windshield: sun-scorched crabgrass and an occasional sliver of the Pacific; the pastel-colored housing developments of Orange County, layered back into infinity like paper dolls. He pulled off the freeway and parked his car at the airport. He removed both passports from the glove compartment and left the mix-tapes and glossy headshots behind. His plane was halfway across the Atlantic already when he remembered that the one time Dietrich had performed in Berlin after the war, people had booed her off the stage. Fleeing the Nazis had lent the vain ambitions of his predecessors a dignity Walter could not claim. Still. They had laid out a one-way path for him and he had failed them. Although what happened that afternoon in the living room in Irvine had nothing to do with Hollywood, he knew no one was going to believe it. The plane had already begun its descent into Berlin when he realized that he was the first of his people to flee in reverse.

23

The first time Hope was pregnant, she was sick from the beginning, throwing up every day well into her fourth month. She was exhausted and plagued by apprehension, privately calculating risk at every turn, staying home so as not to cross the street at the wrong moment or overexert herself. She avoided going anywhere she might have exposed her unborn child to secondhand cigarette smoke or loud noises or germs. What a rotten deal, she thought afterward. Nausea, stretch marks, fifteen pounds and back pain, all that anxiety for nothing. In retrospect now, it seemed sadly ironic that she had been so cautious, as if, by avoiding all manner of external risk, she had forced her body to generate its own calamity. Dave would have said that she was just emotionalizing the facts. But he didn't even know that she was pregnant again. He didn't know that this time she felt totally different. This time, she felt good. Blood for two coursing through her veins! She kept thinking about an article once distributed at the private school where she worked, a study of wealthy children in New York City who drank only expensive bottled water. The children had developed an alarming number of cavities, while their less privileged counterparts in the public schools drank city tap water, which was enhanced by fluoride, and thus had much better teeth. It was a useful metaphor. In the past few days she had worked day and night in the nursery. When she slept, she slept well and when she was awake, the pregnancy made her feel invincible and compassionate. When she walked down the street, she smiled at her neighbors, even when they didn't smile back. When Dave called from Poland, she was neutral, even polite, but did not encourage him to hurry home. When she saw the look on Walter's face at Bodo's restaurant, although she didn't understand a word of what was going on, she took him back to her apartment, where she listened to his story and held his hand.

Across the table in her dining room now she watched his face change color in the dim light of the one lamp that was on in the corner. If his face had been almost white when they came in, it was brighter now, a warmer shade, she thought. The blue of his eyes was by contrast very blue.

"I never told this to anyone before," he said when he was finished. "Not the whole story."

"Why now?"

"Because I don't want us to have any secrets."

She nodded.

"Because I want to start over," said Walter. "When we go back."

She bit her bottom lip. How could she explain to him that she had to stay here?

"This is as good a place as any other to start over," she said.

"Here?"

"If we stand right here on this spot, the whole world will keep spinning past us. We can travel ten thousand miles to California—"

"Six thousand."

"We can travel all that way there but we'll be taking all our problems with us. You came back here, didn't you? How many years ago was that?"

"Sixteen."

"Sixteen years," she said, remembering the beautiful young man on that television show. "Do you think you escaped?"

In a parallel universe, she would have liked to go with him. She could see the two of them in folding chairs on a beach somewhere, zinc on their noses, continuing the same conversation they had here night after night. It was rare to feel so comfortable with another person. In a parallel universe, they might have made it to California together, but in this one she wished he would stay. What could she tell him? *The summer is beautiful in Berlin.* But he knew that. He knew what it was like to watch the sun set long after all the children had gone to bed. He knew how Schillerstrasse looked with green leaves on the trees. She wanted to touch his face, press her cheek against his cheek.

"I have a secret too," she said. "It's time I told you."

He leaned toward her across the table.

"I lost a baby in June. I was seven and a half months pregnant and one day his heart just stopped beating inside me."

"Hope."

It had been hot that day. She had been sitting in an armchair at home, by a fan propped inside one of the living room windows. She had been playing music for the baby, as she often did, not Mozart but pop music, rock and roll, hip-hop; she had her CDs in piles on a table and the armchair pulled up to the stereo, so she could reach everything without getting up. She had been listening to the Talking Heads, rubbing her stomach.

"Feet on the ground, head in the sky," sang David Byrne. *"It's okay, I know nothing's wrong."*

Those lines had been her quote on her yearbook page in high school. She had wanted her baby to hear it and sang along, but when she realized the baby hadn't moved in a while, she stopped singing and stood up. She made one circle through the rooms of her small apartment. It didn't wake him. She turned off the fan and the music and stood as still as she could in the middle of her living room and willed him to move. The sweat on the back of her neck was cold and the apartment was quiet. A siren bleated in the distance, a garbage truck, someone down on the street yelled something to someone else.

"I had to try to deliver him normally even though he was already dead," she told Walter. "I was in labor for forty hours."

"Hope."

"But at the end they had to give me a C-section anyway. They put me under general anesthesia, and when I came to, they had already taken him away. Dave didn't stop them. He said he thought it would be better that way for me, not to see the body, can you imagine? Dave didn't want to see him himself so he deprived me of that possibility too. I never saw my own baby. The hospital just returned the ashes to me with a death certificate."

"He was cremated."

"Yes. Dave signed off on that too. The worst thing, though, was that there was no birth certificate at all. Apparently, it is illegal to issue a birth certificate to a stillborn baby. We were given a record of his death but none of his life, and it was as if the pregnancy hadn't happened at all. He was alive inside me for seven and a half months and then he was gone. Just like that."

She could feel the tears in her eyes, but she did not cry. She did not want to cry about this anymore.

"Do you know the words to that song?"

"Home—"

"Yes."

He sang the first word, now said the rest.

"Love me till my heart stops."

"Love me till I'm dead," she finished. "The climax. It's the best part of the song."

She stood up from the table.

"I have to show you something."

Down the hall, the door to the nursery was closed and she paused in front of it.

"Close your eyes, please."

She had stripped seven layers of wallpaper from the four walls, using the steam machine, an X-acto knife and various blunt, flat instruments. Although the work was still rough, she had uncovered all four original walls, had planned to finish the job with Walter's bread knife, scrape the last bits of paper off the plaster. As it was, the walls were pockmarked and uneven, they would need to be sanded and sealed, but they were glorious. The air was still moist and warm. She had collected the old paper into garbage bags and had set up the Christmas tree there, in the middle of the room. With the little golden clips from the hardware store, she'd clipped real candles to its branches, but had been unable to find any matches. Now she went in first, leaving Walter, eyes closed, in the doorway, and pulled a box she'd taken from The Wild West out of her pocket.

"You can open your eyes now."

The walls were illuminated by the candlelight on the tree. She watched his face as he took it all in: Puss in Boots, Snow White and the Seven Dwarfs, Little Red Riding Hood and the Wolf in her grandmother's cape. A whole wall was devoted to Hansel and Gretel, the elaborate gingerbread house, a winding path through a thicket of trees. He circled the Christmas tree slowly, staring at the luminescent walls, like frescoes in a church.

"What are these paintings?"

"They were here."

"Who painted them? When?"

"I like to think it was the mother of a child who lived in this nursery. It was sometime in the thirties. The last layer I took off was plain newspaper. It stuck to the back of thick wallpaper from the fifties. The date was from January 1939."

Walter touched the trees in Hansel and Gretel's forest, ran one finger along the path to the candy-covered house.

"It's like looking back in time."

She moved closer to him. "Look. I didn't refuse to talk

about my baby because it didn't matter, but because it mattered too much."

"What do you mean?"

"I mean, I understand your grandparents better than you do."

They were standing only a few inches apart.

"Take it from me," she said. "Just because they walked away doesn't mean they didn't care. They cared too much."

"I don't think so."

"They told themselves your mother died because by mourning her, they could keep on loving her. Instead of fighting with her, they said Kaddish in her honor. They celebrated her memory instead of dwelling on their differences. The rituals relieved their pain. They were lucky to have that. Maybe you should try it."

Walter looked up at the fairy-tale characters as if suddenly remembering that he had an audience.

"Most Germans of my generation would love to be Jewish," he said slowly. "Even just a little bit. People are always coming up with a Jewish great-grandmother out of the blue. One of my colleagues at the studio claims she was a rich Jewish woman in Grünewald in her past life. Everyone wants to identify with the oppressed, not the oppressors, to relieve their own inherited guilt. If you ask, almost everyone here will claim that their own family had nothing to do with the Holocaust, that they were hiding Jews in the basement, or in the attic, or under the bed. But if there were as many Jews hidden all over Germany as people claim, believe me, many fewer would have died."

"What does that have to do with you?"

"It's a cliché to discover your Jewish roots."

"She was your mother."

"She was miserable in Germany."

"That was then."

For a moment, Walter didn't say anything. He glanced at the Christmas tree.

"I have lived here most of my life, Hope. I don't think it's possible to be both German and Jewish. Not really."

"They were."

She gestured in a circle, waving to the walls.

"The Jewish mother who lived here in the thirties didn't paint scenes from the Old Testament for her child," she said. "She painted Hansel and Gretel. Little Red Riding Hood. The Wolf. This was her culture too."

Walter stared at the Wolf in the orange light of the Christmas tree.

"What is Kaddish?"

"The mourner's prayer. You light a candle on the anniversary of someone's death to commemorate their life and you say Kaddish."

"I wonder what date they chose for her death."

"It doesn't matter. They lit candles, they said a prayer for her. It made them feel better."

"Right."

"You should try it."

"Light candles for them?"

"Unless you think they are still alive."

He shook his head. His breath was rising quickly in his chest.

"I was in their house, Hope. I was right there in front of them and they told me that I didn't exist."

"But you knew that wasn't true."

He shook his head. "No. I could have been honest from the beginning but instead I hid behind Hans for six months. My character on television. Imagine that."

"You were young."

"By the time I came clean, they were right." He looked at her. "I had already killed myself off."

The candles had burned down into the gold clips that held them to the branches, so that they were shining through the needles, casting patterns on the walls. In this particular light, thought Hope, Walter looked more alive to her than ever.

"You didn't do a very good job," she said.

"What do you mean?"

"You're still here," she said. "I can see you."

24

Walter hadn't walked a red carpet since 1983. The day of the premiere, he lay against the pillows in his dark bedroom and considered the various options. You can glide elegantly forward up the middle, he thought, keeping a wide margin from the screaming fans on either side. Or you can hug the edges, signing autographs while your handlers check their watches impatiently at the end. You can push away the microphones. You can roll your eyes like you would rather be just about anywhere but here. Or you can work it for the cameras and the audience at home, big smiles and air kisses, making the most of thirty seconds in the spotlight. As he recalled, the whole thing was only glamorous on television afterward. Live, the carpet itself was stained and bound with duct tape, the interviewers' makeup as thick as your thumb, and the path was crowded. Producers' wives and children, women carrying clipboards, video technicians and dangerous lengths of wire. The minor players were basically invisible. Nobody at home even noticed those vaguely familiar faces creeping up the carpet behind the big stars. Fans behind the rope screamed right through them, cameras shot around them, occasionally they got caught in the paparazzi crossfire, picking their teeth while the starlet in front struck a pose, but what's the worst that could happen to him, at this point? He would wear a dark suit and a clean shave. He would walk that red carpet like a runway, gaining speed with every step, and take off into the doors of the theater at Potsdamer Platz, to the screening, the party, the airport, to California; he would be clear into another galaxy before the pictures ever made it into the papers.

Hope was not coming with him to California. Where had he gone wrong? It was already early afternoon and although the premiere would begin at six P.M. and he was expected to arrive early, he made no move to get out of bed. Instead, he lay in the dark and reviewed the denouements of the more serious Tom Cruise films for clarity. The drama tended to follow a similar arc. The main character was almost always a cocky young guy, too smart for his own good but unable to focus.

"He has to learn to be himself, but on purpose," said Paul Newman in *The Color of Money.*

He could have been talking about the guys in *Top Gun*, or *Born on the Fourth of July, Rain Man, Jerry Maguire, The Firm.* The traditional Tom Cruise character came into contact with either someone older, wiser and more complicated (Dustin Hoffman, Jack Nicholson, Paul Newman) or a dark collective force (the law firm, the Vietnam War, the sports industry) and the experience forced him to rise to the occasion, to become a better version of himself. The finales were heroic: the Democratic National Convention, the race against time with the Mafia's falsified tax returns, the speech in front of a room of angry divorcées. Walter pictured Tom Cruise at the end of *A Few Good Men*, shouting Jack Nicholson down.

"Don't call me son. I'm a lawyer and an officer in the United States Navy, and you're under arrest, you son of a bitch."

Hope certainly made him want to be a better version of himself. Maybe he should have put a more heroic spin on their flight from the city? He'd clearly made the mistake of being an innocent bystander in his own finale. Tom Cruise had never played a friendly neighbor in his life. In the movie, he and Hope would have arrived home from dinner to find Dave in a headlock on the front stoop, an angry Polish pimp holding a gun to his temple. With Hope screaming in the background and Dave blubbering like a baby, Walter would have had to wrestle the gun away with his bare hands. At the end, they would have pulled away from the curb in a taxi headed for the airport, Dave waving gratefully goodbye. He would have lost his wife but retained his life. It would be something.

When the doorbell rang Walter jumped to his feet, but it was just a messenger with a package from Klara. It contained a script and a note: *This came for you. Read it.* Pity present, he thought, returning to the bedroom. He threw the script on the bed and took the newspaper with him into the bathroom. On the cover, Tom Cruise's first-time visit to Berlin was proclaimed in capital letters: "MISSION POSSIBLE!" Accompanying the headline was a photograph of the movie star descending stairs rolled up to a private plane and waving enthusiastically to the throng of journalists on the tarmac.

Walter was moved to see the actor on German soil. On page two, their shared filmography was listed top to bottom, accompanied by a chronological gallery of Tom Cruise's face. Walter scanned down from the baby-faced mid-twenties, to his present look at forty (longish hair, smooth shave, braces) and shrugged off the comparison to his own parallel trajectory in the opposite direction, exhibited so clearly in the same paper the day before. Recalling the pity and pleasure on people's faces across the restaurant, now, however, he felt strangely calm. At least his worst nightmare had already been realized. Anyway, Tom Cruise knew nothing of his former glory or subsequent demise. Tonight, they would get to know each other. Walter wasn't expecting an actual job offer, or even an audition; just the possibility: a door left slightly but definitively ajar. In the days when he still picked up women in bars, he had had a 1 to 10 system. Ten had been a private phone number scribbled on a napkin, 1 had been a full rebuke. But everything above a 3 had fallen within the realm of possibility: a plan to meet at the same bar next time, a promising smile across a crowded room. Tonight, he thought, he needed a 5. He needed to speak to Tom Cruise tonight so that he could get on the plane knowing that when he got to Los Angeles, Tom Cruise would take his call.

After he showered, he took a nice blue shirt out of his closet and buttoned it carefully. To avoid traffic he would have to leave in a few minutes. The dark blue suit he'd had made at Heike's insistence during her attempted makeover two years earlier was still hanging in its original bag. When he pulled it on, it fit like a glove. He turned to observe himself in the mirror, ran one hand across the monster, smoothed down what was left of his hair. He looked good; thicker, older, but good. He found the laminated VIP pass on the kitchen table and slipped it safely into the inside pocket of his suit jacket and rushed back into his bedroom to look for a tie. He dug through his underwear drawer, the back of his closet, the night table, and found one hanging over the bedpost, still tied in a knot from some game he'd played with Heike at least a year ago. He removed it and undid the knot and sat down on the bed. He was holding the tie open with both hands when his eyes fell on the script lying by him on the bed. *The Wild West*, by Ludwig Schmitz. Walter smirked at the title and peeked inside. After reading page one, he glanced quickly at the clock. He had to get out of here. He was three pages in when he realized that it was Orson's script. When he was ten pages in, he removed his jacket, moved to the armchair by the television, and put his feet up on the bed.

Halfway through the script he checked the clock and turned on the local news: the screaming fans were twenty deep to the velvet rope around the theater. Tom Cruise got out of his limousine with arms outstretched. He made his way slowly down the red carpet, plunged into the crowd, high-fived the guys in the front, signed the teeny-boppers' autograph books; he hugged a woman so excited to see him that she cried. The crowd was still cheering in the background when Walter got up from his chair and went to the window. The night sky over Berlin was unusually clear and he could see over the rooftops toward Potsdamer Platz, where the disk-shaped

Sony theater, a glowing spaceship, was just barely visible. The lights seemed a little brighter than usual tonight, he thought, as if, like the Christmas lights of his childhood, Tom Cruise had brought America with him, as if his presence alone had created a surge in electricity that was flamboyant, wasteful, optimistic.

When Walter first moved into this apartment, Potsdamer Platz was nothing but a bombed-out wasteland between East and West. When he looked out this same window on a winter night, at the same view to the East, there had been only an impenetrable darkness past the Brandenburg Gate, punctuated by the eerie silhouette of the TV tower at Alexanderplatz and the yellow 40-watt haze of the streetlights on Unter den Linden. Now, judging on the view alone, he had moved to a completely different city without leaving this room. He looked around inside. The blue walls were depressing, but they could be changed. He could clean things up, rearrange the furniture, throw stuff out. Perhaps if he turned his bed, when he was lying down he could still look out the window at the sky. The rent was cheap, after all. He could live here for years on his savings. He could do other things. Walter watched the live coverage until Tom Cruise reached the front doors to the theater and turned to wave goodbye to the crowd, then he went back to Orson's script. When he finished it the first time, he read it again. He had just put it down on his lap for the second time when the phone rang.

"You just didn't show up?"

He could hear the sounds of the premiere party going on in the background.

"Tom Cruise thanked you," said Klara. "He said, *Walter Baum makes me sound even better in German than I do in English.*"

Walter laughed. "Not anymore."

"What?" she screamed over the music.

"I'm giving him up."

"Is this about last night?"

"Yes," he said. "But not what you think."

"Did you get the script? The director said to tell you that Til Schweiger pulled out last minute and that you have to save his ass."

"I'll do it."

"Really?"

"Really."

He imagined Klara in the club under strobe lights, the hot crowd throbbing around her, like film in slow motion.

"Let's talk tomorrow," he said.

In the kitchen he found a garbage bag and spent the next half an hour gathering the receipts from his tax audit into it in the living room. Little by little the furniture emerged from the mess, the floorboards and the shape of the walls. He removed the map of Berlin from under books that had flattened it, and hung it up on the wall above the couch. It was no longer possible to see where the historical divisions had been because of all the new cracks and crevices. The green mass of Tiergarten anchored a sprawl of streets, spreading out in all directions from the center. Where only a month earlier the streets had seemed to run off the ragged edges of the paper into nowhere, now they made sense. Thick twists of the *Stadtautobahn* circled the city. The Avus ran out into the blue wilds of Wannsee. The two zoos, the two TV towers, two big airports and three operas were back where they belonged. Walter traced the single road that came in from the East on Unter den Linden, crossed under the Brandenburg Gate and through the park and into Charlottenburg on Bismarckstrasse, just behind his house. He made an X in blue ballpoint at his own address, and he went to retrieve his jacket and tie.

In the bathroom, he examined his face in the mirror above the sink. The circles under his eyes were probably permanent, the furrow in his brow and the lines leading up from his forehead into the thinning crown of hair; but he could work with it. He smoothed his suit and retrieved five small glasses from the kitchen. When she opened the door, Hope was visibly surprised to see him standing there in a suit.

"You look great," she said. "Are you leaving for the premiere now?"

"The premiere is over. It's something else. You're coming with me."

"Where?"

"This is my surprise. Would you mind getting a little bit dressed up?"

She looked down at her sweatpants.

"Okay."

He waited in the foyer while she changed, imagining that he was preparing himself for the camera, as he would become Christmas, when they were shooting Orson's movie in her apartment. When she returned she was wearing a black dress and a yellow sweater. Her face was flushed and she had put on lipstick.

"Now we need a few more things for our journey," he said.

"A coat?"

"No, we won't be needing coats where we're going."

"Walter."

She said it cautiously, as if he were still planning to take her to California. He took a deep breath.

"We need five candles and a box of matches," he said. "Do you have that?"

In the elevator he held the five glasses together with two hands and she had the candles from the Christmas tree—bigger than birthday candles but smaller than dinner ones—and the matches from the restaurant. Walter pressed the button for the basement. They didn't speak as they descended past the lobby into the ground and came out into pitch darkness. He turned on the overhead light so that they could see where they were, a cavelike space with stone walls and an ancient floor, curved ceilings overhead. The air was dank and smelled musty. A narrow corridor was lined with little rooms, each one marked with a number and each door closed by a padlock.

"This is really creepy," said Hope. "Where are we going?"

"Each apartment has a storage room down here," he told her. "You must have one too."

"I don't have anything to store."

He laughed. "Lucky you."

He led her to the door marked "14" and opened the padlock. Inside, there were ten boxes stacked three high in the middle. There was no electricity inside, so he left the door wide open to let in the light from the hallway. He looked over the boxes until he found one marked CALIFORNIA, which had been folded together sixteen years ago, but never taped. When he pulled it open, dust rose from the surface, crumbs of plaster, a cobweb. The photo album he had taken from his grandparents' house that day was the only thing inside. Walter wondered briefly what had happened to everything he'd left behind: his clothes and shoes, his bank account, Sharon; maybe he would never know. He set up two closed boxes for chairs and another in the middle for a table.

"Please come in."

Hope stepped into the dark chamber and sat down.

"What is this?"

"Open it."

The spine of the photo album cracked, giving way after so many years. He had spent the whole flight home looking at these pictures. By the time he arrived in Berlin again, he'd memorized each one.

"She looked a lot like you."

"Thank you."

He arranged the five glasses in a circle on the makeshift table.

"Can you hand me the candles?"

While she looked through the photo album, he rubbed the bottom of the candles until each one was standing, unlit, in a glass.

"Are you ready?" Walter asked her.

"For what?"

"I am going to do it now. I am going to say Kaddish."

"Here?"

"This is the place."

When he lit a match and leaned over the five candles, the warm light illuminated the ninety-year-old stone walls of the room, once plastered and white, now a dingy beige. On the back wall Hebrew letters had been drawn from right to left in tidy lines, in ink and now faded. They covered almost the entire surface. Hope got up from her box and went up to the wall.

"It was a Hebrew school," said Walter.

"A secret one."

"Yes. For the children hiding down here during the war."

"What does it say?"

"I don't know."

"We could ask someone. We could look it up."

"We will do that."

"How did you find this?"

"I wasn't looking for it. When I moved in my things sixteen years ago, it was all just here."

She ran her fingers over the letters.

"There is so much here."

She laid the photo album open on the table to the picture of Walter's young mother, smiling, in a snowsuit, sat down again and smoothed her skirt over her knees.

"Five candles?"

"My parents, my grandparents, your son."

She nodded.

"Do you know the prayer?"

"No. Do you?"

"Unfortunately, no."

"Then I'm going to sing, all right? Whatever songs I can think of. You can sing with me if you want to."

"I'm a terrible singer."

"My voice is actually pretty good," said Walter. "But I haven't performed in front of anyone in a long time."

He started with the lullabies he remembered. *The river Jordan is deep and wide, milk and honey on the other side.* He held the flame carefully to each wick. The first one for his mother, the next for his father, then his grandfather and his grandmother and, finally, for the baby. His voice cracked at the beginning but after a verse or so it evened out. It got stronger as he moved on to fragments of pop music from his youth, whatever he could remember of Journey ballads and Madonna and REO Speedwagon, sung quietly in place of formal prayer. Sometimes Hope joined in, or reminded him of the lyrics, or made requests. He could feel himself sitting up taller on his box, reaching for the high notes. *It's time to bring this ship into the shore and throw away the oars forever.* Walter sang until the candles had burned down, filling the glasses with orange light, and the room glowed.

ACKNOWLEDGMENTS

I owe an incredible debt of gratitude to my agent, Sarah Burnes, for her wisdom and enthusiasm, and to my inspired editor at Riverhead, Megan Lynch. I know how lucky I am.

Patrick Winczewski, the "real" German voice of Tom Cruise, was kind enough to let me into his studio. Let the record show that he could not be more different from Walter Baum.

Many thanks to my first readers: Jordanna Fraiberg, Harvey Friedman, Amanda Herman, Julie von Kessel, Nicole Krauss, Ralph Martin, and Lithe Sebesta. And to Christine Muhlke. And to my ladies in Charlottenburg for the everyday: Yvonne Borrmann, Patti Ferer, Wilma Harzenetter, Penelope Lewis, Charlotte Sötje and especially Gabriela Pardo, *mi comadre*, who picked me up on the playground my very first day there. And finally to my parents, Bob and Sarah LeVine, for embracing Berlin.

This book is dedicated to my husband, Jörg Winger, who has shown me a whole new world.

Anna Winger grew up in Massachusetts and Mexico and was educated at Columbia University. Her essays have appeared in the *New York Times Magazine*, among other publications. She is also a photographer and the creator of *Berlin Stories*, a radio series for NPR Worldwide. She lives in Berlin with her family.